## Praise for Caren Lissner's first novel, *Carrie Pilby:*

"Woody Allen-hilarious, compulsively readable and unpretentiously smart."
—*Philadelphia Weekly*

"Lissner's heroine is utterly charming and unique, and readers will eagerly turn the pages to find out how her search for happiness unfolds."
—*Booklist*

"In language both witty and sweet, Lissner describes the exploits of her 19-year-old heroine, detailing a transformation that is subtle, careful and believable. Instead of completing a total (and predictable) turnaround, Carrie, a genius who has just graduated from Harvard, goes on a quest for a way to live among others, having fun while still adhering to her strict moral code. The results are hilarious and impressive."
—*Philadelphia City Paper*

"Debut author Caren Lissner deftly delivers a novel that is funny, sarcastic and thought-provoking."
—*Romantic Times*

"Caren Lissner will break your heart, twist your mind and bust your gusset, often in the same sentence."
—J. Robert Lennon author of *On the Night Plain*

# Starting from Square ~~One~~ Two

## Caren Lissner

**RED DRESS INK**

First edition March 2004

STARTING FROM SQUARE TWO

A Red Dress Ink novel

ISBN 0-373-25052-5

Visit Red Dress Ink at www.reddressink.com

**Printed in U.S.A.**

## ACKNOWLEDGMENTS

I must first thank Howard Walper, who often Instant Messages me with unsolicited advice on my writing, work, free time and personal life. Everyone should have a friend like Howard. Seriously, he offered amazing insights into this book. I would also like to acknowledge Farrin Jacobs, my editor, for doing such a great editing job and for putting up with me; Cheryl Pientka, whose monumental feats have included putting out fires (literally) and most impressively, putting up with me; and Marc Serges, for being brilliant and also putting up with me; Dawn Eden, for enthusiasm, encouragement and suggestions, and Jeff Hauser, for support and ideas.

I am very grateful to the following for always encouraging my writing: Stacie Fine, Stacie Fine's mom, Janet Rosen, Matt Greco, Eileen Budd, Dan Saffer, Jim Damis, Mary Beth Jipping, Barry Macaluso, Julia Hough, Regina Hill, Shanti Gold, Bridget Grimes, Angela Gaffney, John Prendergast, Neil Genzlinger, Eliot Kaplan, Robert Donnell, Linda Wiedmann, Cheryl Shipman, Dennis and Valerie, John R. Lennon, Jon Blackwell, Michael Malice, Jodi Harris, my parents, my brother Todd, Al Sullivan, Jennifer Merrick, Lucha Malato, David Unger, Joe Barry and everyone with whom I work (and yes, who puts up with me) at the fine Hudson Reporter newspaper chain. Finally, no one is to blame for my writing habit more than the outstanding writing and English teachers I had, just some of whom are included here: Frances Doane, Michael Ferraro, Barbara Kitrosser, Mary Sandholt, Roslyn Schleifer, Walter Hatton, Diana Cavalho, Kristin Hunter Lattany, Cary Holiday and anyone I've forgotten.

# Chapter

1

"It can't be that bad," Gert said.

The D train was careening through the subway tunnel, passing through areas of light, then darkness. Gert was squeezed on one of the long gray seats next to her former college roommate, Hallie. Looming high above them was Hallie's high school friend, Erika, who was tall and always wore huge black boots.

"It *is* that bad," Hallie said to Gert. "You have no idea what it's like out there."

Gert looked up at Erika, who was strap-hanging. They weren't really straps, though. They were metal triangular things. When was the last time they were straps, Gert wondered.

*She's triangle-hanging,* Gert thought to herself.

She'd have said it aloud if Marc were there. He liked corny observations.

Then she felt bad. It was impossible not to think of him in relation to everything. She'd done it for eight years of her life.

"Let me ask you a question," Hallie said to her.

"Fine," Gert said. "Ask me a question."

"You were married to Marc for five years, and you'd dated

him for three before that. In those eight years, did you come across even one other man who, had you been single, you would have considered dating?"

Gert shrugged. "I wasn't thinking like that," she said, "because I was with Marc."

"But," Hallie said, "during that time, did you ever just *happen* to meet a man who was remotely attractive, normal, in his twenties and not taken?"

"No," Gert persisted. "I wasn't trying."

"What about in the course of your regular business?"

"I wouldn't have noticed."

Gert wondered if, in some small way, Hallie and Erika occasionally felt a secret bit of satisfaction that the accident had happened, so they could finally prove to her that the dating scene was just as bad as they'd always said.

But true friends could never wish that on her, could they?

Gert knew they were only trying to help by dragging her out. Everyone was always trying to "help"—like the people who told her that eventually, it would hurt less, or that she was strong and she'd move on. But they had no idea how many times per day she heard expressions, songs or references that reminded her of him. Every time something bad happened to her, or she felt lonely, she thought of him on impulse, as she'd done for most of her adult life—and was reminded again that he was gone. They'd met sophomore year of college, so that was eight years or 2,920 days of memories she had to suppress in order to even feel remotely okay. Didn't people understand that?

The only people who did understand were the women in her support group on Long Island, where she went every week. Among her circle of friends, there was not exactly a surfeit of twenty-nine-year-olds who had lost their husbands. Most of them had not even been married yet. And Gert, who had counted herself so lucky for so long, and who had been far outside the realm of her lonely single friends, was now—because of one horrible day—among their ranks.

It had only been a year and a half since the car accident. That was barely enough time to even accept what had happened. It was also barely enough time to stop having those brief moments when she felt as secure as she used to be, then, in a flash, remembered that everything was all wrong.

But Gert was finally giving in to one of Hallie and Erika's many exhortations to go out. It certainly would be healthier than sitting home all night. Still, her heart wouldn't be in it and her mind wouldn't be on it. She'd just be going through the motions—like she did with so many things these days.

Gert looked at Hallie and Erika. Both of them had complained about dating since college graduation. They always made it sound like war, packed with battle plans and tricks and conspiracies. Gert had been skeptical in the past. Wasn't dating supposed to be fun?

In college, it had been. It went like this: A guy in your class or dorm would strike up a conversation, he'd invite you for coffee or a movie, you'd flirt relentlessly in the study lounges, and eventually the conversations would turn into heated dormroom aerobics. Or in the case of Marc, the two of you were at the bookstore, and he saw you buying a used copy of Calculus for $44.99 instead of $60 new, and he said, "Where'd you get that?" and you talked about how you almost placed out of the class entirely and how you both thought that math was the worst and best subject in the world. It was the worst because it was boring, but it was the best because it always provided finite answers—no room for guesswork or interpretation. You came to realize you both liked things you could count on. You were in the same lecture, so you could study together. You got an A-minus and the first intense relationship of your life.

Gert's other dates, before Marc, hadn't been bad, either. There was cynical Andy, who was obsessed with Ultimate Frisbee and PEZ dispensers. Paul, the head of the political union, called the profs and deans by their first names when he saw them on campus. He went to their office hours even if he wasn't in their classes, because other students didn't take advantage of them and he figured it was a good time to schmooze. But neither of them was as driven or interesting as Marc, a guitar-playing business student who had three red-haired Irish brothers, none of whom looked a thing like him.

Gert's closeness with Marc was what made her realize that someday, she might need to be with someone again. The idea of going through the rest of her life without a person beside her to help her through it was torture. But she couldn't imagine dating right now. No one could possibly have Marc's ideas and expressions, those idiosyncrasies and small kindnesses that made her smile. There couldn't possibly be anyone like him.

Gert looked at Hallie, dressed so scantily in the middle of February. Hallie's dating troubles always had seemed self-imposed. When Hallie had told Gert about the guy who'd said, "I actually drive better after a few beers," Gert couldn't believe Hallie hadn't walked out on him right then. But Hallie had told Gert she wanted to stick with him because he was "sensitive." Next, Hallie met a guy who didn't drive drunk, but had big ears. So Hallie stopped dating him. Gert worried that Hallie was focusing on all the wrong things.

One day Gert actually told Hallie that her priorities seemed skewed.

"You meet a nice guy and his forehead's too high," Gert said. "You meet a jerky guy and you date him anyway and end up bitter when he doesn't morph into a poet. You hate bars but you go to the same ones five days a week. Why don't you just relax a little and have fun?"

Hallie got angry. She said Gert had no idea at all what it was like out there.

That's the phrase Hallie had used: Out There.

Like it was a jungle.

The subway bumped a bit, and everyone grabbed their belongings to prevent liftoff.

"Well?" Hallie said.

"Well, what?" Gert asked.

"Name one decent guy you've met since college who's single."

Gert sighed. "Marc's brother Michael," she said. "He's normal. He's nice. So there *is* one who exists."

"And you'd date him?" asked tall, ponytailed Erika, from somewhere near the ceiling.

"I didn't say I would date him," Gert said. "He's Marc's brother. I'm just saying he exists."

"Isn't he the short one with the mutton chops?" Erika asked.

"No. Eddie's married."

"Is he the one who wears stained overalls and lives in Maine and breeds Sea Monkeys?"

"Patrick doesn't breed Sea Monkeys; he's a crabber. And *he's* married too."

"Oh. So you mean the third brother, the eighteen-year-old."

"Michael's twenty-two now," Gert said.

Hallie and Erika looked at each other.

"So you would date a twenty-two-year-old?" Hallie asked.

"I didn't say *I* would…."

"See!" Hallie said, her voice surging with victory. "That is exactly my point, and something you will learn soon enough. There are no single guys who don't have at least one major flaw, and a flaw, I might add, that would stop you from dating them—even if everything else was great. Why? Simple math. Women are interesting and honest and sensitive. Most men are not. There is only one normal, decent single guy for every five women in this city. This is what's known as the Great Male Statistic. Girls don't want to face the GMS. They want to believe there's someone for everyone. The truth hurts. You only start coming to terms with the GMS when you're twenty-six or twenty-seven. It actually killed Sylvia Plath. She finally found this guy in grad school who she thought was so great, and she married him, and he cheated on her."

"Didn't Sylvia Plath have a history of mental illness since she was an undergrad?" Gert asked.

"Incidental. She didn't kill herself until Ted Hughes cheated. The truth is, the really good men are snapped up quickly. You get into your mid-twenties and it's five to one. Don't give me that look. You don't believe it because you don't *want* to."

Gert was ready to go home. "Then why are we doing this?"

"Because looking for the one in five," Hallie said, "is still better than being alone."

The bar was two blocks from the mouth of the subway. When the women emerged on Bleecker Street, a frigid wind swept through, grazing their bare arms. Hallie wrapped her hands around herself as she walked, but insisted to Gert that she wasn't cold.

"The only way to get into a lasting relationship is to find one before you finish college," said Erika, her dirty-blond ponytail bouncing behind her.

"Absolutely," Hallie said. "Look when both of you met your boyfriends. Sophomore year. And—poof—you had taken them off the market forever. Denied to older women like us."

Erika said, "I gave up Ben at twenty-four, and someone else got him."

"And how long did that take? Five months?"

"Not even," Erika said, looking down at her boots. "Three."

Gert had heard many times about how Erika had met and lost her college boyfriend. Erika and Ben had started dating around the same time as Gert had started dating Marc—sophomore year. But Erika broke up with Ben five years later. She was pretty, a lot of guys liked her, and her friends and family kept telling her not to settle down so quickly. She wasn't sure she was ready to make a lifelong commitment, and she didn't feel hopelessly, madly in love with Ben, the way she'd always dreamed she would be.

So she told Ben she needed a few months off. Better to figure out what she wanted now, she said, than when it was too late. She dated a few guys, realized Ben was much better than everyone she'd met, and called him up one night.

It was too late.

They passed a guy with a huge backpack who was slumped against a building, drunk. A policeman was kneeling down to talk to him. The thick smell of beer-soaked sidewalks and vomit invaded Gert's nostrils. She remembered it from frat parties in college. It was a sad smell—the smell of being among two hundred happy people but just wanting to be with the one who made *you* happy. It was a memory she could do without.

"At least you got to be Ben's first love," Hallie said to Erika. "I'll never get to be anyone's."

"I hate her," Erika said.

"Don't start."

"I'm going to read her Web log tonight and put crap on her message board."

"Again?"

Gert had heard all about Ben's wife, Challa, and her Web log. Challa wrote every few days in her "blog" about her life, for all the world to see. It told of romantic trips, of art classes the couple took together, of how wonderful Ben was with the baby, and of Ben's dream to renovate an old farmhouse in New England where they could raise their family. Erika told Gert and Hallie about the night Ben had sat on her dormroom bed in college and first told *her* of this dream.

"That should be me," Erika always said to them. "She's an imposter, living my life. And here I am, sitting in my pajamas in front of the computer, reading about it."

Hallie, Erika and Gert had problems with the first three bars they passed. Blastoff was playing eighties music. ("Eighties music was never good the first time," Erika sniped. "Just because today's music is so bad, suddenly we think 'Der Kommissar' is good?") Gert passed on the biker bar—too intimidating. Hallie thought there were too many women in Atlantis.

"They should open a really hip bar that refuses to admit women if they're underdressed," Hallie said.

"Aren't you part of the problem?" Gert asked.

"I can't take a stand on it alone," Hallie said. "The stakes are too high. If everyone would just say no to overexposure to the elements, I'd put on a sweater, by gum!"

Gert laughed. Hallie sometimes used funny expressions like "by gum." It did lighten the mood a bit. But these days, it seemed like practically the only time her old roommate said things like that was when she was drinking or drunk.

Gert remembered meeting Hallie on move-in day at college. She'd liked her new roommate instantly. Hallie was a short, chubby-cheeked girl who laughed at everything and constantly poured her heart out about all her unrequited crushes. And just as Hallie was willing to share her problems, she was nosy and would ferret out all of her friends' concerns. If something was bothering Gert, Hallie would be unrelenting in drawing it out of her and making her feel better. The two of them often left a night of studying on their respective beds to head to the corner coffee shop to hash out their problems over espresso. They would leave after two hours with a clear course of action: Call their crushes. Study harder. Hang around over break. Hallie was a psychology major, so she liked helping people deal with their dilemmas.

But toward the end of freshman year, Gert had stopped being able to match Hallie's tales of unrequited longing. Gert was beginning to get male attention, even if she wasn't used to it. A childhood friend of hers told her that she was "college popular" rather than "high school popular"—in her high school, only the beautiful, outgoing girls had had boyfriends, but in college, if you were pretty and funny and easygoing enough, you could do all right. One thing Gert had always had going for her was a calm rationality, a willingness to live and let live. She rarely got bent out of shape over the little things, and it seemed to her that most girls were high-strung. Especially about men. Gert thought that a lot of things guys did were funny, whereas most women found their jokes offensive or just plain gross.

It was like Hallie and Erika—especially these days. They got crazy over every aspect of the dating process, worrying it to death. Hallie was still as good a listener as she had been back in school—but only when Erika wasn't around. When Erika was there, Hallie seemed more concerned with trying to impress her glamorous friend. Gert suspected it went back to high school, when beautiful Erika was exceedingly popular and Hallie was grateful to tag along.

Gert thought that maybe, just as Hallie wanted to help Gert get back into society, she could help Hallie not be so focused on winning everyone else's approval—that of Erika and every man she met. Hallie used to be a lot of fun. But more and more, she acted desperate. Strained.

The three women finally agreed on a bar called Art's. It had a dual meaning that Gert liked. She didn't see a guy named Art, though; just a female bartender with overalls and cropped blond hair. A female Eminem.

There were four stools open at the mahogany counter. Hallie and Erika jockeyed to be at either end, rather than in the middle. If you were in the middle there was no chance of someone sitting next to you. Hallie had done that in lecture halls throughout college, too—always sat just one seat in, so a guy could sit on the end without effort. Nowadays, Hallie also chose the middle seat on airplanes, meaning that seats would be left on either side of her, guaranteed to be taken by people traveling alone. It was Hallie's Law of Maximum Exposure, almost as airtight as the Great Male Statistic: Leave as much surface area as possible so you will come into contact with an exponentially greater number of single people.

Of course, 99.9 percent of the time, the plan failed. On airplanes, Hallie often ended up flanked by someone's grandpa and a woman who looked like Pamela Anderson.

At Art's, a David Bowie song was playing, which made Gert think immediately of Marc, because he'd been a big Bowie fan. There she was, thinking about him again. Whenever she did that, everything else lost focus. She sometimes lingered in such a netherworld for four to five minutes and then popped back into reality and wondered what had just happened. People would be staring at her, wondering why she looked so spacey. But there was comfort in the netherworld.

She tried to figure out which Bowie song it was. Marc would have known. He was a rock 'n' roll encyclopedia. She could count on him for that. It was just one of the many small things she could count on. Whenever they were in the car together, she would test him just to tease him, asking which singer was on, and if he didn't know, he would get all frustrated, and the moment they got home he'd dash up the stairs to look up the song in the *Billboard Book of Top 40 Hits.*

Strains of Bowie were soon replaced by "5:15" by The Who, which also had a memory attached. They'd gone to see the movie *Quadrophenia* together. Gert was unimpressed with the movie, but loved the music. Marc was constantly trying to get Gert, and everyone else, into his favorite bands. It was adorable.

Gert hadn't realized until he was gone just how many different things she had liked about him, nor how much his very existence had become part of her constitution. She wasn't the type to constantly blather on about her boyfriend or husband, but she had always had Marc in the back of her mind, no matter where she was. Now, whenever something reminded her of him, she'd remember what happened and her stomach would drop. She wondered if people who were part of a couple had any idea what a privilege it was to get to spend their lives with the person they loved. Of course, they knew on one level, but did they really *know?*

Erika whined about wanting to sit on an end stool, so Hallie reluctantly offered her one. But instantly, the seat on the other side got taken—by a girl who'd just come in with her boyfriend. What nerve. At least the girl wouldn't be competing with them for the guys hanging out by the dart-board.

Gert picked up the drink menu and looked at it. Wine was eight dollars a glass. It seemed ridiculous for her to spend that much money. Especially now that she was living on a single income.

She looked around the bar and felt sick. Was this the world she'd been left to—squandering money on booze, dressing half-naked, shouting over music, strategizing about where to sit?

Gert felt angry. Angry about everything that had happened. Angry at herself.

Gert knew that thinking about this at the bar didn't make her look very approachable. But she couldn't help it. Obviously she wasn't ready to go out yet. Her initial instincts had been right: a year and a half wasn't long enough. She was too tired, too angry, too sad. Maybe next year.

Then she thought of something.

She could pretend she was back in college, hanging out with friends just like freshman year. She didn't have to be worrying about who was by the dartboard. She could sing along with Roger Daltrey. She could make fun of Erika's ponytail. She didn't have to be looking for a man like her friends were. She didn't want one, anyway.

No worrying, plotting or planning.

Gert craned her neck over the bar and forced a smile. "So," she said to Hallie, "did you fire that girl at work?"

"No." Hallie shook her head. "I will, though."

Hallie was the office manager at a management consulting firm, and her twenty-three-year-old assistant spent half the day calling guys, Instant Messaging guys, checking to see if she had e-mail from guys, and scribbling ratings on the posters of guys she kept on her cubicle wall. On Brad Pitt's arm, the girl had written, "HOT." On Ben Affleck, she'd written, "yumie" (and yes, spelled it wrong). On Josh Hartnett, she'd written,

"Cute!!!" Then, on Robert Downey, Jr., she'd written a simple "OK."

"You can't fire her," Erika said. "She makes you feel better about your own life."

"I know," Hallie said. "I may be twenty-nine and single, but at least I've never put *Tiger Beat* posters on my walls. And now she keeps disappearing every day between 3:00 and 4:00 p.m., and she thinks we don't notice. I don't know where she goes."

"Do you have any idea?" Gert asked.

"No," Hallie said. "My boss is going to have me follow her."

Gert sensed someone sitting next to her. She felt the brush against her shoulder before she even looked. Two men were sitting down. They weren't looking her way, though. They were talking to each other. She snuck a peek. They were both wearing leather bomber jackets. They were average-looking and clean-cut.

"Fresh meat at three o'clock," Erika said.

Hallie took a quick look at the guys, then went back to Erika. "They're short, though," she reported.

"Did I ever tell you that Ben's bitch wife is an inch taller than he is?" Erika said. "I can't imagine what happens when she wears heels. The two of them must look like a circus act."

"Maybe she doesn't wear heels," Gert said.

"Don't be funny," Erika said.

Gert heard the guy to her right say to the bartender, "Just a cranberry juice." The bartender looked at him strangely before going to get the juice.

The guy noticed Gert looking at him. "I'm all for girly drinks," he said, smiling.

"Oh," Gert said. "This may shock you, but so am I."

"What kind?"

"All kinds, as long as there's citrus fruit involved."

"It prevents scurvy," the guy's friend said.

"Health is always important when ordering alcoholic beverages," Gert said.

"So I should order one for you, then," the first guy said.

Gert said, "You could."

Erika whispered to Hallie, "Hook-up at stage right." Gert ignored her. The guys both seemed nice.

"Cranberry juice is…" Gert started, but then she stopped. What she'd thought of was that it was good for urinary tract infections. But that was not appropriate dating conversation. Damn—she was going to have to start thinking like that now. With Marc, of course, she could have said anything. She could have gone to the bathroom in front of him, although she preferred not to.

It was back to square one on everything. Well, at least she was older now. Square two, then.

"Cranberry juice is…good for you," Gert finished.

"It's good for urinary infections," the first guy said.

Erika leaned over Gert's seat and said to him, "Are you a doctor?"

The guy looked at her for a second.

"No," he said, laughing. Erika shrugged and went back to her drink.

"Anyway, there's a reason I can't drink," the guy added.

"What is it?" Gert asked.

"He's on the extra board," his friend said.

Gert looked at them blankly.

"That means I'm on call for work," the first guy said. "But even when I'm not on call, I'm never allowed to drink."

"Are you a cop?"

"Nope."

"Guess what he does," the guy's friend said. "Guess. No one can ever guess it."

"Gert," Hallie called from two stools down. "Do you want a drink?"

Hallie had drained two cosmos in ten minutes. She was giving Gert a look like she wanted to know if Gert needed to be rescued. Gert didn't know why. All they were doing was talking. "No, thanks," Gert said. "I'm okay."

"Gert!" Erika said. "Hallie and I are going to the girls' room!"

"Fine," Gert said. "See you."

"Gert!" Erika called. "Let us know if you want a drink."

Gert nodded.

"Your friends are loud," the guy's friend said in a low voice.

"They're really nice people," Gert said.

"You must be nice to defend them," the first guy said.

"It's the least you should expect someone to do," Gert said, "defend their friends."

"Anyone who has a rule like that," the first guy said, "I'm all for." He smiled. He had a small scar on the bridge of his nose. It looked cute.

"Todd defends *me,* right, Todd?" the second guy asked.

"Yeah, I do," Todd said in an authoritative voice. "Two more guesses."

"You're a treasury officer," Gert said.

"Hey, is that an *Untouchables* reference?"

"Yes," Gert said.

"That's like my favorite movie. How'd you know?"

Gert said, "I just knew."

"Brian, isn't that like my favorite movie?"

"It's like his favorite movie," Brian said.

Erika and Hallie hadn't gone to the bathroom as promised. They were staring at Gert.

Hallie elbowed her.

"Why don't you introduce us?" she asked.

"Oh," Gert said. "Todd and Brian, this is Hallie and Erika."

"Hiiii!" Hallie said, pulling her stool around so that she could see them better. "What do both of you do?"

"I was just trying to guess that," Gert said.

"I'm a stockbroker," Brian said. "But Todd's the one with the interesting job."

"I think stockbrokers are *very* interesting," Erika purred.

"Well, Todd's job is more interesting," Brian insisted.

"He can't drink," Gert added. "So I guessed that he's an officer of the treasury."

Hallie and Erika looked clueless.

"*The Untouchables.* They went after alcohol during Prohibition...."

"That movie rocks," Brian said.

"Oh, right!" Erika said. "Wasn't Kevin Bacon in that?"

"Costner," Brian said.

"Yeah," Erika said. "My ex-boyfriend was into that movie. He married a girl who keeps a Web log."

"How many more guesses you want?" Brian asked Gert.

"One more," Gert said.

Todd pursed his mouth. He had dark hair, a little curly behind his ears.

"Truck driver," Gert guessed finally.

"Close," Todd said.

"Oh...I give up."

"I work for Norfolk Southern," Todd said. "I'm a conductor on a train, and we get twelve hours on and twelve hours off...."

"Those are freight trains, right?"

"Yeah, and you have a couple of guys on each run, one driving and one making sure everything's okay. It's too dangerous to be drinking off-duty, because they could call you all of a sudden to come in. So they don't let you drink at all, ever."

"That's too bad," Gert said. "I mean, if you think it is."

"Nah." Todd shrugged. "I did enough of that in college. It's okay."

"So, Brian, how long have you been a stockbroker?" Erika asked.

"Since college," Brian said. He looked at his watch and nudged Todd. "I think we'd better get going."

"Yeah, we're meeting friends," Todd said. "It was nice to meet you, though."

Gert didn't know if he meant all of them.

"So..." Todd said "...if you have a number, I mean, would you mind if maybe I gave you a call sometime?"

Gert thought about it. There couldn't be much harm. Besides, the practice would do her good. She searched in her purse for something to write on—it had been a while since she'd done this—and finally came up with an inky business card. She scribbled her home number on the back.

Hallie and Erika looked on, concerned.

Then, the men were gone.

"The only person to even talk to a normal guy was Gert," Erika whined in the subway in the wee hours.

"Neither of you would have even talked to Todd," Gert said. "You didn't like that he's a train conductor."

"Well, I *did* like Brian," Erika said.

"Based on what?"

"I don't know. He was cute. So thanks for not helping. You were like, 'I'm taking Todd and that's it.'"

Gert sighed. "I wasn't *taking* him. He just seemed like a nice guy, so I talked to him."

"Why didn't Brian like me?" Erika wailed.

"Maybe Todd only wanted my number so he could call me to get yours," Gert said.

"Well, if he calls, don't give it to him," Erika said. "They were short."

Now Gert knew the truth: Hallie and Erika were single because they were crazy.

"How did you know to mention his favorite movie?" Hallie asked.

"Oh," Gert said. "There's a canon where guys are concerned. Marc was always quoting lines from that movie. If you quote certain things, you can slide right into their conversation."

"What kinds of things?"

"Do you really want to know?"

"We've got nothing to lose."

The canon for guys in their twenties and thirties
    1.  The Simpsons
    2.  This is Spinal Tap
    3.  Star Wars
    4.  Monty Python

5.  Star Trek
6.  The Princess Bride
7.  The Untouchables
8.  The Hobbit
9.  The Matrix
10. Office Space

"Excuse me," Erika said. "Don't you mean, 'The canon for nerds'?"

"No. There are cool guys who like those things."

"Hey," Hallie said. "Maybe we should get together at my place this weekend and rent these flicks."

So they put it on their schedule.

When Gert got home, she was exhausted. Her bed felt soft and wonderful.

She'd spent the last five hours trying to put something out of her mind that she hadn't really wanted to put out of her mind. She'd been in an environment where everyone was supposed to appear carefree and happy, but her feelings had veered between torture and just getting a mild drubbing. Even if the bar scene hadn't been as horrible as Hallie and Erika made it sound, there was a real harshness to it. It was unsettling. It wasn't at all like what she would have done that night if Marc had been there.

If he had been there, they probably would have gone out to dinner, and then taken a walk through Manhattan. Or maybe they would have snuggled on the couch and watched a movie. Even cleaning the house with him would have been better than going to the bar. Playing a rousing round of that silly plastic foosball game he'd insisted on keeping in the living room would have been better. It was too hard to fall in love with someone, learn all of their quirks and passions, assume you'd spend the rest of your life with them, and then suddenly have them snatched away forever.

Slowly, in bed, Gert spread out her bare arms. Sleeping bare-armed, feeling the sheets against her skin, was the closest she got to a caress these days.

She knew she had to stop thinking about what she could have done if Marc had been there. This was the new reality. He never would be.

But did she have it in her to start fighting her way through leather-jacketed and miniskirted crowds in search of a second miracle?

It didn't seem worth it.


Erika brought two bowls overflowing with popcorn into Hallie's living room. It was Friday night. The room had one wide window that was being pelted by the rain. Hallie popped the tops of three Diet Coke cans and a no-frills carbonated fruit punch and let them fizz on the coffee table.

Gert and Erika, sitting on the couch, reached for the diet sodas.

They left one for Hallie's often-absentee roommate, Cat, who was rumored to be making a rare appearance within the hour. Although with meek Cat, who spent weekends with her family on Long Island, it was always hard to be sure.

*Why,* Gert thought, *does it seem wrong for us to be having a slumber party for twenty-nine-year-olds?*

*Because this is not what you expected. You don't have a sleepover party with your twenty-nine-year-old girlfriends. You and your husband have kids, and THEY have sleepovers, and the two of you stand in the doorway beaming, pleased to see the kids so excited, remembering what it was like back then—and thrilled to have your own best friend to sleep with.*

"You know what would be great?" Hallie asked, lying on her stomach on the floor and painting her nails. "If the rain turned to snow, and it piled up, and we were stuck here for three days."

Erika, on the couch, pulled a blanket around herself and shivered visibly. The rain snapped more loudly at the windows. "What would we do?"

"We'd hole up right in this room in our sweatpants and play truth-or-dare and confess our deepest secrets to each other,"

Hallie said, "and order heaping bowls of pad Thai and drink cheap wine."

"I want a *guy* to do those things with," Erika whined.

"Well, you ain't got one, so shut up."

"I'm twenty-nine," Erika said. "It isn't even healthy to be boyfriendless this long. My body needs to be physically touched by a member of the opposite sex."

"Get a root canal."

Gert gazed over the blankets neatly laid out on the floor, and at the popcorn on the table, and really did feel like a kid at a sleepover. She wondered if later Erika would break out the Ouija board, hoping to channel Elvis, and after that the three of them would try to levitate themselves, chanting, "Light as a feather, stiff as a board...."

The door opened, and it was tiny Cat, lugging a doggie bag from whichever pricey restaurant she'd been to with her aunt. Gert had only met Cat a few times. Cat constantly complained, in her squeaky voice, that she wasn't meeting anyone, but turned down every invitation Hallie and Erika made to go out, whether it was dancing at Polly Esther's or rinsing trays at the University Community Soup Kitchen. She was "too tired," or it was too cold out, or she was spending the weekend with her family. Hallie and Erika privately ragged on her, but at the same time, they loved it when she actually did come out with them, because her shrinking-violet existence made them feel good about their own lives. At least they'd had real relationships.

One more thing about Cat was that she wasn't willing to accept any degree of obnoxiousness in boys. If a guy even made a joke about sex, Cat looked intimidated, and she retreated. Gert was glad that Cat stuck by what she believed in, but Hallie and Erika said that Cat would be alone until she was sixty-five. Then she could meet a nice guy who had prostate cancer and just wanted to be her very good friend.

Hallie got up and turned off the light so the women could watch the male canon movies they had rented: *Monty Python's*

*Holy Grail, This Is Spinal Tap,* and number eleven in the canon, *Reservoir Dogs.* Gert was hoping Hallie and Erika would like the movies, but the odds were against it. She'd never had a female friend who had the same sense of humor as she did, except for her high school friend Nancy, who lived in L.A. now.

Even before the movie started, Gert's prediction was proven right. Instead of paying attention to the opening scenes of *Holy Grail,* Erika was fussing over her throw pillows. Hallie was finishing with her nails. Cat had already gone into her room.

Hallie got up and paused the DVD. "I forgot," she said. "Before the movie starts, I have to tell you this. I thought of a great question for the two of you today." She was wearing an orange long-sleeved T-shirt and gray sweatpants that Gert thought looked cute. Even though Erika was around making her nervous, Gert realized that at least this was just a no-pressure girls' night. They didn't have to worry about how they looked or how they dressed. Maybe it could be fun.

"Not another of your profound probing questions," Erika said to Hallie, flicking a piece of popcorn across the coffee table.

"No, this is great," Hallie said, prying and probing as usual. She crawled over to the table and waved her nails to dry them. "Let's say a soothsayer told you that you would not meet the man of your dreams for eight more years."

"Uh-huh."

"Let's say that the soothsayer said that without a doubt, when you turned thirty-seven, you would finally meet someone, fall madly, madly in love with him, and live happily ever after. Would you still date people in the interim?"

"No," Gert said.

"No," Cat said, coming back into the room.

"Probably not," Erika said. "I wouldn't bother."

"Interesting," Hallie said. "So dating is just a means to an end for all of you. It's not about fun or socializing or sex."

"I have enough fun," Gert said.

"I do enough socializing," Erika said.

"I...do enough socializing," Cat said.

"Most people won't admit that," Hallie said. "They won't admit that dating is work. Maybe we should all decide we're going to meet the man of our dreams when we're thirty-seven. Then we'll stop squeezing into tight shirts and walking around half-naked and analyzing every encounter as future husband material. We'll stop feeling the need to put on makeup to take out the trash just in case he's walking by. Maybe we should just assume that we'll meet our dream man at some future point, and stop driving ourselves crazy before then."

"I already met the man of my dreams," Erika said. "He's married to a bitch."

"I already met mine," Gert said. "And then he was gone."

The room was silent for a minute.

Cat said, "Anyone for Ouija?"

The movies ended up largely ignored for the night, as a half hour into the first one, something reminded Erika of Ben, and she said she just had to show Hallie and Gert what had happened on Challa's Web site that day.

Gert had sighed. Erika had the attention span of a Chihuahua.

Standing in Hallie's room by the big bed, they waited for the Web site to load. Hallie's bedroom was mostly black, with a black comforter over the bed and black furniture. She still had the same purple telephone from college, Gert noticed, and she wondered if it still had the same sticky goo around the push-buttons.

Across the computer screen flashed a page with a rich blue background and the words "Challa's Corner." A gliding pastiche of photos swirled across the screen, most of them of Challa, Ben and their baby. On the left was a list of links to things like the Weather Channel and *Elle* magazine.

Gert had to admit to herself that it looked cheesy.

And at the bottom of the screen was the bane of Erika's existence: The Web log.

Standing in front of Hallie's computer, the three women read that day's blog entry from Challa.

Last night was cold out, and we stayed in and put the baby to sleep and made dinner. I cooked linguine and mussels, and Ben tossed a salad. It was soooo romantic! ;) We polished off an entire bottle of red wine LOL!!!

Gert suspected that deep inside, all of the women were thinking that mussels and wine sounded a lot better than soda and popcorn at 11:00 p.m. Gert almost felt her body ache, remembering the effort and passion that went into something as mundane as preparing dinner together.

Erika returned to the home page and clicked a link that said, "Message board." That was where Challa's friends could leave comments like: "Hi, Chall!" "Hey, girl, love the new pix!" "Thanks for helping me waste time at work."

But recently Erika had started to leave messages, too.

She'd used all seven of her America Online screen names to create aliases to post things. Some were meant to annoy Challa, and some were just meant to confuse her. She told Hallie and Gert that Challa deserved it. Why did Challa have to shove everyone else's face in her and Ben's bliss all the time? Erika said that if she herself were married to someone as passionate and artistic as Ben, there was no way she would waste her free time writing blog entries about it.

The three of them read what Erika had posted on the message board that morning.

"You are banal," Erika had written under the screen name Mr. HushPuppy. (She chose screen names completely at random, based on whatever she happened to see from the Internet café while she was typing. That day, someone had walked by in Hush Puppies.)

"Yes, she is, isn't she?" Erika had responded to herself, this time using the name LadyAndTheTrump. "She started a whole

Web site dedicated to herself. Sweetie, you don't need TOO much attention, do you?"

"Challa's a ho and a slut," Mr. HushPuppy wrote.

"Ho, ho, ho, Merrrryyyyy Chall-mas," wrote "JenDurr."

"It wouldn't surprise me if Challa *did* name a holiday after herself," Mr. HushPuppy wrote. "Too much attention isn't enough for this girl. She should be lucky for what she has, not clog everyone else's cyberspace with her binary spittle."

"You're a sick girl, Erika Dennison," Hallie said, laughing.

What really got a rise out of Erika and Hallie that evening was that Challa, who previously had been ignoring the posts, was now getting into fights with the "writers."

"Can't you at least say something meaningful between your insults?" Challa had written back to Mr. HushPuppy. "If you hate me so much, then please don't read this board. I didn't invite you. At least LadyAndTheTrump sometimes has something meaningful to say."

"Ah," Erika said aloud, triumphantly. "She's using me as an example for me to follow."

Gert worried that someday, Erika would take this too far.

# Chapter

2

"This girl, Erika, told me she's just like me, but we're really very different," Gert told her support group on Long Island.

The group was for young widows. Until a few years ago, most of the "young widows" in Gert's area had been in their forties and fifties. Now there was a handful in their twenties and thirties, too. Gert found it worth the forty-five-minute rail jaunt each Saturday morning to talk to people who could understand what she was going through.

She hadn't gone to the group right away. In the weeks after Marc had died, she'd been surrounded by close friends and relatives. They were at the funeral, at Marc's parents' house, stopping by Gert's apartment. Gert needed to be squeezed among a crushing throng of people who knew Marc so well that they understood the profoundness of the loss; people who knew his interests, his kindness, the expressions on his bespectacled face. Only people who knew him as well as she did could understand the depth of the void.

Right after the accident, Gert's mother temporarily moved into Gert's condo in Queens. She had already tried to convince

Gert to move back to L.A., but failed. Gert's best friend from childhood, Nancy, had tried, too. But Gert wasn't sure she wanted to go back yet. All the experts said that you shouldn't make major changes in your life within a year after a death. Besides, deep inside her, she feared that going back home would make her feel even lonelier. At least in New York, there were people like her. Alone.

For a while, relatives stopped by her condo to visit. Co-workers of Marc's from the brokerage firm sent cards and flowers.

Then, slowly, the comforters tapered off. That meant that entire days yawned open with emptiness. Gert would pull herself out of bed, slog to work, get the occasional call from a friend who'd emit platitudes about taking things one step at a time, come home and, if she could stand to do something normal for two hours, watch a movie. In the past, no matter what happened to her, she knew he would be at the end—the end of the phone line, the end of a rough day, the end of the long commute home. Now, only she was there. All she had left to cling to were the vestiges of old routines.

Gert's parents found her a therapist on Fifth Avenue. For the first six months, she went every week and talked to an overly clinical woman who was nevertheless a good listener. But she realized that she would have rather stayed home. What she really needed, she decided, was to interact with people her own age who'd lost a spouse.

Gert knew she wouldn't have found such a support network if not for September 11. Most of the young widows' support groups in the area had sprung up because of that day. Marc had died only four days before that, on the seventh. The funeral was two days later. If it had been two days after that, it probably would have had to be postponed. She'd lost him, buried him and forty-eight hours later the world had exploded.

She found several groups advertising on the back page of the *Voice*. The first day, she had felt intense self-loathing as she walked into the room. All of the women were strangers, and they *looked* strange, too. Strange and sad. They were women who had absolutely nothing in common with her—except for one horrible event. But she had forced herself to hold back her tears. She sat down in a hard school chair in the circle. She listened. And she talked. She found out they all had similar experiences to hers. The other women in the group were prone to dazing out for five minutes at a time for no reason, too. They, too, were still getting sales calls for their husbands and not knowing how to respond. They, too, were incessantly told by well-meaning people that they would feel better soon. They, too, had assumed they would be married to one person for the rest of their lives—and suddenly had had that person yanked away forever.

The only time Gert felt unburdened was when she was in the group. Normally she struggled under the weight of knowing that if she bumped into someone and had to explain that her husband had died, it'd be an uphill battle to deal with their awkward responses, to make them understand how she felt and all of the challenges she faced. The women in the group just knew.

"Where were you when Erika said this?" asked Brenda, a heavyset thirty-five-year-old nurse. Brenda, who had the voice of an evangelist, had become the group's de facto leader. Their group had been started by a social worker from a local hospital, but the social worker eventually had found they were able to run it on their own.

"We were staying at Hallie's apartment Friday night," Gert said. "Hallie was my roommate in college. Erika is her friend from high school. Anyway, Hallie was in the bathroom brushing her teeth, and Erika and I were smoothing out our blankets on the floor, and Erika got serious. She turned to me and said, 'I know you think no one understands what you're going through. But every day when I wake up, I still want to say hi to Ben. He was in my life for so long, and then he was gone. I love him and I never get to see him anymore. So believe me, I know how you feel.'" Gert paused to take a deep breath. "And I know she was trying to be helpful, but having your husband die in a car accident is *not* the same thing as breaking up with him because you weren't sure you loved him and then he ends up with someone else. I wanted to tell her this—"

She broke off.

"But you didn't," said Leslie, a short owl-eyed girl who had been married to a man thirty years older than she. Gert felt sorry for her, imagining she'd taken the first guy to be smitten with her—and then Gert felt bad for being judgmental.

Brenda said to Gert, "You could have told her."

"But she was only trying to help," Gert said.

Michele shook her head. She was thirty-four, a paralegal. "They all are," she said. "But don't you ever want to say, no, this is how it really feels? Losing your husband feels like nothing, dead, like you want to jump back into that week when you had him back, and all you *can* do is look back because there aren't things to look ahead to anymore."

"I can't say all that," Gert said.

"Honey, you need to let someone in," Brenda said. "Don't be afraid of being *real* with people."

*If I was real with people,* Gert thought, *I'd lose all of them.*

The other topics at the meeting were standard: How they'd gotten through special occasions, how they filled their free time, how they were managing their financial affairs. Marc hadn't had any life insurance, except for the $1,000 policy he'd gotten—along with a free Discman—for signing up for a Sony Mastercard. Who would ever have thought to get life insurance for a twenty-seven-year-old? Marc's parents, luckily, paid for the burial and for a year of the mortgage on the condo. Some of the women in the group had had to sell their homes.

"The problem with moving isn't necessarily about money," a woman named Arden said. "I can't pack up his things. Some of them, I haven't touched since he died."

Gert thought of the extra bedroom in the condo, the one Marc had used as a workroom. It held a computer, trophies going back to his high school soccer championships, even Boy

Scout patches. She had barely touched these things since he'd died. Sometimes she wandered into the room and stood there for a while, in a comfortable haze.

"Don't push yourself," Brenda told Arden. "Everything has a time."

"It feels like you're putting him away when you put something aside," Leslie said. "A pipe exploded last year and it poured all over Jesse's Yankees cap, and I had to throw it away. Then I started crying."

Everyone was quiet for a minute.

"But see, they got to the Series," Brenda said. "So he was watching over them."

Leslie laughed. "I don't think he did that."

"See?" Michele said. "We can smile when we remember, not just cry."

Gert's mind started drifting. She found herself wishing that Chase were there. Chase was a quiet girl with short hair and a shy smile who had come to several meetings and then stopped. Chase was twenty-nine, too, and she had lost her fiancé around the time that Gert had lost Marc. She seemed like a nice person, and Gert had hoped they would become friends. But Gert hadn't gotten to the point where she felt comfortable asking for Chase's home number or inviting her to do anything. And then, suddenly, Chase had stopped coming. Gert wasn't sure why. As much as she liked the women in the group, most of them were a few years older than she. She hoped Chase would come back.

People like Chase—fiancées—had it worse than everyone, Gert thought. They hadn't even married their loved one yet. They had had to lose someone they loved before they'd officially become related. They didn't even get to call themselves widows. What *should* they be called? In this day and age, there needed to be a less clunky term than Bereaved Significant Other.

Gert noticed that the people in the group were getting up, and she realized the session was over. She'd been dazing again.

She had to stop doing that.

★ ★ ★

Todd called that afternoon.

Gert was scrubbing the house. When they'd first moved in, they had used a maid service once a week. She'd felt a little spoiled, but all of the neighbors in the condo building used the service, and it was something good to spend their money on when they were making more than enough of it. One day, Marc had been on the phone with his mother and had mentioned something about the maid coming, and his mother had had a fit, saying they were being lazy. Gert knew it was aimed at her. Marc's mother liked Gert, but she could also be hard on her. Gert had, after all, taken over the duty of raising her little boy. Marc's father was a big bear of a man who made bad jokes and always greeted everyone with a new dopey nickname. Marc had picked up this habit, with his own litany of nicknames. He and his father competed over who could make up the worst one. Gert missed Mr. Healy's cheerful face.

Gert had always felt much more comfortable around Marc's father than Marc's mother. Mrs. Healy was overbearing. Everything had to be the best. Marc and his older brothers were driven, all in finance and real estate, all hustling tirelessly. That's how they'd been raised. That's what they got praised for.

Gert pushed thoughts of the Healys out of her mind and moved the mop slowly across the kitchen floor. There was a tiny rainbow near a corner where the sunlight bent through a glass candy dish, and she mopped the spot.

A shrill sound startled Gert. The phone. She stared at it for two rings, then picked it up.

"Is Gert there?" a voice asked.

Gert knew instantly who it was. She smiled. If nothing else, Todd was disarming. Even if she wasn't going to date him, or anyone else right now, she certainly could be friends with him. She had felt incredibly comfortable talking to him at the bar. He was completely different from Marc, though. Marc was sure of himself, maybe even a little cocky. Todd was just Todd.

"It's the Sober Guy," Todd said.

"Ah," Gert said. "Is that what your friends call you?"

"Sometimes," Todd said. "They're always saying, 'Come on, just have one little drink.' They don't care that I'd lose my job. My company is like the CIA. They do drug tests when they hire you that can track marijuana you smoked two months ago."

"Better stick to crack," Gert joked, then winced, wondering if it was too sharp a comment to make to someone she barely knew. It would have made Marc smile, if he were there.

Todd laughed. "So how are you doing?"

Gert hadn't had anyone ask her that in weeks, except her parents, who were still trying to convince her to move back to the West Coast. She'd confirmed their worst fears right after college when she'd married a guy from Boston and moved to Queens.

"Not bad," Gert said.

"What are you doing today?"

"Just cleaning my place."

"I need to do that," Todd said. "My roommate's a slob. Do you live alone?"

"Yes," Gert said, balancing the phone on her shoulder so she could keep mopping. *Yes,* she thought. *I live in a condo with two bedrooms. The second one eventually would have been the baby's room. It's ridiculous that I live here, but I don't want to move.*

"How was your day?" Gert asked.

"Great," Todd said. "I ate lunch at this bar by my old job. And I just had tea, and the bartender looked at me like I was crazy, but I told her I'm not allowed to drink because of work, and you know what she guessed I must be? A brain surgeon. Do I look like a brain surgeon?"

"Anyone can look like a brain surgeon," Gert said.

"Wow. I feel so important now."

"What's your old job?"

"Oh. For a little while after college I was a courier in the diamond district. My friend's family owned a jewelry store.

They needed people they trusted to do those jobs, so we both worked there for a while, walking around the city transporting jewelry and hoping not to get mugged. It was kind of fun, and I got to hang out with my friend's family, who have this old-fashioned business that not a lot of people have anymore. One time, on a Friday after work, they took us to their apartment on the Lower East Side and they had a zillion relatives over and cooked Romanian food. It was incredible."

Gert realized that Todd liked long answers, long explanations. He wasn't concerned about boring her. It didn't mean he was full of himself—just that he wasn't constantly checking to see if he was saying and doing the right thing. He had no affectations, no pretensions.

She liked it.

The other line beeped, and Gert ignored it.

"Do you have to go?" Todd asked.

"No. But I am cleaning…."

"Okay. Well, what I wanted to ask was…do you want to have dinner some night?"

"Um…" Gert said, looking around the room. "I guess, maybe." She realized she was being too tentative. "I mean, sure. Why not?"

"Great," he said. "My schedule gets a little strange. I'm working nights the rest of the week, but I'm free after next weekend. Unless you wanted to get together tonight."

Gert thought putting it off for a week would be wise. She could use the week to work up to it. But looking around again, she realized she didn't have anything to do that night. She might as well go. Todd seemed harmless enough.

"Either way is fine," Gert said. "I didn't have any major plans tonight."

"Really?" Todd said. "Do you want to do it tonight? I don't want to push, but it might be nice to see you before my schedule gets crazy."

Gert was flattered. She accepted.

When she put down the phone, it rang instantly.

"Hey!" Hallie said.

"Hey," Gert said. "You sound excited. What's up?"

"Erika knows this bar where some of the Giants hang out. Do you want to come tonight?"

Gert hesitated. "I could," she said. "But I probably can't."

"Why not?" Hallie asked.

"Well," Gert said, "do you remember that guy Todd, from the bar?"

"Choo-Choo Boy?" Hallie suddenly seemed intrigued. "Did he call you? Did he ask you out?"

"Yes," Gert said. "He asked if I wanted to have dinner."

"That's great!" Hallie said. Gert was glad Hallie was excited for her. "It's at least a start," Hallie added. "When are you going?"

"Tonight," Gert said.

Hallie was quiet for a second.

"Tonight?" she said.

Gert hesitated. Maybe this hadn't been such a good idea after all. "I said I would," she said.

Hallie was quiet again.

"You haven't been out on a date in a long time," Hallie said. "Maybe you should have a powwow with me first to plot strategies."

"Okay."

They met at four outside a coffee shop. Hallie snuffed out her cigarette before entering. The New York smoking ban still wasn't to take effect for two months, but Hallie wanted to practice. Gert was glad for the ban, but kept her opinion to herself. It wasn't that she was a priss; it was just that secondhand smoke gave her a sore throat.

"Here's the thing," Hallie said, sitting down at a square white table with gold flecks in it. The coffee shop was filthy, but cozy. "You know that you can't accept a date for the same night. It makes you seem desperate."

"It's not a date," Gert protested. "It's just a friendly dinner.

Besides, Todd's going to be busy next week. His schedule's going to get crazy."

"With work? Or with dates?"

"With work."

"How do you know?"

"Why would Todd lie?" Gert said. "I just met him."

"I don't know." Hallie shrugged, winding paper from someone else's straw around her pinkie. "For some reason, he just struck me as a little off. I wouldn't be so trusting so soon. Believe me, I've seen what's out there. You have to be careful."

"I will," Gert said, knowing Hallie was only trying to help but wondering how she'd gotten so cynical. Todd was a nice guy, right?

Gert looked around. She noticed that many of the people in the coffee shop were reading the paper. But the women who were reading it kept peering over the top, to see who else might be there.

Hallie said, "I think I've met half the weirdos in Manhattan. And I think Erika's met the other half. I don't want you to get disillusioned."

"Did you ever think," Gert said, choosing her words carefully, "that maybe you and Erika try too hard and obsess too much? You strategize and analyze, and men can probably sense your frustrations."

Hallie looked hurt. "I can't act relaxed and happy with my station in life when I'm not," she said.

Gert wasn't sure what to say.

"Do you remember when I dated Steve for six months after college?" Hallie asked. "While I was dating him, guys hit on me all the time. And of course, I didn't need them, because I was with *him*. They must have sensed that I was happy. And then, after Steve and I broke up and I was miserable, no one ever came up to me. But I couldn't help being miserable. So there's a Spiral Deathtrap of Dating: When you're with someone, you look happy and relaxed, and thus, a lot more people than you need are attracted to you. When you're sulky and alone, no one is attracted to you, and thus, you stay sulky and alone. I can't look content when I'm not."

"I know you can't look happy all the time," Gert said. "Maybe what I'm getting at is that when you and Erika are together, you both come off as less approachable."

Hallie looked beyond Gert, at the wall. "That's not the real problem," she said. "The real problem is that the ratio of women to men around here is too high. I should move to Silicon Valley or Alaska, where the male-to-female ratio makes sense. Or, I could get silicone *implants*."

Gert cringed. "Guys hate silicone implants," she said.

"You know so much about guys," Hallie said to her, "but you've only really been with one."

It struck Gert as odd that Hallie and Erika always claimed to know so much more than she did about men, yet they were still single. They were always trumpeting their dating rules and they were still alone.

*There's a law Hallie should cite,* Gert thought. *Gert's Law of Dating: The more rules you cite about it, the less you really know about it.*

"Anyway," Hallie said, toying with a cigarette she didn't intend to light, "I want you to have a good time with Todd tonight."

Gert smiled. "Thanks," she said.

"But," Hallie continued, looking serious, "don't let your guard down. If a guy seems too good to be true, he usually is."

"Oh, I know it could end up a total disaster," Gert said, waving someone else's smoke away. "But we'll be in a public place. What could happen?"

"You have my cell phone number, right?" Hallie said. "Call me if there's any trouble. Even if I'm talking to Jeremy Shockey, I'll be there for you."

Gert laughed. "I will."

The houses across the street from Gert's were white and connected to each other. From window to window dripped a string of unlit Christmas lights, which normally hung there until just before Easter. On a dark, overcast day like that one, they looked like buds. Flurries coated the barren branches outside and made little hammocks in the corners of the windows. Not much of an accumulation was expected—it was too warm.

Gert stood in the room with Marc's trophies, staring across the street. She saw a little blond-haired girl peeking out a round third-story window. She remembered when the girl had been a tiny baby in a carriage. Seeing the infants in her neighborhood go from carriages to walking on their own two feet made Gert conscious of her age. Lots of things were making her conscious of that lately. She wasn't fond of the reminders.

The girl was part of an extended Greek family who lived in attached houses on the block. Gert's section of Queens, only a few subway stops east of Manhattan, was very Greek.

She returned to her bedroom, to her mirror.

The anticipatory feeling of a date was one of the nicest parts, she had always thought. You knew you were going to see someone you liked. You could scrub extra hard in the shower. You could get a haircut. You could stare at yourself in the mirror. Well, not for too long.

Even though Gert was just going to be friends with Todd, she still felt compelled to at least look half-decent for him.

She stared at her reflection and tried to figure out what she could say to him.

*I rode on a train once.*

Nah, that wouldn't do.

*My uncle used to work for Conrail.*

*Trains are cool. I've got a full complement of HO models.*

Somehow he'd see through the lie. And just because he worked on a train, didn't mean he collected them.

She could hum the song about "getting the train through" from *Sesame Street.* They could talk about kids' TV shows from the 1970s. Marc's oldest brother had been on *Zoom,* which was taped in Boston. That always impressed people of a certain age.

There she was, thinking about Marc again.

She had to stop.

How would she tell Todd about him?

She probably shouldn't mention Marc to Todd right away, she decided. The only way to talk about Marc was to give him his proper due, to tell everything that had happened. He wasn't something you could chat about like the news or weather. If it wasn't the right time to tell everything about him, you shouldn't broach it.

Okay. She needed a conversation topic.

The male canon. Oops—she'd left something off the list when she'd told Hallie and Erika about it: *Fletch*. Guys loved *Fletch*.

What were some lines from *Fletch?*

"Excuse me, miss? Can I borrow your towel? My car just hit a water buffalo."

Didn't really work too well in conversation.

It wasn't a good quote for tonight, anyway. It was too base. Guys didn't necessarily like girls to get too base. Except guys you'd been married to for five years and dated for three, whom you could say just about anything to. Who you could wrestle with at 10:00 a.m. during a blizzard when the city was locked down and the mayor had ordered everyone to stay home. They should have worked on having a baby that day, just like everyone else. They were both waiting for promotions at work. Just one year each at their new salaries, and then they were going to try. There was always more you could have. More, more, more. And all of a sudden, you'd lose the most important thing of all.

"Hi," Todd said, coming into the entrance of Sal's, an Italian restaurant in Chelsea near the movie theater. He was wearing sneakers, but he looked like he'd just gotten a haircut, and he was smiling.

"Hi," Gert said, standing inside the door. The restaurant was moderate-sized, with a family of six chattering near the back. The tablecloths and walls were a rich red. A waitress appeared and led them back.

"I was just on the subway," Todd told Gert, "and some woman insisted I'd gone to school with her brother. She kept saying my name was Cody. The whole ride, she stared at me, going, 'You're *sure* you're not Cody?'"

"You should have showed her your driver's license."

"Imagine if I pulled it out, and it said 'Cody,'" Todd said. "That would be freaky. Like *The Twilight Zone*."

"I loved *The Twilight Zone!*"

"Me, too. The old episodes."

As they sat down, Gert was glad the conversation had started easily. She was also grateful for the dinner-and-movie date. It was simple, it was inexpensive, and it guaranteed that after dinner you wouldn't be asked back to the guy's apartment to watch a video—a common male strategy in college that had meant something else.

"I like this place," Todd said. "The food's good, and the prices are right."

So he was practical. Gert was glad. She didn't like when people tried to impress her with fancy restaurants that provided mouse-sized meals. Marc's co-workers at the brokerage firm had taken them to places like that all the time. She had always left starving.

"So," Todd said, "thanks for coming out on such short notice."

He seemed a little nervous. Gert smiled. "I wasn't doing anything special," she said. Ooh! Her friends would smack her for admitting she was alone on a Saturday. She added, "I could have gone out with my friends tonight, but I can see them anytime."

"How long have you known them?"

"Since college," she said. "Well, Hallie since college. Erika is her high school friend."

"Who was the one with big hair?" Todd asked.

Gert laughed. Everyone had such varying perceptions of looks. Erika had been dressed to kill that night, and Hallie had been practically naked, but what Todd had noticed was big hair.

"I didn't think either of them had big hair," Gert said.

"I didn't mean any offense," Todd said. "Brian was the one who thought so. I didn't notice anyone having big hair."

"That's okay," Gert said. "I think Erika was sort of interested in Brian."

"Girls always like Brian. He's engaged to a woman he works with."

"Then why was he at the bar?"

"Why not? We were waiting to meet friends."

The waitress brought their water, and she stood at the table expectantly. "You ready?" she asked.

"I guess we should pick up our menus first," Todd said, smiling, and the waitress nodded and took off.

Todd added, "Brian lived in England for a year and he said they never give you water when you sit down. You have to ask for it or you'll never ever get it."

"Really?" Gert said. Then, in a barely passable British accent, she added, "That's rather peculiar, don't you think?"

"I rather believe so," Todd said.

"A shame, old boy."

They ordered appetizers and talked more. Todd spoke animatedly about his job. He said his company's trains ran from Croxton Yards in Jersey City up to Binghamton, New York. It was a six-hour run, and usually it was just him on the train, plus an engineer who was driving it. There was a children's hospital that they passed in upstate New York each time, and the kids would always wave out the window at the train. Sometimes, they'd make a sign, like *Blow Your Horn!* This was Todd's favorite part of the run.

Todd said to Gert, "Do you like *your* job?"

Gert told him about working for a marketing and public relations firm that handled only pharmaceutical companies. She had majored in communications in college, but she wasn't sure what she'd do afterward. She'd finally found a job as an assistant at a PR firm. The pay was low and the people seemed phony, so she kept her eye on the want ads. Then she saw an ad to be the assistant to a vice president of a different firm. The pay would be much higher, and the building was right next to a midtown subway stop, but she'd be less focused on creative work and more on meeting her boss's needs. Still, she had been happy enough outside of work that she didn't really care what she was doing during those hours. If she wanted, she could work on a portfolio and move over to the creative side. She actually had wanted to do that for a few years, and had tons of good ideas for product promotions. But for some reason she hadn't gotten around to finishing her portfolio yet.

"Are you guys responsible for the goodies?" Todd asked. "Like the notepads and rubber pill toys and clipboards doctors get with the names of drugs on them?"

Gert laughed. She usually just got blank stares when she told people what she did. At least Todd was creative. "Our company doesn't make them, but it does research to see if they're a good way to increase product name recognition," she said. "We might get twelve people in a room and bring out a tray full of those toys, then take them out of the room and see which ones they remembered."

"Wow." Todd closed his eyes. "I remember…that you're wearing a red shirt and you have long hair, and dimples."

Gert smiled shyly.

The waitress set down a bowl of calamari, along with a huge, soft stuffed red pepper. Gert was hungry. She hadn't eaten Italian food in a while.

They made up their plates, and they ended up talking so rapidly that Gert only ate half her meal. She barely even tasted it. She hadn't expected to enjoy Todd's company so much. He told her that if the train broke down anywhere along the route, whether it was pouring rain or sloppy snow or in the middle of a dangerous city at 3:00 a.m., it was his job to jump out with a flashlight and walk the length of the train to find out where the problem was. "Some of those trains are a mile long," Todd said. "And you don't want to get out and walk the length of a train in a desolate area at 3:00 a.m."

"I wouldn't try it," Gert said.

She told him about the worst part of her job, dealing with her often-cranky boss, Missy, and about the odd cast of characters at her old job. They had been so brain-dead that after a certain point, she'd stopped smiling for fear they'd complain about not getting the joke.

"So how did you end up in your line of work, anyway?" Gert asked Todd.

"Well," he said, wiping his mouth, "it was strange. It wasn't a job that would have occurred to me at all."

"So what happened?"

He hooked some linguine around his fork. "I majored in history in college," he said, "and I wasn't that great a student in school, but history was the one thing I was interested in. I love finding out how things came to be. There are so many stories. I knew I wouldn't have lots of jobs lined up after graduation with that major, though. For a while I led tours in a museum part-time. Then I was reading the help-wanted ads in the paper one Sunday morning, and I saw this boxed ad at the bottom of the page for an information session for a train company, and something kind of clicked. Working for the railroad is kind of a cliché, but I'd never actually thought you could do it."

"It seems like a job people had a hundred years ago," Gert said.

"Exactly!" Todd said. "That's what I thought. But that's what interested me. There's such beauty in trains. Cars and planes and buses change every year, but if you look at a passing freight train, with its string of yellow and orange and brown boxcars, it looks the same as it did fifty years ago. And trains travel through the most historical points in the country, too. They're like moving museums of America. But when I first saw the ad, I didn't know if I should go to the info session. It didn't seem like a job that people who went to college did. I tried to talk myself out of it."

"Yeah…."

"But I realized something: I had majored in history because I loved it. And now I could look into a job I might love, too. My heart told me to go."

"And you went," Gert said.

"And I went. The recruiters actually try to talk you out of it. They tell you about the crazy scheduling, the long hours, the drug testing, and the hard work. But everything they said to scare us off was something that made me want to do the job more."

"That's great," Gert said. "A lot of people don't follow their heart."

"Especially about work."

He asked Gert where she'd grown up. She said she was from L.A., and that her parents were still there. She said she'd come east for college. She didn't say she'd stayed and married a Bostonian, though. She told Todd that her younger brother was still in L.A., and that he'd done nothing for two years after high school and was now waiting tables. She told him about her best friend from childhood, Nancy, who lived there with a husband and two kids. She said she usually talked to her about once a week, and the same with her parents.

Todd told her that the friend she had met at the bar, Brian, was someone he'd known since elementary school. He said he only had a few close friends, but once he got along with someone, they were friends for life.

Gert realized by the time they'd finished dessert that she had gone for more than an hour without thinking of Marc. It was the first time in a year and a half that that had happened. Even when she was sleeping. She'd had a dream two days earlier, in fact, in which she was sure he was right next to her. She could even smell him. Then she awoke. She wanted to crawl back into the dream. She wanted so desperately to fall back to sleep.

When Todd asked whether she still wanted to see a movie, she was glad, because she'd been wavering on it. What she really wanted to do was find out more things about him—not sit in a theater with her mouth shut. But she wasn't going to say that, because then he might suggest going back to his place, and that would ruin everything.

"Well," she said, "it is pretty late."

"That's what I was thinking," Todd said. "I hate to be a wet blanket, but I have to go to work at 5:00 a.m. tomorrow. Could we do it another time, though?"

He wasn't trying to get her back to his apartment! And he wanted to see her again. She hadn't botched the date. What luck!

"Sure," she said. "That sounds good."

"Do you want to take a walk before we head home?"

It was bitter cold outside. He took her hand for a second, without thinking, and then let go when they got near the waterfront. "What's out there?" he asked.

"Water," Gert said.

He laughed. "I knew you were smart," he said. "It looks like an island."

"Long Island?"

"I don't know."

There was a bench facing the water, and they sat down. She wondered if he was going to ask The Question. At what point did guys ask women about their ex-boyfriends and past relationships? It didn't happen on a first date, right? She wasn't sure.

The women in her support group had talked about this: If you met someone new, at what point did you tell him that your husband had died? For the older women, it wasn't much of an issue, because their suitors generally figured they were either divorced or widowed and asked about it. But with younger women, it wasn't expected at all. And Gert had found that when you told someone such news, particularly young people, they often had no idea what to say. Sometimes they just stared at her, stunned. It was almost as if they were waiting for *her* to comfort *them*.

But Todd didn't ask about Gert's former boyfriends. He asked about her friends, her college, her dreams. He told her that he figured that someday he'd have kids, travel and see the world—not by train—and be a good person so that he'd be satisfied when he got old and looked back on his life. He said what was most important to him was to be with the people he cared about and make them happy.

He was simple, Gert thought. Much simpler than Marc.

But he was the kind of guy, she thought, that someone could fall in love with.

Gert found out Todd was younger than she was—twenty-six. Hallie had a "Rule of Twenty-Seven." If a guy was still single after twenty-seven, she said, there must be something wrong with him. If he was decent, it was unlikely that he'd even get that far. So once a woman surpassed the age of twenty-seven, she would always be dating guys younger than her.

Todd was Gert's brother's age, which she found a little strange. It was like dating one of her brother's meatheaded friends. But Todd wasn't anything like her brother. Gert loved her brother, but he could definitely be a meathead sometimes.

They made plans to see a movie the weekend after next. Then Todd gave Gert a quick kiss on the cheek.

She could still smell his cologne and feel the brush of his stubble afterward. She hadn't realized how much she'd missed that.

# Chapter

3

"You can't start dating the first person you meet," Hallie said.

They were at a dingy coffee shop on the Upper West Side, near Hallie's apartment.

"Did Brian say anything about me?" Erika asked Gert. "I don't want to date him…I just want to know why he didn't like me."

"I'll ask the Saturday after next," Gert said, feeling suddenly tired of Erika. She elected to forget the "big hair" comment.

"But you were supposed to come to a party with us on that Saturday!" Hallie said. "You can't go out with him that day. Can't you see Todd on Sunday?"

"He's working on Sunday," Gert said. "He's working for a week straight after that."

"Now she knows his schedule," Erika said.

"They'll have to have their wedding when he's not on call," Hallie said.

"They won't be able to have alcohol at the reception," Erika said, "because Todd can't drink."

"Then I'm not coming," Hallie said. "How can a single girl get through a friend's wedding without alcohol?"

"Will you guys stop!" Gert said. "We're not getting married."

"You act like it."

"You know, all the two of you do is complain," Gert said. "It almost seems like you're upset that I spent an evening with someone nice."

There was silence.

"You know we just want you to be happy," Hallie said.

"Yeah," Erika said. "We know what guys are like. We don't want you to get hurt."

Gert didn't want that either. But sometimes it hurt to get up in the morning. Whatever was coming couldn't be much worse.

Every other Christmas, Gert and Marc had stayed with Marc's parents in their huge warm house in Massachusetts, where all four brothers had grown up. Gert loved that house. It held oodles of guestrooms, a fireplace and long slurpy couches you could fall asleep in. It was in an upscale waterfront hamlet just north of Boston with gaslights on the main streets and shanties near the water. During holidays, relatives practically oozed from the walls: Cousins, nieces and nephews, all asking Gert when she was going to have a baby. She had always said, "Soon."

Nowadays, she sometimes felt like she had a gaping hole inside of her, ready to be filled with something living. She used to look at Marc and think that she couldn't wait to see what kind of person would come from them.

This past year, on both Thanksgiving and Christmas, the Healys hadn't invited her to the house. She and Marc had routinely stayed on the East Coast for one holiday and then gone to her parents' in L.A. for the other. But now, she hadn't heard from Marc's parents in almost five months. She still had their last name. She had been officially part of the family. Yet, suddenly, because of one day, half of her support network was gone.

Going home to L.A. for both holidays had been especially hard. Gert's brother and his girlfriend were there. Gert was alone. After bluffing her way through dinner, she'd gone up to her childhood bedroom, lay on her mattress surrounded by purple walls and cried.

She remembered the times that Marc had stayed with her there on holidays, how they had both crammed onto her single bed in the room with the stuffed animals and purple walls, and how funny that was. He used to scrounge through her closet to find old diaries and report cards and use them to tease her. "'Gert's penmanship has improved slightly, but she needs help following directions,'" Marc read one time in an authoritative voice, linking it to the way she'd botched a bisque recipe the previous weekend. "Oh, look," he said. "A poem: 'I Love My Fish.' Aw, how cute—you drew fins on the 'O' in love, to make it look like a fish! No wonder you flunked handwriting." But as much as he teased, he was unrelenting in wanting to see every single thing in her closet. Gert sometimes felt as though she had actually kept all those things to show someone someday, if she was lucky enough to find someone who cared enough about her to want to know what she'd been like as a kid. And he had. He'd gone through everything, asking incessant questions. Marc was driven in everything he did.

Once, at Marc's house, Gert had gone through his things, too. It was only fair. He had packed most of them away in the basement before heading off to college. She was delighted to find that he had listed the contents of each box very carefully. He was super-organized and super-particular. All his baseball cards were in order, all his die-cast cars were in order. She teased him constantly as she burrowed through the boxes. He'd even alphabetized his comic books.

She also found photos of him growing up. There was one of him at his high school graduation in wire-rimmed glasses, looking younger but just as serious. His short brown hair was neatly cut, and he was wearing a suit and tie. Very neat, very particular, very handsome.

Marc's particularities had extended into adulthood. There was a certain steakhouse near their college in Pennsylvania that he had loved. So a couple of times a year, he would wake up in their New York apartment on a sunny Saturday and randomly decide it was time for a "steak break." He'd drive the two of them three hours back there for dinner. After relaxing and enjoying their meal, they'd drive the three hours home. Marc was such an adventurer, Gert thought. And he took such good care of her, too. But she also knew how to support *him* when he needed it. She filled in all his blanks.

Another thing about Marc was that he was big on looking after his friends. He consistently went out of his way to help them move, to study, to work on projects. A year after graduation, his best friend, the baby-faced Craig, was in Illinois at graduate school teaching economics to freshmen. Marc and Gert took a road trip out there. Marc forced Craig to bring them to one of his classrooms to give them a mock lesson, so they could see exactly how Craig taught his students. Marc delighted in other people's fancies. But at the end of the day, when he needed someone to rest his head against, it was Gert. Heading back in the car, she would look over at him, his Red Sox baseball cap hovering over his tired eyes, and she'd squeeze his right shoulder.

Now she would never go to the steakhouse in Pennsylvania. She'd never get to reach over and squeeze his shoulder while he was driving. And she had no reason to head up to Boston to visit the warm house with the fireplace and the huge slurpy couches.

"It's like you don't just lose *him,*" said Brenda, the nurse, at the support group that weekend. "You lose his whole family. You see them at services and memorials right after, but if you didn't have a baby with him, your in-laws stop needing to see you. It ends up being an exchange of cards on holidays. It's like, for years they cared about you, but it was only because you were part of *him.*"

"We never had kids," Gert said. "I always think that if we'd had kids, I'd still hear from them all the time. They'd be inviting me up there or coming down to visit. Now they act like we were never even related in the first place."

Arden looked angry. "We have this society that makes you feel like it's okay to defer everything," she said. "I have a friend who'd been living with her boyfriend for almost six years. They lost him in the Pentagon, and the two of them hadn't even gotten engaged yet. Six *years.* Now the relationship counts for nothing in anyone's eyes. She feels like she doesn't even have a right to the memories."

Gert thought again of Chase, who'd lost her fiancé in the towers. Chase hadn't been there in six weeks now. Gert wanted to ask Brenda if she had her contact number, so she could make sure Chase was okay. But she knew she probably wouldn't ask.

"You put things off, and poof, you wish you hadn't waited so long," Michele said. "But I have friends who got married and had their kids young, and they always tell me they think they gave up their youth too soon. You never know what's going to happen. You just have to do what you feel is right and not sit around having regrets."

Stephanie, who was a personal trainer, said, "What about my biological clock? I'm thirty-five, and I still can't imagine when I'll be psychologically ready to date again. If I start two years from now, and I meet someone, it will probably be at least a year or two before we get married. By then I'll be thirty-eight. Too old to have kids. For the rest of my life."

"Honey, you can have kids these days till you're fifty," Brenda said.

"No, you can't."

"Yes, you can."

"That's a medical falsehood perpetuated by the media."

"No, it's not."

"Yes, it is. It's…"

Gert wasn't in the mood for this debate. Her gaze moved to the wall of the community center where the meetings were held. There were finger paintings all over it from the daycare program that was in the building. One of the paintings said in round, childish letters, "TODD." Gert smiled, thinking Todd was actually a little innocent and childlike.

She thought of telling the women in the group about going out with him. But she was feeling guilty about it. The women always talked about how they couldn't imagine dating some-one again. What right did she have to have dinner with a man—and what right did she have to actually enjoy it?

"Having a baby alone just isn't something I'm going to do," Arden said.

Everyone else got quiet.

Gert found the silence uncomfortable.

"Well, let's move on," Brenda said. "What else happened this week?"

Gert saw no volunteers among the ten women there. She started reluctantly. "I had dinner with someone," she said. "On Saturday."

The other women leaned closer. "A man?" Brenda asked. Gert nodded. "Your first date since…?"

"Yes," Gert said. "But it wasn't really a date. Just a friendly dinner. I met him when I was out with friends, and he asked me to dinner, and I figured I might as well try, just to see what it was like."

"And how was it?"

She shrugged. "His name's Todd. He seemed nice…."

"But he's not your husband," Brenda said.

"No," Gert said, shaking her head. "No one could be. And he's very different from Marc. But in a way, I was glad. If he was anything like him I'd have felt like I was cheating."

"Don't ever feel like that," Brenda said. "Don't any of you feel like that."

"There's at least room in our hearts for new friends," Michele said.

"Are you going to see him again?" Leslie asked.

"I think so," Gert said. "It's strange, but I feel like I want to learn more about him. But just last week we were all saying how we couldn't possibly imagine dating again. What right do I have to go out with *anyone* when it's only been a year and a half?"

They all got quiet.

"I have a confession," Michele said. "I know I said I couldn't date for years. But sometimes, when I'm in bed at night, I miss being held."

"I do, too," Leslie said.

"It's odd," Brenda said. "I think the better your relationship was with your husband, the more you probably will need to find that closeness again. It's just that the idea of being with a stranger repulses us. What we really want is to be with our husbands. But it's impossible. Right now, a fantasy seems better than a real person."

"When are you going to see him again?" Arden asked.

"Next weekend," Gert said.

"Those friends you mention," Brenda said, "make sure you don't let their notions of dating and five-nights-a-week partying push you. If you need four months to get to know this guy, to get to the point when you so much as want to kiss him, you take four months. Gert has to do what's right for Gert."

Gert smiled. Brenda often lapsed into social worker–speak.

"Are those girls younger than you?" Michele asked. "When you talk about them, they seem like it."

"No," Gert said. "But sometimes, I feel about five years older than them."

"It's not that you're five years older," Arden said. "It's that they're emotionally five years younger than you. If you're between twenty-five and thirty-five and you've never been married, you get to subtract five years from your age. So your friends are twenty-three or twenty-four. And if you have children before you're thirty-five, you *add* five years to your age."

"What if you're a widow?" Brenda asked.

"You add a hundred," someone said, and all the women laughed.

★ ★ ★

At work, someone had left a card on Gert's desk. It was a congratulations card for a guy who worked on a different floor. Gert was supposed to put ten dollars in it for a wedding gift.

Gert hated these cards. Hallie had told her once that in China, it was the opposite. In China, if something great happened to you, you took everyone *else* in the office out to dinner; they didn't take you. That made sense—after all, you were the lucky one. You were the one who was getting married or promoted.

Marrying the person you loved was not a struggle. The struggle was being able to keep going after you'd lost yours, or not finding one at all. The people who needed cards were those who weren't engaged, those who weren't about to have a baby—those who were miserable, single, alone.

"Congratulations," Gert wrote unenthusiastically in the card, and stuck in her ten dollars.

She got up, sauntered down the hall and pitched the card onto the desk of Leon, the long-haired fiftyish nihilist proofreader. "No backs!" Gert said, and raced back down the hall.

"Awww, I *hate* these!" she heard him say.

As she ran, she looked at the tops of buildings: The GE building, the Paine Webber building, some brown towers she didn't know the name of.

At work, the people were mostly older. She had always been glad that she'd been married and hadn't counted on work as a social outlet. No one in her office went out after hours. The only person there whom she really had thought of as a friend was her boss, but even that had changed over the last few months. Missy was in her mid-forties and still dressed sexily, always in skirts and off-black panty hose. She had an evil sense of humor. But for the past few months, she'd had mood swings that could have registered on the Richter scale. Gert thought it had to do with relationship issues. The rumor was that Missy was having an affair with the chiseled young guy on the ninth floor who worked in the mailroom. There were elevators near the back of the building that could be stopped between floors without setting off alarms.

What else could she say about Missy? Missy had been saying for years that she was going to get separated from her husband, Dennis, but she never had. Gert had met Dennis at the office Christmas party. He was a sad sack. He hated dancing, so he always stood near the buffet table watching Missy dance up a storm with every guy in the company. Gert wondered why Dennis didn't try a little harder to keep up with Missy, looks-wise. Not that he should have had to. But he could have at least tried.

After fobbing off the congratulations card, Gert sat back down and stared at her in-box. The accounts that her boss handled involved baldness remedies, skin creams and hemorrhoid preparations. Not really Gert's preferences, but she had, from time to time, thought up some pretty funny campaigns for all of them. Watching British comedies with Marc often got her thinking creatively. Someday, Gert could take over those accounts if Missy moved to others. Or she could move to other accounts if she had a portfolio of creative work. But Missy was there to stay, and Gert had put off starting creative work for a long time. There were only so many things you could do at once. She'd been fulfilled enough in the past and had never really expected to get most of her satisfaction nine-to-five, anyway. She went out with Marc's co-workers, took road trips to see friends, celebrated milestones with both of their families—siblings' graduations, new babies—cooked together, bought a condo. She had felt feminine doing these things, even. Now she felt like she had to be the man *and* woman in dealing with every daily chore and struggle.

Before Marc died, she had been toying with some portfolio ideas that he'd encouraged. But after the accident she'd been uninspired to do anything that disturbed the stasis of other facets of her life, particularly work. Tragedy could certainly make you lose interest in the fast track.

\* \* \*

"Oh my God!" Hallie sang into the phone to Gert that night. "You have to get over to Erika's apartment. We're reading Challa's Web site!"

Gert was in bed, kicking her heels and watching a romantic movie that was making her feel more depressed than romantic. She had to be careful with forms of entertainment these days. Things that were romantic made her miss Marc. Things that were witty made her miss Marc. Things with action made her miss Marc. She was on a long main course of light and fluffy.

"I was watching a movie," Gert told Hallie.

"What movie?"

"*Before Sunrise,*" Gert said.

"Oh my God, you never saw that?" Hallie asked. "That was ten years ago."

Marc would never have seen an Ethan Hawke movie. Especially one about Ethan taking his brooding self on a train through Europe. Gert thought about all the movies she could catch up on now, and then hated herself for the thought. She often thought about the movies Marc would have wanted to see, the ones that were coming out that spring: Both the *Matrix* and *X-Men* sequels. Every single time she heard about them, she felt bad, thinking about how excited Marc would have been. If he were there, they'd be strategizing about how to get to see them both on their opening days.

"I guess I just never rented it," Gert said of *Before Sunrise*.

"Well, I don't want to take you away, but you have to see the Web site," Hallie said. "We're going to order dumplings for dinner and plot strategy."

Gert was getting tired of the movie, anyway. Maybe watching other people's evil machinations would take her mind off her pain. She was going to have to force herself to recover, even if it meant pushing herself into uncomfortable situations.

"That sounds good," Gert said, pulling herself up.

On the N train, Gert remembered the corollary to Hallie's Law of Maximum Exposure: If you're single, being outside is always better than staying in, even if you have nowhere to go. You could meet someone getting on the bus, or standing in line buying your shriveled bagel.

Gert decided that Hallie should either forget these dating rules completely, or put them on a list and publish them. Even if they were myopic and pessimistic, at least someone would find them funny. Maybe Hallie could post them on a Web site for bitter wymyn.

Erika's apartment was a studio in Harlem. It hadn't always been hers alone. Erika had gotten it with a friend right after college. They had hung a blanket across the room to separate it. Eventually, the other girl got married and moved out, and Erika was earning enough money at the design firm to allow her to take the big step of living in the prewar hovel alone.

It was the coziest apartment Gert had seen in Manhattan. Two of the walls were exposed brick, and there was artwork everywhere. Some of it was stuff Erika had bought, and some was stuff she had designed. Gert knew that both Erika and Ben had been big fans of modern art. Ben had always wanted to be an architect, although from what Gert heard, he had never ended up going to graduate school.

Gert knocked on Erika's front door. She heard cackling inside, then steps. When the door swung open, Erika was there, looking pretty and smiling at Gert. Her blond hair was streaked with a few dark lowlights, and it was back in a ribbon. Graphic designers always dressed well.

"Gertie!" Erika said, and she threw her arms around her and hugged her. Gert felt a surge of warmth. She realized why Hallie always wanted to please Erika. If Erika was in a happy mood, she could make you feel like the most accepted and wanted person in the world—like you were as glamorous as she was. "I'm so glad you're here," Erika said. "We need you."

Maybe Erika wasn't so bad.

Gert followed her to the far corner of the room. Hallie was

already sitting in front of Erika's enormous Macintosh. It had little color printouts taped to it. They were impressive designs.

"This is great!" Hallie said. "This is so great!"

"What?"

"Take a look."

Gert peered closely at the screen.

## TO WHOEVER KEEPS POSTING THE OBNOXIOUS MESSAGES

I know your the same person because their all coming from the same server I checked it out. Even if you use diff. screen names you can't fool me. Your unintelligent and unoriginal to. You obviously don't like me and I'm not sure what I ever did to you, but tell me and maybe we can come to an understanding about it otherwise I'll delete every one of your postis.—C.S.

"You have to help me," Erika said to Gert. "We need to write some posts, but from different computers. You have a computer at home, right?"

"Yeah…" Gert said uneasily. She didn't like where this was going.

"I need to create more screen names and send messages from different servers," Erika said. "That way, it won't be coming from just mine and the Internet café. It'll really drive Challa nuts. I'm going to write that I'm some girl who had an affair with Ben on a business trip."

Hallie's mouth dropped open, and her gaze moved from the screen to Erika's face. "You've mentioned that before," she said. "But you said you'd never do it."

Erika said, "This girl is living my life, and wasting Ben's. She's stupid and needs too much attention. She took my whole life. *I* should be having kids with him right now."

Gert felt nervous. "What if you write that," Gert said, "and she takes the site down?"

Erika was quiet for a second.

"Don't you understand?" she said, her voice rising. "Don't you get it? That would be the most wonderful thing in the world."

Erika sounded ready to cry. Gert felt embarrassed for her, so she stared at the floor.

"If Challa took this stupid site down," Erika said, "then I wouldn't have to maniacally check it every day to see what Ben's doing. I wouldn't have to know everything that's going on in his life. But I just have to. I have to figure out what he's doing now, and whether I did the right thing. I just *wish* the site didn't exist. But if it does, I have to check it."

Gert considered suggesting that Erika *pretend* the site didn't exist. But she knew people couldn't trick themselves in matters of the heart. Hell, she'd certainly tried. She had dutifully repeated positive messages as her therapist had instructed. "If I get through today, I'll have accomplished something." "Marc would want me to be happy." "There was nothing I could've done." "Everything happens for a reason." These were the lies she'd told herself.

"I know you guys think this is crazy," Erika said. "But Ben and I honestly had something. I can't just forget about it."

As the three of them sat on the subway heading toward Gert's condo, it occurred to Gert that she should have pretended her computer was broken. They would have believed her. There was a nasty computer virus going around called the "Kiss Virus." It looked like an e-card that said, "KISS…" but when you clicked the link, it said, "…your hard drive goodbye!"

Gert told herself it wouldn't be so bad. Maybe Erika would just blow off steam for a few minutes and be done with it. At least Erika and Hallie were helping Gert get out of her apartment. She had to cut them more slack. This was Erika's strange method of getting closure.

Gert knew about closure. It was a favorite topic in the support group—those women who wished they'd said more to their husbands before they'd died. Gert had her own fantasies, in fact, about that day, all the ways she should have stopped the chain of events that led to Marc's death.

"Did you tell Gert about your date?" Erika said to Hallie, pushing a newspaper away on the subway seat.

"Oh, it's barely worth telling," Hallie said. She turned to Gert. "This guy from work set me up with his friend the other night. He's into seafood, so we went to a seafood place."

"Sounds good…" Gert said.

"Well, it started off that way," Hallie said, "but…two things. One, he wore a Tweety Bird shirt. It had an emblem of Tweety on the shirt where an alligator would be."

"At least he's different," Gert offered.

"Yeah, but," Hallie said, "he's totally obsessed with Bugs Bunny and Warner Brothers cartoons."

"That's like a secondary male canon thing," Gert said. "A lot of guys are into Bugs Bunny cartoons. Remember Marc's best friend, Craig? He had all the tapes."

"I do remember Craig, and I know some guys are into Bugs Bunny," Hallie said. "But would they wear Tweety Bird on a first date?"

"I guess not," Gert admitted.

"I think the more I go out, the more easily I get irritated by guys who don't make an effort," Hallie said. "I spend so much energy worrying about impressing them, but they don't even do the basics to look half-decent."

"What was the second bad thing about him?" Gert asked.

"Oh. He kept saying things about us being on a first date, or pointing out that things were awkward, even when I didn't feel that way," Hallie said. "Like, our meals came, and the minute I put food in my mouth, he said, 'So, have you ever gone camping?' And I said, 'No, I guess I was never really into that.' And he was quiet for a second, and then he said, 'Wow, this is awkward.'"

"There should be a rule," Erika said, putting her finger in the air, "that if you actually point out that something is awkward on a date, you immediately get ejected from your chair."

Gert was glad that she had felt comfortable with Marc, and then with Todd, right away.

"I guess I'll go on one more date with him," Hallie said. "Everyone deserves a second date."

"Not everyone," Erika said.

"I'm perfecting a top-secret innovative method to meet men, anyway," Hallie said. "No more of these horrible blind dates. Both of you will think I'm a genius when you hear my idea."

"You said something about this last week," Erika said. "Tell me already."

"I'll tell you soon," Hallie said. "I promise. I'm working on it. You'll both love it."

Gert didn't know whether to look forward to it or dread it.

Erika was tapping away at the keys of the computer in Marc's trophy room.

"My new screen name is Baltimora," she announced. "It's in honor of the group that sang that 'Jungle Love' song in the eighties, which was on the radio when the alarm went off this morning, so now it's stuck in my head. And boy, this'll drive Challa crazy."

"I want to write some," Hallie said. "You said I could write some."

Gert walked over to her window and pulled down the shade.

"The two of us can argue with each other!" Erika said, cracking up. "We'll both say that we're flight attendants who gave oral sex to Ben on his business trip to Texas, and that he was the best customer we've ever had."

"That's mean," Gert said, wondering why she was trying to give Erika the benefit of the doubt. "What if you were married to him and living your life, and some girl kept writing this stuff to you?"

Hallie and Erika got silent.

"Gertie," Hallie said.

"Gert," Erika said, "if I had married him and was as happy as this girl seems to be, I would not need so much freaking attention that I'd write a Web site about myself every day. She needs to appreciate what she has instead of rubbing our noses in her syrupy slop."

Hallie and Erika switched off writing messages, and they laughed hysterically. At the end, the exchange said:

THIS SITE IS STUPID AND P.S. LEARN TO SPELL. BEN IS A LITTLE "TO" SMART FOR YOU.—Baltimora

Hey, leave them alone. The two of them are happy. Ben told me so when we did it in the bathroom on Continental flight 221 to Houston.—XSGIRRRL

WAS THAT TO "BUSH" INTERCONTINENTAL AIRPORT? GET IT—BaLT.

We're lucky Ben has so many business trips. He showed me this site to tell me how annoying his wife is. Don't get me mad, honey, or hack hack hack! —XSGIRRRL

"They could file a harassment complaint on you," Gert said.

"It's a public forum," Erika said. "There's no law against calling someone annoying on their Web site. Besides, the worst that can happen is that Challa feels as bad today as I do every day."

Gert suddenly understood. Erika wanted to jar Challa a little, make her less smug. Deep inside, Gert couldn't help but know what Challa's life was like. When she'd had Marc she never thought about being alone, about how hard it could be. Now Gert saw women walking with their husbands or complaining about their boyfriends, and she wanted to shake them and say, "Do you realize what you have?"

"I'm going to go back to using the Internet cafés to send these next time, anyway," Erika said. "They're less traceable."

Gert was still pretty concerned about what Erika might do next.

# Chapter

## 4

*I am definitely too old for this,* Gert thought.

*I am too old to have get-togethers with friends who sit around and make "boy lists" like something out of a Judy Blume book, and rate every guy we ever dated on a scale of one to ten. I'm too old to wake up every Sunday morning and look out my window at all the couples getting into their cars to drive to the suburbs to visit their in-laws while I'm going to stay home in my pajamas reading the newspaper.*

"Hey, I know what we can do," Hallie said on her couch, flipping through *Cosmo.* "Let's take the Purity Test."

"You guys gave me the Purity Test last week," Erika said. "I got an F."

Gert was on the far end of the couch, looking at the photos in *Entertainment Weekly.* Hallie's wicker basket of magazines was always a good distraction.

Hallie laughed. "Let's play truth-or-dare, then," she said.

"As if there's something you *haven't* done," Erika said, stretching out on the rug.

"Speak for yourself," Hallie said. "I guess you want to go first."

"Maybe I want to do a dare instead," Erika said, pulling a low-fat Pop-Tart off the table.

"Well, we'll just play 'truth,'" Hallie said.

"You always pulled this in high school," Erika sighed. "Okay. Give me a 'truth.'"

"How many naked male members have you seen in your life?" Hallie said. "*Not* counting relatives."

Gert couldn't help but think of her own answer. It was a pretty low number. But she'd never really minded....

"Come on," Hallie said. "How many Johnsons have you seen *au naturel?*"

Erika said, "Less than...ten. No, wait. Less than eleven."

"Gert?"

"It's Erika's turn," Gert said. "We don't all have to go."

"Everyone has to answer in 'truth,'" Hallie said.

"According to rules, which Hallie just made up," Erika said wryly, polishing off half of the Pop-Tart.

Gert thought about adding on a few but decided to go with honesty. "Less than...three."

"You guys are hedging," Hallie said, exasperated. "How are we going to learn each other's secrets if we can't be honest?"

"Well, *you* answer it," Erika said. She shot Gert a smile. It felt nice to be liked by her.

"I've seen nine and a half," Hallie said simply.

"Nine and a *half?*"

"Yes."

"But—"

"No follow-up questions allowed," Hallie said. "I answered mine. We have to move on now. Rules are rules."

Heading home on the subway, Gert heard cars honking and an ambulance in the distance.

She thought of some "truth" questions she'd really like to ask Hallie and Erika.

*Did you resent me while I was married? Are you worried because there's a possibility with Todd? And about Todd: Am I supposed to feel okay when I see him this weekend? How have you dealt with being alone? How can you be happy if you're not with someone you love? Hanging out, eating your favorite foods and trading "truths"—is this what passes for happiness when you're single? If neither of you ever fell in love again, would you find a way to compensate with other hobbies and activities—grow a new limb?*

Gert had thought about asking them directly. But they seemed to only want to play games and joke around. Everything was a joke to them. She didn't want it to always be this way. Maybe if she got Hallie alone again they could really talk. It wouldn't happen with Erika around.

When Gert picked up her mail, she wasn't surprised to see mostly junk mail. Her personal mail had slowed to a trickle since the advent of e-mail. She still got magazines, since she hadn't had the heart to cancel Marc's two-year subscriptions. But today, there was something in a fancy beige envelope. It was partially hidden inside the curled Macy's circular.

Gert pulled it out. It was addressed to "Ms. Gert Healy."

She stood in the foyer, on the ridged black mat, and tore it open. She first had to step aside to let Mr. Schroeder and his schnauzer get by. The two of them looked alike.

*Mr. and Mrs. Donald Barnett*
*Request the honor of your presence*
*At the marriage of their daughter*
*Jennifer Ann Barnett*
*To Michael Howell Healy*

And then a date.

Marc's youngest brother, Michael, was getting married.

Gert felt stunned. How could this happen so fast? How

could she be so far out of the loop to not know of the engagement of Marc's youngest brother?

Michael was Gert's favorite out of the brothers. For some reason, Gert and Michael had had a special bond. It probably was because he was sweet and shy, not driven like the others. Michael was confused about what he wanted to do with his life, back in school. He thought he might major in communications some day, like Gert did, so they'd talked about that. Michael also was inexperienced with women, so when he'd finally begun having girlfriends in college and bringing them to family gatherings, Gert had taken extra care to make sure they felt welcome. There had been a time when she, too, had been the new girlfriend at family dinners. She brought them into conversations, asked them about themselves, winked at them in a show of female-outsider solidarity. Michael always seemed to appreciate it.

Gert wondered if Michael was still considered her brother-in-law. Did your husband's death instantly mean you were no longer officially related to his family? What were the rules on that?

This was silly. Of course Michael was her brother-in-law. But if she and Marc had gotten divorced, he wouldn't be anymore. So maybe not.

She didn't want to think about it. The dark clouds kept coming. Marc's absence was like a nightmare that repeated every day.

She stood in the vestibule and stared at the invitation, her eyes following the dark swirls of black ink. The wedding was only a month away. She'd certainly go. She was happy for Michael. But when she went to his wedding, whom would they seat her with? Marc's brothers and their wives? Michael's friends? A table of Random Single People? She'd seen tables like that at weddings in the past, but hadn't paid them much mind.

Gert sat on the living room couch and went into one of her dazes for a while. She left the rest of the mail unopened on the little table. She was lost in thought about Michael's wedding. Everyone would be dressed up, happy. If she were there with Marc, and the accident had never happened, she would be, too.

She never would have spent a moment thinking about the possibility that in a second, it could all be taken away.

Would she feel uncomfortable at Michael's wedding? Should she go there and ask the Healys why they hadn't invited her for the holidays last year? Try to reopen a relationship that was slowly sealing itself off? A wedding should be a happy occasion, not a venue for confrontation. If only Marc were here, the two of them would both be so happy right now, looking forward to this chance to see Michael get married and remember their own wedding in Boston. Their wedding had been a great convergence of all the things and people they loved.

She thought of calling someone. The support group had told her that she had to open up and trust people. Hallie had been so good at working through problems once. She remembered in college asking Hallie if she should keep dating the Ultimate Frisbee guy, who was nice but whom she didn't feel attracted to. Hallie had told her something she remembered to this day: Trust your feelings, not just your brain. Gert hadn't had enough experience with men at that point to think she should turn anyone down, as long as they were nice enough.

Hallie had been there for other problems, too—failed tests, awkward alliances. But of course, after a point, Gert could go to Marc first, or Nancy on the phone. Hallie's eventual underlying notes of bitterness began to make Gert ambivalent about telling Hallie the whole story. Gert tempered any good news she had when she told Hallie. She knew Hallie couldn't match it; she didn't want her friend to be jealous.

But Hallie hadn't given up. She'd always made a point to stay in touch with Gert somehow. Gert needed to make an effort, too, she decided.

Gert reached over to the end table and picked up the phone. She dialed Hallie, but there was no answer. Hallie was probably out with Erika, Gert figured.

She tiredly picked up the rest of her mail. There was a card from a magazine telling her she should renew quickly, even though the subscription didn't run out for ten months. She was tired of being lied to by subscription departments. Although in the early nineties, Marc had gotten a renewal card for his favorite magazine, *Spy,* and it had said, "The end is near." He'd renewed, and two months later, the magazine had folded. Apparently Marc hadn't taken the message literally enough. Gert had told Marc to call and get his money back, but Marc said that it was only fourteen dollars, and for all the laughs *Spy* had given him over the years, they could keep it.

Next in the mail was a DSL offer. Then there was yet another postcard from a gym advertising a discount for new members. Maybe they should offer free DSL, Gert thought. If those two industries joined forces, thousands of trees could be saved.

Lastly she got to a picturesque postcard from a cruise line.

It was the cruise she and Marc had taken four years ago. Going on a cruise was something they'd talked about since graduation. So finally, he'd given her one as an anniversary present. It was the best vacation they'd both had. It was like a fantasy. There were schedules each day of silly activities, boundless food to gorge themselves on, a rec room, and private time to talk, play cards, or just watch the sun set from the deck. They could stay in their room all day or go out and socialize. One night, on the deck at twilight, he'd told her how much he loved her. He'd brought with him a card he'd sent her not long after they'd started dating, which he'd just found in their closet. In it, he'd written that he'd always been skeptical of the idea of spending the rest of his life with one person until he met her. He told her what he loved about her—that she was emotional yet sensible, sensitive at times, witty at others.

Gert told him what she loved about him, too. In fact, she often had. She'd never suffered from the regret some women in her support group had—feeling that they hadn't told their husbands enough that they'd cared about them—because she always had. There were other things for her to feel guilty about, but not that.

Gert's memory of the cruise smashed headlong into the

wicked blip on her radar that was reality. She was in the present, trying to figure out how she would get through Michael's wedding. She couldn't imagine going on another cruise like that, ever. How did people vacation alone, anyway?

The phone rang, making Gert jump because she was right next to it. She put down the mail.

"Hi," Hallie said. It sounded like she was walking.

"Hi," Gert said. "Where are you?"

"On the way home. I was getting a haircut. Why'd you call my home number and not my cell?"

"I didn't want to interrupt," Gert said.

"Yeah, you would have interrupted a lot," Hallie said. "I was actually having sex with the guy with the half penis."

"What was that about, anyway?"

"Oh, nothing, I made it up to get over on Erika. She's always one-upping me—" a honking taxi drowned some of her out "—I confessed it this morning. You know what? I think she was jealous."

Gert shook her head. She wondered why they were always so competitive and jealous.

"So what's wrong?" Hallie said. "Are you nervous about seeing Todd this weekend?"

Gert felt a little better that Hallie was concerned. She got into a more comfortable position on the couch. Across the room was a photo of Marc sitting on his dormroom bed in his wire rims, looking natty and handsome. "I got a wedding invitation from Marc's youngest brother."

"Wow," Hallie said. "And you feel like they're all moving on without you."

Gert bit her lip. That wasn't even the main problem. She didn't know why she thought she could talk about this.

"Gert?" Hallie asked.

She didn't want to cry. She hadn't cried in front of Hallie since college.

She should have thought about it more before she picked up the phone.

"Gert?" Hallie said. "Are you okay?"

Maybe she should cry, break the tacit tension between them. But instead, Gert swallowed, tried to stabilize her voice. "Yes," Gert said.

"You don't have to talk," Hallie said. "Catch your breath."

Gert felt a little better.

"Here. I have a Magic Eight-Ball on my key chain," Hallie said. "I'll tell you what the Eight-Ball says. Ready?" She paused. "The Magic Eight-Ball says, 'Take your time. It's okay.'"

Gert laughed, despite herself. "The Eight-Ball doesn't have that on it," she said. She knew she could talk without crying now. Maybe she just hadn't tried enough with Hallie. "I just feel like," Gert said, "I'm not sure, technically, if Marc's relatives are my in-laws anymore. Two years ago, they were my family. Now, all of a sudden, they're not."

"But they must *feel* like they're your family," Hallie said. "They invited you to the wedding."

"*Michael* invited me. I'm not sure how the rest of them feel."

"Wow," Hallie said.

"Losing Marc was bad enough, but there are all those extra things that go with it," Gert said. "And he's not here to help me through them."

"I guess I don't even think of some of these things you must be going through," Hallie said.

"Most people don't," Gert said.

"I know," Hallie said.

"You could always ask," Gert said.

"I'm afraid of making you feel worse."

Gert knew that this was what everyone feared. But it was more hurtful to not take the risk.

"Not everything has to be funny all the time," Gert said. "Sometimes it's *okay* to be sad, or serious, if it's the right thing."

"I know," Hallie said. "I don't mean to always make jokes."

"We used to talk in college," Gert said. "A lot."

"We had *time* in college," Hallie said, her voice partially drowned out by a passing truck.

"I know," Gert said.

"What happened?" Hallie asked.

"We both realized we were becoming adults and needed to find someone to spend the rest of our lives with," Gert said.

"That becomes the priority, doesn't it?" Hallie said. "It's your number-one job as soon as you graduate. Once you've found someone, everything else falls into place. But until we do, it has to be top priority."

Neither of them said anything for a minute.

"So are you going?" Hallie asked.

"Where?"

"To Michael's wedding."

Hallie was going to talk about this. Gert was glad. "I think so," she said. "Maybe it won't be so bad. It's a happy occasion, right?"

"Right," Hallie said. "They'll all be thrilled to see you. I'm sure they will. Hey, I have to get on the subway now. Let's talk about this more when I see you. You're still going with us to the reading tomorrow night, right?"

Hallie and Erika were going to a reading by a guy they'd gone to high school with, although they'd hardly talked to him back then. He had just self-published his book and placed his own ads for it in *Harper's*. Gert thought it was sad that someone thought he had so much to say and couldn't find a publisher. But Roddy Brown had gotten lucky. His self-arranged readings in Manhattan were starting to draw crowds.

"I'll be there," Gert said.

"If the reading goes too late," Hallie said, "we'll talk on the weekend. We'll have to compare notes after your date with Todd anyway."

"You'll be out with Bugs Bunny Boy, right?"

"Ugh," Hallie said. "Don't remind me."

"Well," Gert said, "I think you should really give him a chance. You might be surprised."

There. Gert could be helpful, too. Despite her paltry dating experience.

"I will," Hallie said. "And thanks."

★ ★ ★

Gert had joined a gym a month ago, and already she was sure that the guy who worked there had it in for her.

She'd be sitting on the bike, pedaling furiously, listening to music, and he would come over and say something to her really low. She'd take off her headphones, and he'd say, "I just wanted to make sure your seat's comfortable."

He never did that to anyone else. At least, it didn't seem like it.

"It's fine," she'd say.

Then she'd be running on the treadmill, and he'd come over and say, "Are you sure those are good shoes for you? They don't look like running shoes."

Gert didn't want to talk to anyone while she was working out. Working out was personal. It was like someone talking to you while you were on the toilet. Which an annoying girl named Dawn at work always did. Dawn would come into the rest room, and if she saw someone's feet under a stall, she'd say, "Who's in theaahh?"

"My shoes are fine," Gert told the guy at the gym.

It was Hallie who had first suggested joining a gym. Hal--lie had told Gert it was a great way to work out aggression. Gert didn't really believe that that was Hallie's main motivation for going to the gym, though—Hallie went, like everyone else, because she thought it made her more attractive. No sense lying about it. When Gert had been married, neither she nor Marc had joined a gym. They both had had better things to do.

But now Gert had free time, and she was sinking into the realm of the rest of the world—the world that worried too much about how it looked.

The more Gert thought about her new place in this universe, the more aggression she had to get out. Which made the gym perfect.

Now, as she engaged in the monotony of the StairMaster,

the annoying gym guy was on her back again. "Do you want to know how to do that better?" he asked her.

"I know how to climb stairs," she said evenly.

The man was clueless-looking, with tight, curly hair and oversize glasses. He was in his forties. He didn't look built, but he was lean, and she figured he'd studied about training more than he'd actually done it.

"Okay, ma'am," he said simply, and walked away.

Gert felt bad. It wasn't his fault that he was a pest. He was only trying to help. But really, she wished he would leave her alone. She didn't want to be at the gym. She wanted to be at home talking to Marc. Or just listening to him breathe.

The reading was packed that night. It was on the second floor of a chain bookstore in Chelsea. That floor was so crowded that a store employee stood at the foot of the stairs, refusing to let anyone else up. He was wearing a headset and carrying a clip-board. Above him, on the balcony, a similarly attired employee was handling crowd control, his buttocks pressed back into the green metal bars that prevented people from falling.

Gert had agreed to meet the girls after her workout. Erika was dolled up in heavy makeup and a skirt. So were most of the women there. Everyone had seen Roddy Brown's hand-some jacket photo. It wasn't only the photo that had lured them. The text beneath it said, "Roddy Brown lives in Manhattan with his dog, Rufus. He eats Frosted Flakes for dinner." Single male writer + New York + lives with dog = personal ad.

"But I *know* Roddy," Erika told the guard. "We went to high school together."

"He knows you're coming?"

"He'll be surprised. I haven't seen him in forever."

"Well, he'll come this way when he's finished," the guard said. "You can see him then."

A girl in a pink jacket pushed forward. "I'll be out of your hair in one second," she told the guard, "but can you please give him this?"

It was the girl's business card, and she'd written on it, "Roddy—Love the book! Call me."

"Let's get out of here," Erika said to Gert and Hallie. "He's not worth this kind of trouble."

At Kafé Krunch, the girls sat in the back room in a dark corner on a pair of orange couches, waving marshmallows over a flaming Sterno can. They had bought the "s'more-gasbord" from the counter, and in order to make it worth the eleven dollar price, they had snuck in their own extra ingredients from the Food Emporium—an extra Hershey bar, marshmallows, graham crackers—and planned to stay an hour.

Hallie stared into the flame, which was the only bright thing in the back room. She poked a half-melted Hershey bar into the fire and drew it out.

"Who needs men when you can have chocolate?" Hallie said.

"Yeah, right," Erika said, bringing her knees to her chin. She sucked at the singed husk of a marshmallow. The small flame made her face glow, but it also made it look a little contorted.

Gert relaxed on the soft couch. She enjoyed the quiet back rooms of New York dessert cafés. They were definitely better than bars. There were comfy chairs, enough darkness for anonymity, and plenty of slackers trying to figure out what to do later. She stared at the ceiling. There was a pencil sticking out of it. She didn't know if it was a prank or decoration.

Erika was facing Gert and Hallie. Her makeup was on perfect, but it hadn't helped her get to her target, Roddy.

"Why do I do it?" she asked, putting her face in her hands. "Why did all 700 women at the event have the same exact idea I had? Why aren't there any decent men left who don't have a fan club a mile wide?"

Hallie shook her head, poking a piece of Hershey bar into the flame. "I know," she said.

"In high school, hardly anyone talked to Roddy Brown,"

Erika said, her face glowing orange and yellow. "He was a geek. I bet he never kissed a girl until he was twenty-one."

"You should have gone for him *then*," Hallie said.

"Who you tellin'?" Erika said. "I thought he'd be happy to see me tonight. But any remotely normal guy in this city ends up with a line of girls waiting to meet him that's longer than the one for Space Mountain. They were leaving him their business cards. And I was almost just as bad."

"I'll bet if *I* self-published a book, there wouldn't be a crowd of guys at a reading waiting for *me*," Hallie said.

"Damn straight," Erika said. "We need to fix the criteria. How can we make guys pursue women for their literary aspirations, and women only pick men after the men spend three hours on their appearance?"

"I know what to do," Hallie said. "We'll pay half the single women here to move to Alaska. Then the rest of us might start being treated with respect."

"I know who I'd pay to go to Alaska," Erika said. "Challa."

*Next topic,* Gert thought. Erika's obsession with Challa was really worrying her.

"Check this out," Erika said, becoming visibly excited. "I've been writing messages to her as Vicki Vale. Challa's too stupid to recognize the reference. Ben loves Batman. I can just see Challa running into their bedroom, wailing, 'Ben, this bitch Vicki Vale keeps leaving messages on my Web site!'"

Hallie laughed a little, and steamed skim milk issued from her mouth.

"Ben's so creative," Erika said. "I *know* him. I can't imagine he's truly happy with their dull life. Sooner or later he's going to get tired of it, and I have to know what the right time is so that I can be there. Otherwise I'll miss out."

Gert thought that maybe she could subtly help Erika. She still saw some good in her. "Do you have any contact with Ben?" she asked.

Erika's eyebrows narrowed a bit. She looked straight at Gert for the first time that night. Behind her, at the far end of the room, a group of guys was coming in wearing baseball caps. There were too many overgrown frat boys in town. Gert couldn't imagine dating one of them. Marc actually had been in a fraternity, but at least he didn't act like he was still in one after graduation.

"I find a reason to e-mail him every few months," Erika said, "just so he knows I still exist. I'm actually due to send another one. There's an exhibit coming to the Whitney that I know he'd like, so I was thinking of e-mailing him about that."

Gert felt bad for Erika as she listened to her talk about Ben. Erika always became more animated when she talked about him.

"A few months ago," Erika said, "I bumped into one of his friends, this guy Don, so I e-mailed Ben to tell him. Ben usually writes back after a few days, but he keeps it short and emotionless. It's like a new rejection every time. Last time he was like, 'Hi. That's great you saw Don. I hope you have a great new year.' The end. There's never any hint that we spent five years together."

"Maybe he doesn't want to seem like he's leading you on," Gert said.

Erika's face tightened. "Why does he have to worry about 'seeming'?" she asked. "We shared five *years.* It's almost as if Challa's looking over his shoulder and might leave him if she caught him showing any emotion toward me. Can't he at least miss me a little bit?"

Gert didn't know what to say.

"Hey," Erika said, becoming excited again. She looked at Gert and Hallie. "You guys both have dates on Saturday. Gert has Todd and…"

"I have Bugs Bunny Boy," Hallie said. "*You* can go on the date if you want."

Gert thought of Todd and felt a bit nervous.

Erika looked at Hallie. "Look on the bright side," she said. "At least Bugs Bunny Boy isn't half as bad as that guy you went out with who spent your whole first date talking about why there shouldn't be a Black History Month unless there's a White History Month."

Hallie laughed. "True," she said. "But Bugs Bunny Boy is neck and neck with the British guy who I really liked and slept with and then he told me that he was moving back to Britain in two weeks."

Erika shook her head.

"And at least Bugs Bunny Boy isn't as bad," Hallie added, "as the guy who, the minute he met me for dinner, pointed at the tiny white spot on my blouse and said, 'Oh, you got some deodorant on there.'"

"Yeah," Erika said, "and Bugs Bunny Boy is definitely not as bad as the guy who was annoyed that you had a cough, so every time you coughed, he coughed, because he wanted to show you how irritating it was."

Gert wondered if they were making all these guys up, or if dating was really this bad.

Suddenly all three heads swung to the left. One of the frat boys, tall and good-looking, was standing next to Hallie.

"Any of you girls have a light?" he asked in an unplaceable accent. His friends were behind him, waiting for him.

Gert looked up. She kept matches in her purse because Marc had always told her to. It seemed a little silly, now that she thought about it. She held out the pack.

"I guess that'll do, right?" the guy said, smiling.

He looked like he was about to leave, but Erika called out, "So, what's your name?"

The guy seemed startled for a second. "Rick," he said. He had five-o'clock shadow. It was attractive.

"I'm Erika," Erika said, reaching over the couch to shake his hand. But he shifted a little, still seeming like he wanted to go. Erika continued, "That's Gert, and that's Hallie."

"Nice to meet you." He shook their hands, but then turned to walk away.

"So," Erika called out. "Where are you from?"

He turned around again, but kept walking backward. "New Jehhh-sey," he said. Then he took off with his friends.

Erika looked deflated. All the guy had really wanted was a light. Erika's whole body seemed to sink in her seat. Gert felt sorry for her.

"I need chocolate," Erika said. "And give me another graham."

"None left," Hallie said.

Erika dug into her pocketbook for eleven dollars.

# Chapter 5

"So," Gert said, laughing during dinner, "the guy with the clipboard wouldn't even let us up the stairs."

She and Todd were on their second date, at a restaurant in Little Italy. Gert had never actually been in Little Italy before, although she'd certainly heard good things. She was sure that if she stayed in New York for another eight years, she still wouldn't get to all the neighborhoods. Two months ago, in fact, she had visited Columbia University for a focus group on women who had lost a spouse, and she was amazed at what she saw when she wandered a few blocks north to 122nd and Broadway: To her left, a verdant park that held Grant's Tomb, and ahead of her, the part of the subway where it exploded up into an elevated line bedizened with lights. On both sides were Gothic buildings and grassy fields and backpacking students, and it looked completely different than only fifteen blocks earlier. Tonight, she'd felt the same way when she'd started following Todd's directions to Little Italy. She'd begun to doubt them, because up until the last block, she'd been surrounded by the stores and unintelligible signs of Chinatown. Then she'd turned a corner and been thrust into a wonderland of bright lights, iron balconies, roaring laughter and rich tomato smells.

Todd smiled while Gert talked about her friends. He was a great listener. Better than anyone she'd met in a while. It was refreshing to talk to someone who didn't know anything about her, who didn't pass judgment or cut her off. He seemed genuinely interested.

She thought about how Marc used to tell her about his day. She'd always listened to his adventures in pursuing clients. He was the consummate salesman. She loved watching him relish the chase.

"I know Hallie and Erika are your friends," Todd said, "but it seems like there's a tension between you."

Gert found it interesting that she'd been on only two dates with him and he'd already picked up on that. "I have more friends, but they're in other parts of the country," she said apologetically. "I probably should make more of an effort to understand Hallie and Erika. It's just that they get so crazy about everything, especially dating. They analyze every aspect of it to death. And they get jealous of people in good relationships, too."

Todd was wearing a soft sweater. Gert figured he'd gotten it as a gift once from a girl. Most of the men she knew tended to prefer button-down shirts that were comfortable and easy to clean.

"You seem more easygoing than they are," Todd said.

"Yeah, well," Gert said. She knew guys liked that about her, but she suddenly felt modest. "I don't want to bore you all night with my sad, sad stories of my sad, sad friends."

"I don't mind," he said, arranging his fork and knife. "Talk about whatever you want."

The waiter came with their waters. They passed on drinks and said they needed a few more minutes to look at the menu.

Gert remembered that Hallie had told her to make sure she didn't just talk about herself on a date. "So," she said to Todd, "what's new with you since we last met?"

Hallie was right, Gert could tell. Todd leaned back. "Let's see," he said. "Since I last had the very distinct pleasure of being in your company—" Gert couldn't help but smile "—I got one raise, one invitation to a friend's wedding and one rent increase."

"That's great!" Gert said. "I mean, about the raise. Not the rent increase." She raised her empty wineglass. "To the raise."

Todd clinked it with his empty glass. "To the raise."

Gert put her glass down and said, "You must be doing a good job, if they gave you a raise."

"Nah." Todd shrugged. "It's mandatory after a certain point. It's not a big deal."

"But they still wouldn't give it to you if you weren't doing a good job, right?"

"Right," Todd said.

"So I'm sure you deserved it," Gert said.

"Thanks." He looked bashful. She liked that he could be bashful. That, and the tiny scar on the bridge of his nose.

"I guess the raise will all go to counteract the rent increase, though," Gert said.

"Not all of it," Todd said. "Some of it will go to counteract my friend's wedding present."

"Who's your friend?"

"Howie Wald," Todd said. "We went to sleep-away camp together the summer before sixth grade."

The mention of a wedding reminded Gert about Michael's wedding. There was so much about her that Todd didn't know. Couldn't know yet. It seemed nearly insurmountable. But it was something she'd have to deal with. She'd have to explain her past to every new person she met…eventually.

Gert tried to remember what Todd had just been talking about. Oh—sleep-away camp. "That's cute that you still talk to your elementary school friends," she said.

Todd looked a little embarrassed again—probably because she had called him cute—which was, well, cute.

"You still talk to one of *your* elementary school friends," Todd said.

"Yeah," Gert said. "But not so much, anymore. Since she got married and had kids."

Todd shook his head. "Married people," he said. "You have to give up on them. They get married and disappear down their gopher holes."

"I wouldn't disappear," she said, careful not to give anything away.

Todd smiled. "You know what?" he said. "I believe you wouldn't."

She felt undeserving of the faith. She had actually disappeared somewhat.

"I can't blame them, though," Todd added. "If you have a wife and kids to take care of, the last thing you want to be doing is hanging out with your pals, drinking beer and quoting *Caddyshack*." He looked at her. "Tell me something great that happened to *you* this week."

She wanted to think of something. But she couldn't. *He's going to think I'm boring,* she thought. *This is hard. Think of something.*

"I…I haven't really done anything," Gert stammered.

"Come on," Todd said. "I'll bet you're one of those people who does lots of great things and never tells anyone."

Gert smiled.

"It seems like you're very, very patient with your friends," Todd said. "Treating people with respect is something a person should be proud of."

It had been a long time since anyone had complimented Gert on just being herself. "Thanks," she said.

"What about your boss?" Todd asked. "You said she's hard to deal with. Did you get through the week without her yelling at you?"

"She was away."

"So, yes."

"No. She called to yell at me. But other than that, work was fine."

"Well, here's an accomplishment," he said. "You were willing to see me again, goofy train guy."

"You're not *that* goofy," Gert said.

"Sure I am."

"Come on," Gert said. "I'll bet that what you said about me is true of you—you do lots of nice things and never tell anyone."

Todd said, "I do." He reached across the table, took her hand, and kissed it. "I'm not going to tell anyone about that."

"So that was our secret?" she asked.

"Yes."

The waitress appeared and startled them. But Gert was a bit relieved, because she was unsure what to do next. What if he wanted to give her a real kiss, later? Could she do it?

What scared her a little bit was, she thought she could.

As they ate, Todd told her about his hometown—Emporia, in southern Virginia near the North Carolina border. It had train tracks running through it, which maybe had been the first thing that made him like trains. When he was a kid, he'd found a cache there of old receipts from a railroad company. He still had them. They were on very thin forms, filled in by a typewriter. He liked collecting old train memorabilia.

Gert told him what it was like to go to high school in the suburbs of L.A.

"There must have been a lot of competition for school plays," Todd said.

Gert said there was, but she wasn't into acting, although she had been in the chorus in *West Side Story*. She asked Todd if he'd ever been in a school play. He said he'd been in *Oliver!* in seventh grade.

"I had no lines," he said. "Everyone in my music class was in the play. So I told my parents not to bother coming. But they came anyway. And you know what? When I looked out and saw them there, for some reason, I was really glad they were there. Is that weird?"

"No," Gert said.

"I think it's one of the biggest signs of caring," Todd said, "when you tell people not to do something for you, and they do it anyway. We did this other thing in school that year, a trip to Williamsburg, and both my parents agreed to chaperon…"

Gert liked watching him talk. She didn't even hear everything that he was saying. She just liked the way he said it—always so full of enthusiasm, so unaffected. When he got into a story, he'd start talking faster, full of intensity, and then, when he finally stopped, he'd look a little guilty—as if he'd taken too much liberty. But he was clearly moved by the little things.

"It's interesting that both of us have parents who are still together," Gert said.

"I know," Todd said. "I guess we must be better adjusted than most kids."

Gert smiled. "I wonder what the secret is for people to stay together."

"I'm not sure," Todd said, "but it probably has to do with finding someone who really, really amazes you."

As they were walking back to the subway, he stopped her and gave her a quick kiss on the cheek.

"I'm glad I met you," he said.

"Me, too," she said.

"Do you want…I mean, if you're not busy…to do something next weekend?"

"Sure."

"He just gave you a quick kiss?"

Gert was having drinks with Hallie and Erika at the small café that was attached to the Cinema Classics theater in the East Village. It was the theater that showed *The Wizard of Oz* once a month at the same time as it played Pink Floyd's *Dark Side of the Moon* album, to allow people to decide if the rumor was true that they were in sync. Gert and Marc had gone one time when Gert's brother was visiting, and Gert hadn't been convinced, but the guys liked the music so they'd stayed for the whole thing. Three hours of watching *The Wiz-*

*ard of Oz* with no dialogue at all, just Pink Floyd music, was a little much for Gert. She knew that Floyd was high in the male music canon, but that didn't mean she wanted to listen to it for three hours while watching a bunch of dwarves wave their lollipops.

"And," Hallie asked, "how was the kiss?"

"It was nice," Gert said. "He's just the sweetest guy."

Erika stirred the leftover ice in her margarita glass with a straw. "What happens if you order your drink without ice?" she asked. "There was more ice in our drinks than drink."

"They only give you like half the drink," Hallie said. "It doesn't work. So when are you going to see him next?"

"Next Saturday, for dinner," Gert said.

"And *after* dinner what are you doing?" Erika asked.

"Probably a movie."

Gert was more nervous about that, because she wasn't sure what was expected on a third date in the real world.

Erika raised and lowered her eyebrows.

"Well, I know you think he's sweet," Hallie said, "but be careful."

"Yeah, Gert," Erika said. "Have you even Googled him yet?"

"No," Gert said. She felt like that was intrusive.

"I was supposed to go on a date with this guy once," Erika said, "but first, I Googled him. I found out that there were fifteen posts on www.spankme.com."

"It was lucky you Googled in time," Hallie said.

"Why? We dated for three months."

Gert looked around the room. It was small and rectangular, with a few refrigerators full of bottled juices. Free weekly newspapers were piled by the window in front.

"Hey!" Erika said to Hallie. "When are you going to tell us your top secret innovative method of meeting men?"

Hallie looked startled. "Oh," she said. "Well, I can tell you now, if you promise not to tell anyone."

Gert looked at her, interested. She hoped Hallie *could* use it to meet someone. Then Hallie wouldn't be so angry.

Hallie looked at the ceiling. "I thought of this while I was walking through Times Square one day," she said. "This guy was about to pass me, and he was carrying a bunch of advertising storyboards, and he was just the right height, and he seemed interesting. There was just something about him I really liked. Just this instant attraction. And I thought of something to say to him, but he had walked past me already, and I couldn't think of a way to do it. And I thought, if I was a guy and he was a girl, I'd just jog up and ask for his number, and that would be it."

"Exactly," Erika said, setting her jaw, as if she'd been burned about this for a while. She tucked a wisp of her hair behind her ear. "So? What do we do?"

"One day," Hallie said resolutely, "we're going to take matters into our own hands."

Gert cautiously sipped her Coke.

"The three of us are going to hang out in Times Square, and if we see a man we think is attractive, we'll go up together and ask if he's single," Hallie said. "Then we'll get his number. That's it."

*Something honest!* Gert thought. *Daring, but honest. But is there a catch?*

"The reason that dating is so frustrating," Hallie opined, "is that when men ask us out, they already know they're attracted to us, so they've already gotten past a big step. We, on the other hand, are the ones being asked, so we're not always attracted to them right away. We have to sit at the table waiting for some sort of feelings to kick in. And if they don't, the guys gets mad. Why do men always get to make the choices?"

"They shouldn't," Erika said, shaking her head. She wiped melted ice from the table. "You're right."

"So will you guys do it with me?" Hallie asked.

Gert didn't really want to drag herself through it, but it seemed at least a little healthier than watching Hallie and Erika feel like victims all the time. "I'll help," Gert said. "As long as I don't have to ask for any numbers."

"Fair enough," Hallie said. "Erika and I will do the real pursuing. But we need your support." Gert smiled. She felt okay about them again. She certainly did go back and forth.

"I'm in, too," Erika said. "There's power in numbers...." But her voice trailed off. She was watching something near the window. There were two men at a table, discussing the weekly paper.

Hallie followed Erika's gaze. "They're short," Hallie said.

"I don't care," Erika said. "They're cute. Watch and learn."

Erika got up and slinked toward the front door. But at the last minute, she suddenly stopped and pointed to one of the articles in the paper the guys were reading.

"I can't bear to look," Hallie told Gert, shielding her eyes with her hand. "It's too embarrassing."

Gert laughed. "So, you saw Bugs Bunny Boy last night?"

Hallie winced. "It wasn't good."

"Why not?" Gert had been hoping this would work out. "Was he wearing Warner Brothers again?"

"No," Hallie said. "He was wearing Disney. But that wasn't the worst of it. He had this horrendous flu and kept sneezing all over me." Hallie shivered visibly. "I feel chilled just thinking about it. I can still picture his sweaty forehead, with his bangs sticking to it. He was wearing a black turtleneck with Donald Duck. Why would you go out when you're that sick? He has no common sense. I could never find that attractive."

"Maybe you could look at it as, he was horrendously sick and still wanted to be with you," Gert said.

"Delirium is one excuse for his behavior," Hallie said.

Gert noticed that Erika was talking to the men. She focused on Hallie again. "Why don't you give him one more chance? He doesn't seem that bad."

Hallie shrugged. "I don't know," she said. "I need more than 'He doesn't seem that bad.'"

They were both quiet for a second. Gert read the little pink movie schedule on the table. She tried to think of another topic. Work. "Has anything happened with that girl at your office?" she asked.

Hallie lit up. She shook her head. "They wanted me to fire her on Friday for disappearing," Hallie said. "And of course, when I went to fire her, she had disappeared. I was busy by the time she got back. I'm going to follow her Monday and see where she goes. My boss thinks it'll be better if we have more cause."

Erika returned. She shielded her hand with her body and showed Gert and Hallie what she'd copped from the guys.

It was a business card.

It said, "Eden Youdani, Resident," and it was from Mount Sinai hospital.

"He's a doctor?" Hallie said.

"The cute one was," Erika said, sitting down. Hallie glanced toward the men's table, but they had just left. "The other one mentioned a fiancée."

"That definitely makes him uncute," Hallie said.

"Here's the thing, though," Erika said. "Dr. Youdani wears a yarmulke."

Hallie looked back again. "I didn't notice."

"Because he was facing us."

"That means he's religious," Gert said. "Would he date someone non-Jewish?"

"Probably not," Erika said.

"So…?"

"I didn't tell him I wasn't," Erika said, a sneaky expression crossing her face.

Hallie said, "Are you going to call him?"

"Of course. He's a doctor!"

"But what happens when he finds out you're not Jewish?"

Erika shrugged. "Why should he have to find out?"

Gert thought that Erika was going to just keep hurling herself after impossible men. Maybe it was a way to avoid meeting anyone new. That way, she could keep dwelling on Ben.

In some ways, Gert understood. It was hard to compare everyone to your fantasy guy—especially if he'd once been real.

"But he *will* find out you're not Jewish eventually," Hallie said.

"That's fine," Erika said. "Eventually. I'll just avoid revealing my religion for the first few dates. People are too polite to ask. They beat around the bush with, 'What did you get for, uh…Christmas, or Chanukah….' I can figure my way around that. By the time he finds out, he'll be enamored and it'll be too late. A nice, responsible doctor is the one thing that might get my mind off Ben." She sighed. "It's terrible when you liked someone so much that they raise the bar for everyone else. They doom you to sky-high standards."

Gert definitely understood that. "Dr. Eden Youdani doesn't know what he's in for," Hallie said.

That night, Gert and Todd talked on the phone. And they began talking on the phone every day.

"They put us up in a hotel whenever we make a late run," he told her via his cell phone on Monday. "I'm staying in Binghamton tonight. One year we got hit with a sudden storm that dumped two feet of snow. I was stuck for three days."

"That actually sounds romantic," Gert said.

"It might have been," he said, "but I was stranded with only Bernie the engineer. And there's only so much cable you can watch."

"What else is there to do in Binghamton?"

"Get a drink in a bar and watch the snow," he said. "Well, a nonalcoholic drink."

Tuesday, he called and said the kids at the hospital in New York had made a sign that said, *Hi, Train!* He said he'd smiled for hours after seeing that.

Wednesday, he said, "My little brother has a girlfriend who he's actually been seeing for more than two months."

"He sounds like *my* brother," Gert said.

"It's weird when younger brothers start to grow up."

"It is."

Thursday, Missy gave Gert extra work at the last minute. Gert had to stay at work later than expected. She felt agitated, but she was happy when Todd called around six.

"She was snapping at me all day," Gert said, talking low and cupping the phone lest someone from another department walk by and hear. "I'm tempted to do a lousy job and run home, but people depend on our work. They need to know about new drugs they might need."

"You feel such a responsibility for what you do," Todd said.

"I only do what everyone should do," Gert said.

"You're modest, too," Todd said.

The support washed over Gert like a warm massage.

"Did anything happen on *your* job?" she asked, remembering again what Hallie had told her.

"Well, not mine specifically," Todd said. "But we found out that down in South Carolina, a conductor saved a three-year-old girl. She'd wandered out of her backyard and was crawling on the tracks and they were only able to get the train down to five miles an hour, so the conductor jumped out and ran ahead of the train and pushed her off."

"Wow!" Gert said. "Is that what you guys do?"

"We hope we never have to," he said, "but sometimes, it happens."

He left her feeling as if she couldn't wait to see him on Saturday.

First, she had to get through Friday.

And she wasn't sure, waking up Friday morning, if she'd make it.

She had had another really intense dream that night about Marc. It wasn't anything specific—they were in the car, going somewhere—but the important thing was, he was there, and the future was infinite. She had woken up suddenly, before the end of the dream, and for the first few seconds, she tried to tell herself that maybe the accident was what she had imagined, and Marc's being alive was real. She had felt so settled and happy in the dream—the way she had always been before.

The prevalence of dreams about Marc, and her depression during daylight hours over what had happened, varied so much with circumstances. They arose depending on the weather, what she'd eaten, where she was in her biological cycle, the tasks she had before her, which music was on, the day of the week, the time of day. Usually she didn't even know what the stimulus was, or whether there was more than one. There might be blocks of time during her day when she felt okay, even hopeful. Then she would suddenly remember how happy she had been up until a year and a half ago, and the contrast with how she felt now—empty, robbed—was almost too much to bear.

She hadn't even realized at the time how happy she'd been, because it was just the way she always felt. And along with it was the underlying assumption that it would always be that way. For many years she saved newspapers with important events— both she and Marc did—with the assumption that they'd give them to their kids someday. It was just a given. Now there was something missing inside of her, some inner stable core.

Lying on her stomach in bed, Gert turned over on her side. She could call in sick today. Why not give herself a break? Toying with calling in sick sometimes helped her for a few minutes in the morning, even though, in the end, she usually decided to save it for an emergency. Her mom had once told her, "It's okay to take a mental health day," but she always talked herself out of it.

She looked up at her alarm clock. It was 7:29.

The worst time to wake up was one minute before the alarm was about to go off. Now she would have to lie there helplessly and wait for the explosion.

The numbers hit 7:30.

"Crappy the Clown! Crappy the Clown! Crappy the Clown!" yelled a morning DJ. This was the worst morning show in all of New York. That was why Gert kept her clock radio on it: Having to listen for one second urged her right out of bed.

"Where's Crappy's lovely assistant? Abigail Van Urine, come hither!"

Gert got up and snapped it off.

★ ★ ★

That day at work was more miserable than she'd expected.

"Did you sign for my FedEx yesterday?" Missy asked, coming in at ten, her hair in disarray. She didn't look as perfect as usual.

"Yes," Gert said, looking up. "I put it on your desk."

"Where on my desk?"

Gert would have to stay out of Missy's way today as much as possible. Best to keep off her radar when she was acting like this.

"In your office," Gert said.

"No, I know where my desk is. Obviously it's in my office. But where on my desk did you put it? Come show me. There are half a million things on my desk. Where on my desk?"

The day before, Gert had seen something come over the fax machine: A copy of a rough draft of a divorce agreement Missy was working on. It was to be a no-fault divorce. Gert didn't know if Missy's husband even knew about her plans. If Missy was having an affair with the mailroom guy, Dennis certainly didn't know about *that,* either. Maybe the FedEx had to do with all of this.

"I put it in front of your chair," Gert said, getting up.

Missy, face-to-face with Gert, said slowly, "From now on, if you get something important, hold on to it and give it to me directly."

Gert had been leaving things on Missy's desk or chair for years. She didn't know why there was a sudden change.

Missy turned, and Gert followed her into her office. Missy's office was a mess. The desk faced the door, with her chair leaning back against the window. Missy was the only person Gert knew who actually positioned herself so she wouldn't be able to look out the window.

But Missy was right. There was no FedEx on the desk.

"I thought I left it there," Gert said.

"Jesus, Gert. When you see something important come in, put it in a safe place," Missy said, seething. Gert willed herself to keep her mouth shut and looked at the ground.

But Missy was still looking at Gert. "Are you going to give me some privacy, or what?" Missy finally said.

Gert started toward the door.

"Close that, please," Missy snapped.

Gert walked out, sat down in her chair and returned to the survey forms she was supposed to be working on. But she bristled. She remembered how good Marc had always been at comforting her after a day like this. A dinner, a hug—it almost had made it worth the pain. Now she just had work to do, and no comfort in sight. It was still a day until she'd see Todd.

Usually, Gert noticed only the buildings of midtown when she looked down the hall, but today she looked down and saw Dennis, Missy's husband. He looked basically the same as at the Christmas party three months ago, except that now his mustache was better trimmed. He reminded Gert of Cliff Clavin from *Cheers,* but was even less intimidating.

Gert noticed the wrinkles in his forehead and his gray hair and she suddenly felt bad for him. He was probably a nice guy who had met Missy when they both were very young. Then she'd outgrown him, outsocialized him.

He stopped at Gert's desk. "Is Melissa Hathaway in there?"

Gert found it odd that Dennis didn't recognize her from parties. Clearly, interpersonal skills were not his bag. "I think so, but I can call," Gert said. "Who should I say is waiting?"

"Dennis."

Gert picked up the phone. "Melissa? Dennis is here to see you."

"Dennis my husband? Here? I'm supposed to meet him at Arthur's."

Gert didn't know what she was supposed to say. She hated it when Missy yelled at someone else through her. "Well, he's here, so—"

"Tell him I'll be out in fifteen minutes."

Gert put down the phone. "She's tied up," Gert said. "She'll be out in fifteen minutes."

Dennis didn't move. "Fifteen minutes? Can I borrow your phone?"

He reached for it.

Finally some balls, Gert thought. She could only sit and look on.

"What's her extension?"

"It's 512."

Dennis held the receiver and punched in the numbers. He looked at Gert. "Why isn't it working?"

Gert took the phone from him, pressed an "8" first, then Missy's extension, and handed it back to him.

"I'm coming in there," Dennis said into the phone. "I have an early meeting, so we need to talk now."

Missy came outside immediately. She said, without any emotion, "Gert, come in here. Dennis, I'll be out in a minute."

Gert walked back into Missy's office.

Missy looked a bit more calm. "Find the envelope before I get back," she said, sounding almost human. But then she added, "And by the way, if you *did* put it here, go ask the cleaning people if they moved it."

Then she stomped out.

*If* she put it there?

She'd told her she had. What more evidence did Missy need? She'd worked for Missy for four years and should have accrued a bit of trustworthiness by now.

As soon as Dennis and Missy were safely in the elevator, Gert returned to Missy's office, on a sudden hunch, and pulled back the office door. The missing envelope was lying there, on the floor, under some other papers. Missy often threw things behind the door so she'd remember to bring them home with her at night. She kept a pair of boots there, too, and an umbrella. Missy had apparently thrown a bunch of documents there and had not gone back to look.

Gert sighed and brought the FedEx back to her own desk. It was fairly flat. She saw that it was from a law firm. She didn't open it, although she was dying to know what was inside. She imagined it was kinky photos of Missy and the mailboy in the elevators. This didn't cheer her up, though.

Suddenly Gert's phone rang.

She patted it for a second, fearing it was Missy. Finally she picked it up.

"All clear?" Todd asked.

She was thrilled to hear a friendly voice.

"All clear," Gert said. She relaxed in her chair, lowering her voice to a whisper. She put the FedEx into her drawer, where it would be safe. "Missy just went ballistic on me."

"She really is a Heckle and Jeckle, isn't she?" Todd asked.

Gert laughed. "Jekyll and Hyde."

"That's what I meant," Todd said. "I've been watching too many cartoons. I'm sorry you're having a rough day. You sound really beat."

"I am," Gert said. "Completely wiped."

"Do you want to push our dinner up to tonight? Maybe it would make you feel better."

Todd sounded a bit seductive this time. It was a different Todd. She liked it. "That sounds *sooo* nice," she said. "But I thought you weren't getting back till tomorrow."

"Hold on." She could hear a horn. Then he got back on. "I'll be in right after dinnertime, but I thought that might be cutting it too close. I'll be a mess and unshowered. But if you're willing to see me a mess and unshowered, I can do it."

"I'll bet you look cute when you're a mess and unshowered."

Todd laughed. "I'll let you be the judge," he said. "Is eight-thirty okay?"

"Sounds good."

When she hung up, she was hopeful, where a second ago, she'd been down. Now she couldn't imagine how she would be feeling if Todd hadn't just called.

In fact, she couldn't imagine getting through another hour of work without having something to look forward to tonight.

She was glad she didn't have Missy's life. Glad she wasn't in a loveless, miserable marriage. How did women like Missy let that happen? How did men like Dennis let it happen? How did anyone let it happen? Was it so worth not being alone that you'd spend years with someone you didn't even like?

Perhaps.

She was so excited about dinner that when Missy breezed back in later and then ran out again for a meeting, Gert forgot to tell her she had found the envelope. When Gert left for the weekend, it was still inside Gert's desk.

Todd had decided that for their third date, they'd go to the restaurant of a French cooking school. Todd figured this would be a good way to get good food at a reasonable price.

Marc had been simple about food. He liked his burgers and beer and wasn't much for fine dining.

At the restaurant, Todd was seated across from her, wearing a white dress shirt. She liked the way he looked in it. His shoulders looked strong underneath.

"I like eating in French restaurants," Todd said, opening his napkin. "It's certainly cheaper than going to France." The restaurant looked to be full of young people who seemed to be out for the same thing: quality eats at restaurant school prices.

A waitress came to take their drink orders. Todd asked what a good wine was for someone who had a rough day. The waitress said, "All of them." Todd told Gert she should have one, even if he couldn't drink himself. Gert smiled and decided on red wine.

They picked up the dinner menus. Gert noticed that even though the place was staffed by students, it was still pricey. But she decided she wouldn't offer to pay. Todd was swooping in to save her from a miserable day, and she would let him.

She looked at him. He was reading the menu intently. She wondered if Todd ever had trouble at work. It never seemed like it.

"Do you have any enemies?" Gert asked. Then she wondered why it had come out so funny.

Todd laughed. "What? That's a random question. Has some varmint been 'round these parts looking for me?"

"No," Gert said. "You just seem like such an easygoing person that I can't imagine anyone being mad at you."

"Well," Todd said, "I guess if you're a guy, there's always someone who picked a fight with you along the line. There was one time when I was at a frat party and some guy saw me talking to a girl he liked. I didn't even know he liked her. He was drunk, so he tried to pick a fight. And stupid me, I fought back. It's instinct, I guess. He hit me, I hit him, and we both ended up at Student Health."

"Were you hurt?"

"He got me in the nose," Todd said. "I still have a scar. The other guy had a bruise on his cheek. The dean told us to stay away from each other. The whole thing was stupid. I think the guy just came there looking for a fight."

A waiter placed a basket of rolls on the table. Gert noticed that they were shiny. She wondered if they were sweet. Shiny rolls usually were sweet. She'd learned that when she was eight. Her father's friend had opened a diner in Anaheim, and they'd driven down to it. Gert immediately loved the place, because instead of the usual dull dinner rolls, they'd brought out a basket of sweet rolls and warm cinnamon buns. Both varieties were soft and delicious—better, even, than Gert's subsequent burger and fries. Gert's parents told her not to fill up on rolls, but she ate three, and she decided they were the best rolls she'd ever tasted. After they all left, Gert kept agitating for her parents to take her there again, and her father reported this to his friend, but she didn't tell them that the inspiration was just those warm, sweet buns. A few months later, the family finally went back to the diner for Gert's birthday. But when the waitress came, she only brought out a basket of regular dinner rolls. What had happened? Gert was disappointed. She just ate her food in silence. Why did good things have to change so quickly?

Todd looked at her. "What are you thinking about?"

"Nothing," she said.

"Come on," he teased.

"It's boring."

"I doubt it. Tell me."

"Well," she said uncertainly, "the rolls just reminded me of something from childhood."

"Oh," he said. "What did they remind you of?"

"When I was eight," Gert started slowly, "we went to this diner. My father's friend owned it." She told him the whole story. "So I had chocolate pudding for dessert, but I missed those sweet rolls."

"Why didn't you ask where they were?"

She shrugged. "I guess I was too shy."

"It's easy to be like that if you're a kid," Todd said, sitting back. "That reminds me of this ice-cream place they used to have near Busch Gardens in Virginia. Instead of just dropping a few sprinkles on top of your ice cream, they would pour them throughout the whole cone, under and over and in between, and my brother and I thought that was heaven. We spent half our lives complaining about how most places only put sprinkles on top, and how you could lick them off in a second. So my mom drove us up there once a year. It was about forty-five minutes from us. Then one time we went up there, and they didn't do it. In our case, my brother *did* ask them why, and the guy at the counter said they didn't know that the old owner had done it that way. They'd changed owners and no one had told the new ones."

*The true test of a relationship,* Gert thought, *is if you can tell someone the most boring story in the world about yourself, and they'll still have something to add.*

The waitress returned with Gert's wine. Then a waiter with long, scraggly hair took over to recite the specials. But he had a thick French accent, and Gert could barely make out what he was saying. She listened patiently, not wanting Todd to pick up on her ignorance.

"Was it just me," Todd said after he left, "or did you not understand a word of that?"

Gert laughed. Todd was so honest. She'd never seen him try

to cover up when he didn't know something. "The only thing I understood was 'strawberry crème torte.'"

"Do you like strawberry crème tortes?" Todd asked.

"When they're available."

"Well, we'll have to get you one."

He looked at the menu. "Another thing we have to try is the escargot."

"Have you ever had it?"

"No," he said. "That's why we have to try it. Only once, though. I don't intend to get addicted to snails."

"Why not?" she said. "They're probably easy to hunt for. They can't get away."

A waitress came and asked if Gert wanted more wine. She looked at Todd, who said, "Yes." The waitress asked if Todd wanted any, but he passed.

"So," he said, "you have to answer the same question that *you* asked *me.*"

"What?" Gert asked.

"Do you have any enemies?"

Gert laughed. "Well, I never got into a fight at a frat party."

"Anywhere else?"

She thought about her condo association. They met each month on the roof deck, and they always seemed to bring up petty complaints about whichever neighbor wasn't there. Gert had been ready to scream the last time it had happened. Marc had gone to the meetings in the past.

She suddenly had a thought. She still hadn't told Todd about Marc. She'd do it after dinner. But she didn't know how he'd respond. She almost wished she'd told him right away. Now it would be strange.

She looked at him. He was younger than her. What did he know of tragedy? It might only scare him off.

She tensed up—just when she was trying to wind down from a tough day.

Todd looked at her quizzically. She tried to remember what he'd asked.

"Oh, enemies. Uh, I guess I don't have any enemies," she said finally. "Well," she added hastily, "some girl in third grade pulled my hair."

"For a reason?"

"Yeah, I'd stepped on her by accident, so she pulled my hair. I cried, and the teacher yelled at her. That's the whole story."

He was still looking at her. She nervously took a few sips of her wine.

He waited for her to finish drinking, then smiled at her. "So, do you feel better now?"

"I should hope so. It was twenty years ago."

"No. Not about that girl. About today."

She actually was starting to, again. She felt like she had finished a long cry and was catching her breath. "I do," she said. The waitress came and refilled her wineglass. "I know I shouldn't let Missy get to me. But it's the most frustrating thing when your boss yells at you when it's not your fault, and you can't say anything back because you want to keep your job."

"And then you fantasize that if you didn't really need the job, you would just tell her off," Todd said, "but if you didn't need the job, you wouldn't *be* there."

"Exactly," Gert said. She was glad he understood.

"So how did it end up with the FedEx?"

Gert put her wineglass down. "Oh my God!" she said. "I forgot to tell her!"

"What?"

"I found it when she went to lunch."

"Where?"

"Behind her door. I meant to tell her. She came back and left again."

"Well, tell her on Monday," Todd said.

"She might have needed it for this weekend," Gert said. "I have to tell her. She'll kill me."

"No she won't."

"*Probably* not, but she does things on whims sometimes. And what if she needed it?"

"Do you have her cell number?" Todd asked.

"At work I do, but I can't get in. What am I going to do?"

"Tell her Monday."

"But I should find a way to tell her *tonight,*" Gert said.

Todd said, "Relax. Don't worry about it."

Gert felt her voice rising, but she couldn't help it. "I can't not worry!" she said. "I should have told her."

"But there's nothing you can do about it."

He smiled.

"I need to try," Gert said.

She didn't smile back.

"It's the weekend. Relax a little."

He was still smiling.

"This is important!" Gert said. She felt the back of her neck get hot.

Todd seemed confused.

"Is everything that easy for you?" Gert said. "You think you can just smile and make everything okay?"

Now he looked perplexed.

"This is something worth worrying about," she said. "Not something you can just smile about and it goes away!"

He held up his hands. "But if there's nothing you can do…"

"Maybe there is!"

"Do you want me to call Information?"

"Right. A top executive keeps her home number listed."

Todd took out his cell phone. "What's her name?"

"Hathaway. But she won't be in there."

He dialed. "First name?"

"It might be under Dennis."

He asked the operator and waited. "There's a D. Hathaway on Central Park West," he said.

"That's them! Call them." She handed him a pen from her pocketbook.

He scribbled it on a slip of paper and dialed. Then he handed her the phone. Gert listened.

"Hi. We're not home," said the machine. "Please leave a

message with your name and number and we'll get back to you."

"Missy, if you're there, I found your FedEx," Gert said. "I forgot to tell you. I put it in my top drawer at work. I hope that's okay. If you have any problems, call me, all right?" She left her cell and home numbers, hung up and handed the phone back to Todd.

He lowered his head as she looked at him.

"I guess I overreacted a little," she said softly. "I'm sorry."

"It's okay."

"I just got worried for a second."

"It's fine," Todd said, shrugging.

But she thought *he* should concede a little, too. He had told her to calm down when she was talking about something important.

*How would he act in a crisis?* Gert thought. *What if someone he loves was in an accident? Is he one of those people who's never experienced real tragedy, and he always assumes everything is naturally going to work out just fine?*

*Can I really be with someone who doesn't worry about anything? Maybe when I tell him about Marc, he'll just stare at me like everyone else does, not knowing what to say. Maybe he'll try to make that seem all right, too.*

"Are you okay?" Todd asked her.

It seemed pointless to argue now. "Yeah," she said.

But she still thought he should apologize, too.

During dessert, Gert started to feel a bit better. She carefully carved the strawberry crème torte with her fork. She looked up and saw Todd smiling.

"What?" she said.

"Nothing," he said. "You just look happy. I'm glad."

They finished and retrieved their coats from the back. Gert turned to look back as she was leaving. She saw Todd hand the coat check guy a five.

"That was nice of you," she said when he got to the door.

"Oh," he said, looking at his coat. He seemed a little embarrassed. "I did coat check one summer during college. People don't give you anything, because they resent having to check their coats."

"I would think they'd give a lot."

"No. They don't. And he probably was a student, so he needs the money."

Todd could be frugal, but he could also spend money when the situation called for it. Gert was pleased. She decided she'd been too hard on him tonight. So what if he'd been slow to catch on to her concern about the FedEx? He'd also been intuitive enough to save her day. She thought about what she'd be doing right then if he hadn't called. She'd probably be sitting on the couch at home, her feet up, watching horrible TV sitcoms and crying.

He didn't know everything about her yet, but at least he was trying to be nice. He put his hand on her back for a second as they went out the door. His hand felt warm.

"You know, it's still early," he said as they walked past some boutique stores.

"It is," Gert said. She looked at him. "You know, you really helped me feel better tonight. Thanks."

He stopped under a streetlight, then leaned in and kissed her.

It felt warm, wonderful. She looked up at him.

He stood there. "Can I do that again?" he asked.

"Only if you promise never again to order me to calm down when I'm upset."

He looked at the ground. "I'm sorry," he said, shifting his feet. "I shouldn't have done that. It just, it upset me to see you so worried."

"Sometimes it's okay to be worried," Gert said pointedly. Even if she was still tingling from the kiss, she had to make sure he got the point.

"You're right," he said. "You're absolutely right. I wanted to make the problem go away, and that was stupid."

"It's okay."

He looked across the street, and so she did, too. There was a small theater showing an old Hitchcock film.

"You want to go see that?" Todd said.

"I've seen it," Gert said. "It's my father's favorite."

*"The 39 Steps?"*

"Yes," she said.

"You know what I always wanted to see?" Todd asked.

*"North by Northwest!"* Gert said.

"Yeah!" Todd said. "How'd you know?"

"I've always wanted to see it, too. It's strange that neither of us has."

"We could rent it," Todd said.

Gert thought about it. She wasn't worried about sitting next to him on his couch anymore. Their dates normally ended so early that it might actually be nice to be physically close to him for more than two seconds.

She thought about what it would be like to say no. He'd leave, and she'd be on the subway heading back to Astoria alone. The thought of it pained her. In fact, the need to not be alone right then gripped her.

Todd said, "My roommate's probably home. We have separate rooms, but we'll hear him walking in and out of the apartment."

"I don't have a roommate," Gert said. "But I live in Queens."

"I don't mind," Todd said.

Of course he didn't.

Sitting next to Todd in the subway, Gert looked up at the ads. The cartoons with AIDS were at it again. There had been an ongoing serial in the New York subways for years about two cartoon characters who had AIDS. There was a Spanish version, and in that one, AIDS was called SIDA. *Sindroma Inmuno Definiciencia Adquirida.*

Not the most romantic thing to read on a date.

Gert felt shocked. She *was* on a date. No denying it. And now she was bringing a guy back to her apartment. Her and her husband's place. A guy she'd only known for a few weeks.

But they were just going to watch a movie, right? It didn't have to mean anything more.

Marc was on her mind though. This was disrespectful. And unfair to him. Why should she get to have fun when Marc couldn't?

She remembered the photos of Marc all over the condo. And all the other things that would tell Todd abruptly that she'd been married before.

She'd have to tell him as they were walking toward the condo. It was ridiculous that she'd put it off for this long, anyway.

No more stalling.

The first time Gert had visited Astoria, Queens, she'd been surprised. Marc had told her it was a low-cost alternative to Manhattan: just a few subway stops east, with wider streets, big diners and bigger families. In their neighborhood, the elevated subway station towered three stories high on blue metal stilts, its shadows engulfing factories and real estate offices and restaurants that served giant salads with slabs of feta and long, hairy strips of anchovy. The houses rose on sloped roads, each foundation a foot higher than the last. A few blocks west, a glistening bridge spanned the East River into the more gentrified neighborhoods of Manhattan.

The subway train came to a stop. Todd took Gert's hand when they got off. It had been so long since someone had held her hand.

They crossed the concrete platform and trotted down the stairs, past a group of teenagers who were going up with skateboards. They headed under the station and heard loud echoes and rumblings above.

The streets were dark and cold, but there was no wind. Todd began massaging Gert's hand with his thumb. A faint sensation passed through her body.

A group of people was howling from off somewhere. They sounded like hooligans.

"I'm glad I'm not a teenager anymore," Gert said.

"Me, too," Todd said. "I had no idea what I wanted."

"I do now," Gert said.

"I do, too," he said, and he swung her hand. "But we can still act like we're teenagers if we want. *Aaaaaoooooo!*"

Gert laughed and howled, "*Aaaaaoooo!* Hey, that feels good. Maybe I have some werewolf in me."

He stopped and kissed her quickly. "Nope."

"You can tell by doing that?"

"Werewolves don't have soft lips."

When they reached her block, Todd said, "Every time I feel like I've been everywhere in New York, I see somewhere new."

"I was thinking that the other day," Gert said. "When we met up in Little Italy."

"You'd never been there?"

"Just near it."

"I took the subway once for four hours, just to get to as many neighborhoods as I could," Todd said.

Gert smiled to herself. It was an interesting thing to do— a Todd thing. Gert swung his hand, feeling daring because of the wine.

The condo building was four stories high, with a sloped roof. Gert wondered whether Todd could tell that it was condos and not apartments. She'd have to tell him the minute they got inside.

But when she got to her front door, she said, "Just hold on a second. I have to clean something up."

She slipped in, leaving him in the hall, and looked for photos of Marc in the living room. Todd would just have to be kept in suspense for a few minutes more. She had to tell him before he saw the photos.

Gert spotted the picture near the TV that showed Marc smiling at their college graduation. It stabbed at her heart.

For a second, she was ready to cry. What was she doing?

Todd was in the hall.

She closed her eyes and gulped, turning the photo toward the wall.

She knew Todd was waiting. She turned over the other one of Marc standing outside their house with his friend Craig. Then she went to the door.

"Sorry," Gert said. "I just hadn't planned on company today."

"I know," Todd said. "Don't worry. Wow, this is nice."

Gert looked around the living room. It was big, square, minimally decorated. For a place in New York, it *was* nice.

She gave Todd a tour, but she left the door to Marc's trophy room closed.

She would put off telling Todd about Marc until after the movie. No sense putting that into his mind and ruining something they'd both waited a long time to see. She could tell him right afterward.

Todd sat on the couch. Gert put the DVD in. She thought about how far to sit from Todd. A few inches? What was the line between cautious and frigid? Another tough dating decision. How did Hallie and Erika do this all the time?

The room was dark. Gert was close enough to Todd for him to put his arm around her. She didn't stop him. She felt okay about it. In fact, after about twenty minutes, she decided it was safe to lay her head on his shoulder.

When he pulled her closer, her whole body sighed. It had been so long since she'd been held. She couldn't help it.

She closed her eyes and just listened for a while, to the movie and to Todd breathing.

They stayed like that for more than an hour. Todd didn't make any other moves, and Gert was glad. She wanted to keep it simple. No more confusing choices.

Eventually, though, Todd took her hand. He massaged the

inside of it again, slowly, his fingers tracing the ridges above her palm. Soon, she couldn't concentrate on the film. He tickled the inside of her hand, then massaged it more. It felt wonderful.

She opened her eyes and watched his hand moving. His fingers moved deliberately. He was so slow, so painstaking about everything he did.

She closed her eyes and imagined that those hands gave good backrubs. She was so relaxed that she didn't think she could ever get up.

But he was being a gentleman, so she decided she should keep watching the movie. If he was going to try to be good, she shouldn't be having impure thoughts. Even if she could blame the wine.

It occurred to her that maybe she was being selfish, since he'd been massaging her hand for twenty minutes and she hadn't reciprocated. She took his hand, then moved her fingers into the tender valleys between his.

He kissed her on her head. She liked it, but then she went back to watching. She didn't move. He didn't, either; just held her tighter. They both kept their eyes on the screen.

When the movie faded out, she didn't get up. She didn't think she could. The credits rolled but neither of them stirred. She was nervous and excited. She didn't know what might happen next.

He moved her hair back from her face, and leaned down to kiss her.

She lay on her back and looked up at him. Then she put her hands on his face and brought it down to her. She was feeling something she hadn't felt in a long time, and she didn't want to stop.

The need to not be alone clutched her as hard as anything ever could.

Hours later, she woke up. She was in her bedroom, and it was dark. She hazily looked around.

What had happened tonight?

Missy, Todd, wine, dessert—

She heard someone sleeping beside her.

Uh-oh.

Now she remembered.

She'd wanted it to happen. She admitted it to herself. It wasn't the wine, or being lonely, or desperation.

But had she gone too far?

"I'm glad I met you," Todd whispered suddenly. She was startled. She'd thought he was sleeping.

"Oh." She turned to look at him.

"You're so beautiful, and so smart…."

She couldn't think of a thing to say.

"My friends were really down on women for a while," he said. He was still whispering.

She smiled. "Your friends couldn't have been as down on women as my friends are on men."

"Everyone pretty much sucks, don't they?"

"That's why we hide inside," Gert said.

"I intend to." He reached for her shoulder and squeezed it.

"I think that when people get lonely," she said, "they try to find someone to blame. But there isn't really anyone to blame. It just takes a long time to find the right person."

"Some people are better at it than others," he said. "I can't imagine anyone not getting along with you. Well, except for that girl in third grade."

"Tell that to my boss."

"I would say that the issues are on her side of the net."

They were quiet for a minute. She stared at him in the dim light. His hair was in tufts, and he was wearing a T-shirt. He looked cute, relaxed. He usually did.

"How long were you alone?" Todd asked.

Gert was surprised. It was The Question. She still hadn't told him about Marc.

"Uh, a year and a half," she said. Why hadn't she told him?

"And how long did the two of you go out?"

"Three years."

"Wow—"

"So what about you?" Gert broke in. "You mentioned you had a college girlfriend."

Todd thought. "We were together for six months after college. She moved to Seattle. It wasn't worth keeping up over the phone."

"Did either of you want to move with the other?"

"I guess it wasn't that serious."

"You didn't have any girlfriends after that?"

Todd shrugged. "It didn't work out. My schedule's too erratic."

Gert didn't say anything.

"Okay, so that's not the whole reason," he conceded without being challenged. "I guess I just didn't meet anyone I liked enough."

"What about at work?"

"There aren't many women who sign up to heave eighty-pound parts around a railyard," he said. "And the ones who do aren't that appealing."

He looked at her. "So what about you? Why did you break up with your boyfriend?"

Gert didn't say anything.

"Never mind," Todd said. "You know what? I don't know why I brought it up."

"No…."

"I hate going through laundry lists of exes. Why does everyone feel compelled to do it?"

"But I *will* tell you…"

"It's like you're asking someone how little room they have left to care about you," he said. "It's stupid. We'll talk about it another day. It's late anyway." He yawned. "It doesn't matter. You're here now."

"Okay…."

He closed his eyes. She watched him, feeling glad he was there.

But she also felt scared. She'd withheld the truth one more time.

She couldn't keep doing that. It was almost like lying.

Still, for one last night—maybe for the last night in a long time—she'd be not a widow, but just a twenty-nine-year-old single woman.

She shifted a bit and squeezed his arm. She'd missed holding on to a strong body. Even if they'd gone too fast, even if tomorrow Todd thought her too easy or clingy or serious and ran away, she desperately needed to cling tonight.

When she woke up, something was missing—that awful dread, that lead ball in her stomach.

Todd's eyes were already open. "I didn't want to wake you," he said.

"No," she said. "It's nice."

But she sensed something different. Todd was farther away on the bed. He was staring at her. Maybe she was being paranoid.

Or maybe he'd seen something. A picture of Marc. Or something of Marc's. He could have peeked in the medicine cabinet and seen Marc's old prescriptions. It could be anything. Marc's brothers had come to take some of his things from the condo six months after he'd died, which had been rough on Gert, but they'd called and offered to come, at the prodding of their father. It had to be done. She'd kept most of his clothes, though; she'd folded and stored them neatly in the closet, just the way he would have wanted. Even the black socks that had turned dark green when he goofed up the wash, she'd put in a drawer. Sometimes, she even wore Marc's shirts, the unisex stuff. It was weird for her to wear some of his clothes, but if there was one thing the support group had taught her, it was that she had the right to deal with life's challenges any way she wanted. If Marc had to be taken from her in a crazy accident, she could do crazy things like wear his shirts.

But now Todd was here. He looked happy, and he made her *feel* happy. He was not like any guy she had ever met. And there was still much more to learn about him. The possibilities both excited and intimidated her.

But what if he had seen something? A man's razor? His pill bottles? Notes?

There was no polite way to ask.

He reached over and brushed her hair out of her eyes.

"It was nice waking up with you," he said.

At the diner on the corner, the one that caught all the sunlight, they sat in a booth by the back window. Todd was back in his clothes from the night before, except that he was wearing Marc's Celtics cap from their living room. He had asked Gert if he could wear it because his hair was a mess. She couldn't tell him it was Marc's. She wasn't sure she liked Todd wearing Marc's cap. She felt kind of lousy about it, actually.

"Are you a fan?" he asked, sipping coffee. Behind him, outside, someone was trying to pull a yellow Labrador puppy along, but the dog wanted to sniff the sidewalk.

Gert said, "My dad is." She hoped that would be the end of it.

"How does a guy from L.A. become a Celtics fan?"

*When first we practice to deceive…* "He's half-Irish," Gert said, and she sipped her own coffee. She should tell him about Marc now. Right now. But a mellow morning-after breakfast didn't seem like the right time.

The waitress arrived. Todd ordered Sugar Corn Pops. She had to laugh. What was wrong with men? Marc had ordered cold cereal at diners, too. They were in a place where they could get fifty breakfast dishes, and men just wanted cereal.

Gert ordered an omelette, toast and hash browns.

As Todd turned to watch the window and the man with the dog, Gert looked at his profile. She liked looking at Todd.

Her cell phone rang. Todd raised and lowered his eyebrows. Gert made a funny face. He laughed.

"Gert!" Hallie said. "Where are you?"

"Um, eating breakfast."

"Thank God," Hallie said. "I thought you'd rush into things with What's-His-Name."

"Nope." Gert reached over and dabbed a spot of coffee off Todd's chin.

"You'll never guess who Erika's writing weird e-mails to now," Hallie said.

Gert wanted to get off the phone. "Who?"

"Eden."

"The doctor from the café?"

"Yes," Hallie said. "Eden Youdani. They haven't gone out yet, but they've been trading e-mails like mad. She's afraid to meet up with him because he'll figure out she's not Jewish, so she keeps writing him these flirty e-mails but saying she's too busy to see him right now. He asks her questions about herself and she only answers the ones she wants to. She says when they finally go out together, she's going to get him drunk and seduce him, so that by the time he finds out she's not Jewish, he'll be too satisfied to care."

"Good plan," Gert said absently. Todd was opening his little box of Corn Pops.

"So tell me how your date went with Todd," Hallie said.

"I will," Gert said. "But I'm walking out the door. Can I call you back?"

"Yeah. Call and tell me what happened!" Hallie hung up.

Todd said, "Who was that?"

"Hallie. She wanted to know how our date went."

"Did you tell her about the unbridled lust?"

"Ha."

Todd said, "It's too bad you need to rush off to yoga."

She cringed. There *was* a yoga class at the community center, but she was going for the support group. Another lie she'd told. "It *is* too bad," she said.

"You want to take a ride on a train one morning?" Todd asked.

This sounded interesting. "One of yours?"

"No, I'd get fired. But there's a chocolate festival they have every year in the spring, and they charter an old-fashioned train to get there."

"Chocolate!" Gert said. "I'm in. Where is it?"

"Hackettstown, New Jersey."

*"Hackettstown?"*

"I know it doesn't sound too good, but you'd be surprised what you'd find in New Jersey."

"I've been through New Jersey," Gert said. "It wasn't a surprise."

"That's why you have to take a train," Todd said. "Anyone can drive down the Turnpike and see rotten-egg–smelling industrial plants. But if you take a train through the back woods, it's a whole different world. There were these coal trains that used to go from Pennsylvania through western New Jersey and New York state, the Erie-Lackawanna trains. You take that route now, you pass through the ghost towns and mills and forests that they ran through one hundred years ago. It's the way the country used to look. There's this green viaduct in West Jersey, with all these arches over a huge ravine…you just have to see it. I get to see places no one ever sees."

She could see in his eyes how much he loved what he did.

"I'd do anything for good views and chocolate," she said.

He smiled. "I had a clue. I saw the fondue pot in your kitchen last night."

She tensed up again. It had been a wedding gift. She was hiding so many things.

"I…I mostly use it for cheese," she stammered.

"I've never had cheese fondue."

"Only chocolate?" she said. "Interesting. I make a mean Swiss mix." She hadn't cooked much since Marc had been gone. He'd liked putting wine in everything. Like cheese fondue.

"Sounds great," Todd said. He sipped the milk on his spoon.

"I'll make you some," she said, wanting to take it back as soon as she said it. But then she thought about it. Maybe if she invited him to her place for dinner, she could tell him about Marc. Then she wouldn't have to say it in a crowded restaurant or while a movie was on. Yes. That's what she would do.

No more excuses.

"I'll make dinner for you this week," she said uncertainly.

Todd looked interested. "That sounds good."

# Chapter

6

Gert stared at her reflection in the bathroom mirror at home.

Nothing to feel guilty about.

Right?

She opened the medicine cabinet. There were none of Marc's things there, or anywhere in the bathroom. He was definitely clueless.

Which meant she *had* to tell him Thursday.

She admitted to herself that it wasn't just that the timing had been wrong. She was scared to death of telling him, and of his reaction. She didn't want Todd to disappoint her.

Todd was three years younger than she. The fact that she had already started to build a life with someone else, had already pledged her life to someone else, might scare him off.

But by not talking about it, she was betraying Marc. If Todd couldn't take it, that was his problem. Marc was the biggest part of her. She'd met him before she was old enough to drink, old enough to really know what the world was like. He was on her mind all the time. If Todd really liked Gert, he'd have to accept that important part of her.

But was it so wrong that she'd waited?

Erika was going to wait awhile to tell Dr. Yarmulke that she was Christian. You didn't hit someone with the hardest things about you first. Hallie had told her about that—the Dating Disclosure Law. When you met someone, you let them get to know you, let them get to care about you…then, and only then, did you roll out the red carpet so they could step over the tacks.

"Gert, you are clinging to this guy who you have nothing in common with!" Hallie said on the phone later that day. "Marc you went to college with. You two had memories. This guy has nothing to offer you. I know you're excited because you just met him, but believe me, you'll get bored with him. Did he even go to college?"

"Yes," Gert said, playing with a loose strand of gold thread on her couch. "You just assume he didn't because of his job." Gert wondered why Hallie was so suspicious of Todd. He hadn't done one thing to indicate he was anything other than a good guy. "What difference would it make if he *hadn't* gone to college, anyway?" Gert asked. "I *like* him."

"I know," Hallie said, "but what do the two of you talk about?"

"Everything," Gert said. "Everything. He's just the nicest guy."

"There are a million nice guys!"

"But you always say there are none."

Hallie was quiet.

"You know, you and Erika have these weird standards," Gert said. "If someone wears the wrong shirt or doesn't have the right job or is too short or too fat, you blow them off. How do you expect to ever meet anyone that way?"

There. She'd said it. What she'd been thinking for years.

Hallie paused. "You want to know the truth?" she said.

"Yes."

"I don't have weird standards."

Gert wasn't sure about that.

Hallie said, "My standard is, I want to feel happy when I'm with someone. Is that such a weird standard?"

"No," Gert said.

"You're right," Hallie said. "If you ask why I'm not interested in someone, I might say their nose is too big, or they don't know how to dress, or they're too thin or too fat or too plain. But the truth is, I only notice those things because of the real reason— that I'm just not feeling anything. But people don't want to hear that. They always want an explanation. So I have to come up with something concrete even though feelings aren't like that. If I *did* meet a guy and I felt happy with him for whatever reason, I wouldn't give a rat's ass what he wore or how tall he was or what he did for a living. But when I'm with someone and it just doesn't feel right, *that's* when I start noticing the bad haircut or Chicago accent or unibrow. And it's true that tomorrow I may go home with someone who you think is totally wrong for me. And the next day I might meet a perfectly nice guy who you think I should feel excited about, but I don't. But if I do go home with someone, it means for a change, something feels right. For a change, I'm feeling hopeful. I just want to feel *happy* when I'm with someone. Is that so wrong?"

Hallie did have a point, Gert thought. She shouldn't have to justify not being attracted to someone.

"It's not wrong," Gert said, slowly. "I want to be happy, too."

They both were quiet for a minute.

Hallie said, "I know. I know you do."

"I'll make a confession," Gert said. "You're right. I *am* rushing into things with Todd. I'm not *good* at being alone. I don't even know how to do it. But it's only because it feels right, like you said. If you talked to Todd, you'd know. He's just the neatest guy."

"But you haven't even been to his apartment yet," Hallie said. "You told me so. How do you know he's not living with someone?"

"He lives with his roommate, Doug," Gert said.

"How do you know it's not Dot?"

"Hallie!"

"I'm just looking out for you," Hallie said. "It happened to Erika. *And* a girl I work with. I wouldn't be a good friend if I didn't warn you."

Gert took a breath. "It just seems like sometimes," she said, "when you say these things to me, it's more out of resentment. You and Erika both."

Hallie was quiet again.

"Well," Hallie said, "I think it's not too hard to see that we do get jealous of you. You go to a bar, you get a guy. It's always been that way. Guys just like you."

Gert didn't know how to respond to that.

"With Marc, with Todd…with other guys in college. You have something. I don't know what it is, but you have something. I wish I did."

Gert held her tongue.

"Do you know what might make me and Erika feel less resentful?" Hallie asked.

"What?"

"If women who got into early relationships, like you, acknowledged that they were lucky, rather than blaming single women like us for being single," Hallie said. "I know you think it's our fault that we haven't met anyone, and you've practically said as much. But you have your own standards, too; it's just that they've never had to be tested. Have you ever dated someone bald?"

"No."

"Or shorter than you?"

"No."

"Or of a different religion?"

"No…."

"Or much older than you?"

"No…."

"Or of a different race?"

"No."

"Or a guy with facial hair?"

"No. I haven't."

"Or a guy who didn't have a job?"

"No."

"Or…"

"I get the point," Gert said.

"Everyone has standards," Hallie said. "Yours may be different than mine. They're probably more liberal. But deep down, you still have them."

"I probably do," Gert admitted. But Hallie and Erika were still too picky, right?

"Do you know how you might help all of us?" Hallie asked.

"How?" Gert asked.

"If Todd is really such a great guy, then he probably has great single friends. Have you ever once thought of asking Todd if he has any friends that might come out with the two of you and me and Erika? Did that ever occur to you at all?"

"I thought you wouldn't be interested," Gert said.

"Of course I would!" Hallie said.

"Okay," Gert said. Maybe she *could* help. "Do you want me to see if Todd knows of any good single friends who might be interested in coming out with us and meeting you?"

"Well," Hallie said, "now that you mention it, yes."

That night, Gert called Todd.

"I could introduce her to Brett Stoddard," Todd said. "But he's a dog."

"What do you mean, 'He's a dog'?" Gert asked. "He's ugly?"

She heard Todd turn on the water then shut it off and thought of Hallie's comment about her never having been in his apartment. She tried to put it out of her mind. Why let Hallie make her paranoid?

"No, he's not ugly," Todd said. "I mean, like when women say, 'Men are dogs,' Brett Stoddard's a dog. He brags all the time about his methods for bagging women. He knows exactly what to say to get women to fall in love with him, and once they do, the challenge is over and he dumps them. He asks them a million questions about themselves, he takes their side in any argument, and every once in a while he quotes the only two poems he knows. One is by Shelley, and…I forget who the other one is. But he pops them into first-date conversation, and women go crazy. They're so thrilled to be with a guy who quotes poetry that they sleep with him by the third date. After they sleep with him, he dumps them. And on to the next."

"Well, what does he want?" Gert asked. "It can't be sex, if he stops seeing them after he sleeps with them."

"I think it *is* sex, but I think it's also the challenge," Todd said. "I guess part of sexiness is elusiveness."

Gert got quiet. "Then I guess they're right," she said.

"Who's right?"

"Hallie and Erika. With all their dating rules. Maybe they're right."

Todd was quiet for a second.

"We're talking about Brett Stoddard here," he said impatiently. "Girls who want to be with guys like Brett Stoddard should play games. Girls who want normal, nice guys, who have real emotions and don't try to hide them, should not play games. If you want a guy who plays games, then you play games."

Gert smiled to herself. "You know, you're a good guy."

"That's definitely a violation of your friends' rules, to tip your hand like that," he said.

"Well, I want a guy who's real," she said, "and not Brett Stoddard."

On Sunday morning, Gert lay in bed until 11:30 a.m. It had been a long weekend already. FedEx battle with Missy on Friday, date with Todd Friday night, conversations with Hallie and Todd Saturday. Today, she had a day of rest.

She thought she should get up and buy the Sunday *Times* before all the copies were gone. She remembered how reading the paper with Marc each week, trading sections on the couch, was one of the most intimate things they did. Once, they were in their pajamas reading the comics and somehow started arguing over whether the leafy item in Dagwood Bumstead's sandwiches was spinach or lettuce. Gert said no one put spinach on a sandwich. Marc said it was too dark to be lettuce. That led to a discussion of the fact that neither of them had ever made, or eaten, a Dagwood sandwich. Marc had immediately insisted that it become a project. They went to the supermarket that afternoon and loaded up a cart with turkey breast, ham, tomatoes, lettuce, spinach, Swiss cheese, provolone, pickles, bologna, salami, mustard, mayonnaise, bread and eggs to hard-boil. In the kitchen, they worked side by side, laughing and daring each other to go higher. Their creations nearly toppled over. They ate as much as they could, but it was hard to get their mouths around them. Eventually, Gert and Marc fell onto the couch together, sated. It was the kind of thing you would only do with a significant other.

She missed him, remembering his little projects. No matter who else was in the picture, she'd always want him back. *Always,* she thought. Was that terrible? How could she reconcile it?

When she stepped outside, Gert's block was alive and full of chatter. The Greek family from across the street was dressed up, headed to church. A gaggle of Indian kids was running around with a scruffy mixed-breed dog. Frosted spears of grass were springing back to life. Gert breathed the cool air. On the corner, a blue moving van was parked, its back ramp lying on the ground like a tired tongue.

That was when Gert saw the girl. And her boyfriend.

The girl was in her early twenties. She was pretty and slight, wearing tight burgundy nylon pants and a long-sleeved football shirt. Her boyfriend, clad in a green college sweatshirt with white lettering on it, was smiling and needling her. "Easy…" he said, watching her pull a plastic chair off the truck. "I want you to know that I'm behind you one hundred percent." The girl glared at him. "Don't stop now," he said. "Remember, you said you didn't want my help. Wait—butterfingers! Butterfingers!" The chair teetered. "You're doing great," the guy said, laughing. Finally the girl put the chair down and went to swat him, half smiling, but he caught her wrists, and she struggled, laughing.

Gert gulped and looked away.

She had never been the jealous type—especially after watching Hallie and Erika turn it into an Olympic sport. But now, seeing these two probably moving in together for the first time, made her feel something in her throat. She had been that girl. How long ago? Five years? Six?

Doing something as simple as unloading the chairs from a moving van, finding some excuse to tease and make physical contact. Knowing that it was just the beginning. The beginning of forever.

If only she could snap back to the time when she was unloading the moving van with Marc. If only she could think of a way to keep him this time.

# Chapter

## 7

Missy floated into work on Monday morning looking chipper as ever, in a navy blue suit and skirt. She was the queen of perfectly fitting suits.

"Morning," she sang, putting her key in the door to her office. "How are you?"

Gert wondered about the change of mood. She thought that probably, when Missy had gone to lunch with her husband on Friday, they'd made up. Then they'd a weekend of makeup passion. That was why Missy was so happy. Guys probably had a lot of incentive to make up with Missy.

"I'm fine," Gert replied.

"Great," Missy said, throwing the door open. "Did you find my FedEx?"

"Yes," Gert said. "Didn't you get the message I left?"

Missy stopped in the doorway.

"What message?"

"The one I left at your house," Gert said.

"How could you have my new number?" Missy asked.

"I used the one that's listed."

"Under…?"

"Dennis Hathaway."

Missy gasped. "I'm never there anymore! You left Dennis a message? What did you say?"

"That the FedEx was in my top drawer…."

"Never call his home again!" Missy seethed, and she immediately went into her office and slammed the door. Gert looked at the phone on her desk and saw Missy's line light up.

Gert opened her top drawer, and her other drawers. The envelope wasn't there.

Had Dennis gotten her message, come in this morning and swiped the envelope?

Missy came back out. "Do you have it?"

"It's not here," Gert admitted.

Wordlessly Missy returned to her office and slammed the door again. Gert wondered if she'd get fired.

There was no way she could look for another job now. She just had too much to deal with without looking for work.

She set her jaw and tried not to cry. She stared at the buildings across the street. They looked fuzzy, then straightened out. She was tired of misery. To hell with Missy and her stupid FedEx. Missy hadn't said a nice word to her in months.

Gert noticed the light on her phone still blinking. Missy must be on with security, telling them about the purloined envelope. Gert checked her drawer again. It was nowhere to be found. She steeled herself for the blowup.

She closed her eyes. She didn't know if she could hold her tongue this time.

"I'm going out to file a police complaint!" Missy said, storming out of her office. Then she stopped and turned to Gert. "You know what? You did me a favor. I am actually glad he had the nerve to do this. *So* glad!" She disappeared down the hall.

Gert breathed.

Missy's line rang the minute the elevator closed, and Gert picked it up.

It was a young, male voice. "Is…Melissa Hathaway there?" it said. It sounded faux-professional, like a young kid calling school pretending to be his parents. It sounded like the mail-room guy. Gert had met him once, when he'd delivered some documents to Missy, although she wasn't sure if the documents were just his excuse to see her.

Missy must have spent the weekend with him, Gert thought. No wonder she had come in happy.

"Would you like me to take a message?" Gert asked, trying to keep a straight face.

"No. I'll call back later. Thanks, ma'am."

Gert put the phone down. She felt better. Missy must be living with Mailboy now. Her moods must be shifting based on how things were going with him. It was like in seventh grade, when Gert's crushes could make or break her day—but Missy wasn't thirteen.

Gert thought that this would make a funny story to tell Todd. That had been her first thought.

She realized she was thinking about him when he wasn't around. That was a good sign, right?

Yes, very good.

But it was only three days until she was to tell him about Marc. She got nervous again and had to stare at the buildings to relax.

Hallie was picking mushrooms off her pizza. They had decided to meet for lunch at the gourmet pizza place around the corner from Gert's office. Hallie had called her at work that morning to say she'd felt a little bad about their conversation the other day. Gert had agreed.

The pizza place was where Gert let herself indulge whenever work was going badly. A slice there was four dollars, but a slice, festooned with fresh veggies, was a meal.

"I did what you said," Gert said, rescuing a dangling strand of saucy cheese. "You were right. I should have thought about helping you more, if you were lonely. I asked Todd about his single friends."

"You did?" Hallie said, smiling. "Thanks!"

"Yeah," Gert said. "You know, you really were right about some things. You and Erika were helping me meet people, but I didn't help you."

"It's not your responsibility," Hallie said, shrugging. "It's just hard out there. It's just...I'm scared about being the last one alone."

"I know," Gert said.

Gert thought that Hallie also looked like a girl who was scared, like she'd lost her mother in the mall. Like a girl who had been wanting things since she was little and was only just realizing she might not get them.

Maybe they'd both get through this stretch of loneliness somehow.

"Todd has one friend you might like," Gert said. "But there's a caveat."

She told her about Brett Stoddard.

Hallie was thrilled. Because, she said, if she knew Brett's tricks and seductions, she'd know what to do.

If he was going to play games with girls, Hallie could play, too. She wouldn't act overeager with Brett. If the two of them got to the fabled third date, she wouldn't sleep with him. When he recited the two poems, she'd look pleased but not fall into his lap. When he acted indignant about the way other men treated women, another move Todd had told Gert about, she'd smile, but not kiss his butt. For once, she had insight into a guy's mind. And Hallie would do everything she could to take advantage of it.

"I'll have the upper hand," Hallie said. "For a change, I'll know what I'm getting into. I won't have to do the ridiculous guesswork, constantly worrying if I'm giving too much or too little. Do guys do that? I get tired of it."

"Well," Gert said, "I can set it up so we go on a double date. But you can't harass Todd or anything."

Hallie laughed. "Give me a little credit," she said. "I won't ask Todd if he secretly lives with a girl."

"Stop!" Gert said, slightly nervous again.

Hallie said, "I won't. And I won't have to. Half the reason for us to *meet* Todd's friends is to tell for sure what kind of guy he is."

"What do you mean 'us'?"

"Well, Erika can come along, right?"

Gert sighed and rubbed her forehead. Suddenly she had a headache.

"She can bring Dr. Eden to this," Hallie said. "If there are more people there, it'll give him less of a chance to ask her about religion. And then she can get him drunk and seduce him like she wanted. It'll be perfect."

Gert wondered what it was that made Hallie always need to be accepted by Erika. Erika could turn cold in a second. Maybe that was it—the ones whose attention was harder to get were the ones you worked more to have. Erika had once seemed to be going places. There was the graphic design career—she was one of the few people Gert knew who was happy in her job— and she had once had the hunky, artistic boyfriend. No wonder Hallie looked up to her.

"Has Erika stopped writing the stuff to Challa?" Gert asked, hoping maybe Erika was getting a little better.

"Still is," Hallie said. "She's trying to alternate it with e-mails to Eden, but it's not the same thing." She leaned closer. "I know you don't believe this, but Erika and Ben *were* perfect together. I went up to Lehigh to see a basketball game with them once, and they had their eyes on each other the whole time. They weren't even watching the game. She just made a stupid mistake. I swear, Gert, they were a perfect couple. She did one dumb thing and now she's paying for it."

Gert wasn't convinced. If Erika had loved Ben the way Gert had loved Marc, she wouldn't have dumped him.

"So when do you want to do this triple date?" Hallie asked.

Gert chewed a piece of pepperoni. "We can't do it Thursday," Gert said. "Todd and I are cooking dinner together."

"Wow," Hallie said. "Sounds intimate."

"It has to be," Gert said. "Because that's when I'm going to tell Todd about Marc."

Hallie dropped her soda straw. "You haven't told Todd about Marc yet?"

"There was never a good time," Gert said.

"Gertie!" Hallie said. "You have to tell him!"

"I know," Gert said. "But I'm scared."

"Scared he might freak out?"

Gert nodded. "A lot of people our age aren't used to hearing something like that. Todd especially. I didn't tell you this, but Friday night, we almost had a fight."

"About what?" Hallie said. She actually seemed concerned. Gert sensed that on some level, Hallie, despite her jealousy, wanted things to work out, if only to provide hope to her that a healthy relationship could be found in the city. Even if Hallie also didn't want to lose her friend again.

Gert told Hallie about the FedEx battle.

"You did let Todd off easy," Hallie said.

"Well, he said he was sorry," Gert said. "And he sort of resolved it."

"How?"

"He tried to call Information for Missy's number."

"I don't blame you for not thinking of that," Hallie said. "Who in their right mind lists their number?"

"Exactly," Gert said. "Anyway, I'm trying to be patient with him. Sometimes you have to let guys learn how to deal with you."

"This time you're right," Hallie said. "You did the right thing with Todd. And you've hit on one of my dating laws without knowing it: The Male Training Rule."

"The what?" Gert asked.

"I have two friends who trained their last boyfriend how to behave, and both times, after they broke up, the guys married the very next girl they dated. So those girls got him in top form. When you train a guy, ten times out of ten, some other girl ends up being the beneficiary of your largesse. So the rule is, never train a guy. If you think he has potential to change, and if his issues aren't that bad, deal with them quietly until you're engaged or married, and *then* set your foot down. That way, he won't be able to run to someone else."

Gert smiled. "I was thinking the other day that you should write a book of these rules. Law of Maximum Exposure. Great Male Statistic…."

"The Great Male Statistic isn't a rule," Hallie said. "It's a statistic."

"The Male Training Rule," Gert said. "Rule of Twenty-Seven."

"Don't forget the Iowa Paradox."

"What's that?" Gert said.

"You haven't heard it? Weren't you there— Oh, that was Cat. Well, it's like this. Have you ever heard people say, 'It's hard to meet people in New York'?"

"Oh, yeah," Gert said. "All the time."

"But that's stupid, right? Because where are you supposed to go, someplace where no one lives, like Iowa? Then you won't meet anyone. You can like, stand in the middle of a cornfield in your overalls and pigtails, and you're not going to find a husband. I guess people say that about New York because New Yorkers are busy and aloof. But if there are nice single people in Iowa, you'll hardly meet any of them. Thus: The Iowa Paradox. You can live in New York and pass one thousand rude single people on the sidewalk every day, or you can move somewhere rural and have a choice of three polite ones at church."

"Which side of the paradox is it best to stay on?" Gert asked.

"I'm here, aren't I?"

Heading back up to work, Gert watched the number change on the elevator. She hoped Missy wouldn't be there. It would be nice if Missy had taken off for the afternoon.

Gert sat down to input some numbers into the computer. She thought again about compiling her portfolio. She was in a better mood.

One time, she and Marc had had a good laugh about alternative slogans for hemorrhoid creams. He'd contributed "Something new to wipe your ass with." She told him not to give up his job on Wall Street. But she had, back in college, liked to think of new advertising and marketing ideas. It might be worth it to try again.

She could take an hour or two a day to work on her portfolio, maybe talk to the other account supervisors about what to do. She could always move to a different firm if Missy didn't want to let her out from under her thumb. That was a plan.

A school of fish swam across Gert's computer screen. She clicked it and faced a blank page. She would force herself to come up with ten hemorrhoid cream slogans or publicity ideas, right now. Since it might be the only way to get her out of being what was basically a glorified secretary.

Let's see. What could she come up with?

*When your moody boss flares up, give her a kick in the rear.*

Gert's phone rang a few hours later, while she was rereading her list, satisfied.

"I have to tell you this!" Hallie said, out of breath. "We canned that girl at work!"

"Your assistant?"

"I followed her," Hallie said, lowering her voice. "My boss gave me permission. Guess where she goes every day at 3:00 p.m.?"

"To have sex?" Gert asked. She surprised herself. But it had just seemed like the most obvious answer. She'd been thinking of Missy and the elevators.

Hallie laughed. "Where's your mind? No. MTV Studios. She ran the three blocks every day to watch them tape *Total Request Live* through the windows."

"With all the teeny-boppers who stand there?"

"Yes," Hallie said. "Erika and I are meeting at the Internet café after work to celebrate. Want to come?"

Gert hadn't done anything with the both of them in two weeks. But why end such a wonderful streak?

"The Internet café?" Gert asked. "Is she going to be writing stuff to Challa?"

Hallie sighed. "Yes," she said. "She's really upset today. Remember Erika told us there was an artist coming to the Whitney she wanted to see? Well, I swear to God, Gert, Erika just checked Challa's Web log from work, and in one of the entries, it said that Challa and Ben were in New York all weekend and went to the Whitney to see this artist! And Erika didn't even know. It just shows how well she knows him. When she sees stuff like that, she thinks more and more that she made a mistake."

Gert felt bad. It was hard to get over someone when you remembered just how good a couple you were. "She should just stop reading the blog," Gert said.

"She can't help it," Hallie said. "I know you think it's crazy, but she said something to me before that really touched me. She said, 'Everyone says this feeling will go away, but it never ever does. I've tried to kill it, but it doesn't go away.' And I don't think it does. She tries to pursue a lot of guys, but no one she's met has come close to the way she felt about Ben."

"I can understand, sort of," Gert said. "I do like Todd, but then I think of Marc, and suddenly I can't feel as much for Todd anymore. And I had a dream about Marc on Friday."

"Again?"

"Yes," Gert said. "I guess Erika's holding on, too. We just have to accept that people are going to stay in our hearts even when they don't stay in our lives."

"You know," Hallie said, "they make all these antidepressants. They should make a pill that stops you from loving the people you can't have, and makes you attracted to those you can."

"Oh, God," Gert said. "I'd sign right up."

# Chapter 8

Gert ran as if she was being chased by a rabid pit bull. She ran as if she was representing the U.S. in the Olympics. She ran as if she was late for final exams.

Annoying Gym Guy appeared next to her. He hadn't bothered her in a while. She kept her pace on the treadmill.

He said something that she couldn't hear.

"Excuse me?" she said, lifting her headphones. The gym had just installed CD players in the treadmills, and she was glad. It was easier than clipping a Discman to her waist.

"You seem disoriented," Annoying Gym Guy said.

"I had headphones on," Gert said. "I couldn't hear you."

"Is your workout going okay?"

"It's fine," she said, staring straight ahead.

"I didn't mean to bother you, ma'am."

*Then don't,* she thought.

She slowed down the treadmill so she could walk. Every time she thought about what might happen that night, she lost her resolve.

Todd was coming at eight for dinner.

If she scared him off, she'd be alone again. She really liked Todd. She wondered if there was any way to mitigate what she was about to tell him.

She would just have to tell it to him straight.

On the subway, Gert slumped forward in her seat, exhausted. The first section of the *New York Times* was lying beside her, smudged and dirty. She picked it up.

The cover held stories about Iraq, the depressed economy and a twenty-one-year-old kid who'd just been elected mayor of the town of Lola, Indiana.

Gert read the Lola article. Then she looked at the story beside the jump. It was one of those "*Times* Neediest Cases Fund" stories. The *Times* ran profiles of people throughout the city who needed help through the paper's charity fund. The idea was that if you sent the money to the fund, rather than tossing it to a sea of administrators, it went directly to the poor. And you would know, from the article, who the people were who needed your help.

### Bronx Tale Turns To Bronx Tragedy

It wasn't love at first sight for Sherell Lewis and Martin Charms. Lewis acknowledges that there was a long period during which she barely said hello to Charms, her next-door neighbor, each morning when she was leaving for work and he was coming home. But after they stopped to chat in the doorway one day, they began dating. Their long work hours and different schedules made their time together short, but soon they realized they were in love.

They saved a few hours each weekend to be together, with Charms feeling lagged from night shifts at a book factory and

Lewis worn out from cleaning apartments for a local maid service. For eight months they saw each other twice a week.

Then, on one moonlit night on the roof, Charms asked Lewis to marry him.

They moved into Charms's tiny one-bedroom apartment. Eventually they had a son. A daughter followed. Money was tight, and so was space, but they worked hard to stay afloat. Charms switched to a day job as a cook so he could spend time with the family at night. Lewis accepted a promotion to assistant manager at the cleaning company. Charms's mother moved in to help with the children during the day. She slept in the living room in a small bed. They pinched pennies, but they were happy.

In November Charms's mother had a stroke.

When she came home from the hospital, she was bedridden. Lewis and Charms tried to cut their hours at work. But when Lewis asked the manager of her maid service for different hours, he said he needed to save money due to the economic downturn and had been planning to eliminate her position. He let her go.

Charms doubled his hours at the restaurant, trying to keep up with his mother's bills that Medicare didn't cover. Lewis did some baby-sitting in her home, but taking care of three or four children wore her out.

A month later Charms's mother died. The burial left little for child care or even the next month's rent.

Charms kept his shift from eleven in the morning to midnight at the grill. Lewis stayed home with the children. One afternoon she got a call in the middle of the day from Charms's boss. Charms had had a heart attack.

Gert put down the paper. The Neediest Cases stories were all like this. Part of her wanted to believe they were exaggerated. How could so many bad things hit one person at the same time?

She had always believed somewhere in the back of her mind that after a person suffered a tragedy, fate left them alone for a while. People who got leukemia didn't then get Parkinson's disease. But she knew that realistically, mankind had no compact with God limiting heartbreaks to one per customer.

As hard as Gert's tragedy was, she was conscious of the fact that there were people who had suffered a similar tragedy and had no support network to deal with it.

Gert didn't like acknowledging such things. Dealing with her own problems was hard enough. But she forced herself to stare at the picture of Sherell Lewis with her children. How did you lose your job, then your mother-in-law, then your husband? There was too much sadness, she thought. How did some people go on?

She wanted to send her money. She folded the article and put it into her purse.

She thought of how much she'd hedged on telling Todd the truth about her own tragedy. *Too bad,* she thought. If she had to deal with tragedy, and if Sherell Lewis had to, then Todd could, too.

But she didn't want to be angry when she told him. It wasn't his fault that the girl he'd met at a bar was a widow.

*Start at the beginning,* she thought. *Don't overload him.*

She moved her finger over the folded article sticking out of her pocketbook.

She'd never donated money to anyone she didn't know— not in her entire life. Thinking about it, she realized that Marc never had, either.

Why hadn't they?

Whenever they'd had extra, they had always spent it on things like the maid service. The only time Marc had donated anything was the $1,000 he'd given to their college alumni association. It had gotten them a nice mention in the class bulletin and helped the class set a record.

At home, Gert sat at the kitchen table and gazed at the yellow refrigerator. The fridge was the oldest thing in the condo.

It had half-torn Barney stickers on it, left from the family who'd lived there before.

Gert looked around the condo. Except for a print of the falling leaves she'd put up in the living room, the walls were fairly bare. It was because Marc was a minimalist. He hadn't really liked to have things on the walls. He wasn't into art in general, except as an investment. He'd gone gallery-hopping with Gert and some friends in SoHo on one sunny afternoon, because he said it seemed like a "New York thing to do." His pet peeve was government funding for the arts. "Who's the government to tell us what's good?" he'd asked. Gert had agreed on that point. Marc liked music, but as far as visual art, he just couldn't be moved.

It was something she'd accepted about him. He was quirky, but he definitely tended toward the practical side with certain things.

Gert got up and put the fondue pot on the table. Todd was bringing some of the groceries. They were first going to have bread and cheese fondue and follow it up with shrimp cacciatore.

When the doorbell rang, she was lost in thought, playing out how best to bring up Marc.

Gert buzzed Todd in, checked her hair in the mirror. *Don't chicken out,* she thought.

Todd laid a paper shopping bag on the table. He looked happy. He was wearing a brown lamb's wool sweater with bits of pink and dark brown in it.

Gert smiled, pinching his shoulder. "Admit that a girl bought that for you," she said.

"How'd you know?"

"Men never have taste in sweaters." She tried not to be nervous.

"Wrong," Todd said. "We just don't buy them because we don't want to hand-wash them. We buy them when we have girlfriends so we can trick them into doing it."

"Sexist."

"But you *like* it."

"Sure. We love scrubbing your smelly sweaty sweaters." She pushed the container of shrimp into his hands. "Peel some shrimp."

She stood there a minute.

"I have something to tell you."

"This is never good."

"It's not anything awful, but every time I've wanted to tell you, something came up."

He looked up.

"It's just…I was married before."

She'd practiced it, but now she'd still stumbled when she had to say it to his face.

He stopped peeling shrimp and turned to face her. "What?"

Gert didn't say anything.

"You're divorced?" He put the shrimp down and looked as though someone had smacked him in the face. "Why didn't you tell me?"

"I didn't *not* tell you. At first it didn't come up…"

"But we were talking the other night," he said. "I know you said something. What was it? You said you'd dated your last boyfriend for three years."

"We *did*."

"A husband isn't a boyfriend."

"We did date for three years first."

"That's like lying."

"I didn't lie to you."

"It's a half truth."

"*Now* you've found something worth worrying about," she said, thinking of the FedEx incident.

"Why didn't you tell me?" he said.

"I didn't *not* tell you. I—"

"What if *I* told you I was divorced all of a sudden?"

"I'm not divorced."

"You mean you're still married to the guy?"

"No," Gert said. "He's—" She couldn't look at him. "He died in a car accident," Gert said.

Todd took a deep breath.

"…a year and a half ago."

"I'm sorry," he said.

"I wanted to tell you," she said. "I was scared."

He looked at her. "Maybe we should sit down."

As the shrimp thawed on the table, Todd and Gert sat side by side on the couch. The side of her left leg was touching his right. She wasn't sure how much he wanted to know.

He said to tell him everything.

"We were married for five years," Gert said.

"Where did you meet?"

"In college."

She told him about meeting Marc in the bookstore. She told him about their first date, to a school play that his friend was in, and how he was good at supporting friends' projects. She talked about the first moment she realized how much she cared about him: during history class one morning, when she kept seeing his face, and thinking of things he'd said without even trying. She kept flashing back to their dates and smiling. She realized this was something beyond a crush or casual dating.

"Go on," Todd said.

"We graduated and moved to New York," Gert said. "I was at his apartment all the time. His parents were kind of old-fashioned. They didn't like that much. But it was silly to live apart. I moved in, and we got engaged."

She told him a little more. When Marc had the accident, he'd been on the way to a doctor's appointment. He'd taken off work because he was sick with the flu. According to the police, he'd drifted into another lane and been hit head-on.

Gert didn't go into her feelings of guilt, or all the reasons Marc's mother might be angry at her. She had trouble thinking about them herself.

When she finished, Todd was silent for a few seconds.

She waited for him to say something. *It's too much for him,* she thought. *I knew it.*

He said finally, "It's a lot to tell someone you just met."

"I know it's a lot," she said. "I just didn't know how you'd react. What you said when I told you—'I'm sorry'—that's all you have to say. But some people don't say anything. They're afraid of saying something wrong."

He looked at her uncertainly. She had no idea what he was thinking or what he would do next. Would he walk out? Pretend everything was fine then leave after dinner?

Finally, he said, "You're pretty brave."

"I don't think so." She tried not to cry.

He leaned over and hugged her. She held in her tears, which wasn't easy. Todd took her hand. He was quiet for a long time. Finally she had to break the silence.

"What?" she asked.

"Nothing," he said. "I'm just processing it. It's a major thing about you that I didn't know before. It's just not what I'm used to."

"You think I am?"

"I'm sure you're not."

"When I got married, I thought I'd be married forever," she said. "I never thought I'd have to date again."

"Well," he said, looking at her, "I'm glad you did."

"Are you sure?"

"Yes," he said. "You hungry?"

"God, yes."

After they'd eaten, they were back on the couch, resting. He had dimmed the lights, but she could still see the serious expression on his face.

"Will you show me your pictures?" he asked.

"What pictures?"

"Your family. Um, your wedding."

"You really want to see those?" she asked.

"I want to know about all the things you care about."

Gert had three photo albums. The purple one contained old pictures her mom had given her before college. She'd put them into the album the first week she'd gotten to campus. Hallie had helped. That was how they'd gotten to know each other so quickly—Hallie had learned about Gert's past right away.

The second album was from college. There were freshman year photos showing the guys on her floor hanging out in the dorm lounge, and later photos of her, Marc and Marc's fraternity brothers.

The third album was her wedding album. It was white, with gold around the sides.

Gert started with the purple album, the family one. She held it on her lap, and Todd looked on. The sides of their legs were again touching.

Todd looked slightly ambivalent, as if part of him really didn't want to be confronted with his predecessor. But they'd get through this.

"These are my parents, when they were young," Gert said, turning the pages of the purple album.

"He looks like that guy from *Welcome Back, Kotter,*" Todd said.

"Epstein? You're not the first to say that. But he doesn't look like him anymore."

"That look doesn't do it for lawyers," Todd said. "Is he sensitive about that? Should I call him Mr. Epstein?"

"Don't," she said. "This is me as a baby."

"You look like Telly Savalas."

"It's gotta be the hair."

"Okay, Miss Savalas."

"This is my brother Henry."

"Now, *he's* got hair."

They moved on to the college album. There was a picture of Marc painting his off-campus apartment. There was one of Marc and his best friend Craig hamming it up with their short-lived college band, Crusty Oatmeal Spoon.

Craig was coming to New York soon, Gert remembered. They were going to do lunch. It would be good to see him.

"You don't have to go so fast," Todd said.

Gert slowed down. "I just don't know how much you want to see," she said.

"I want to see everything."

She felt a lump in her throat.

"This was Marc's house off-campus," Gert said. "Sophomore year. When I met him."

"I like the color."

"I know! It's a strange green and most people didn't like it, but I thought it was great. So I guess you and I have something in common."

"Hopefully more than one thing," Todd said, putting his hand on her knee.

"These are Marc's brothers," she said. "Michael's the one who…" She had to stop herself. She hadn't told Todd about Michael's wedding. She knew she couldn't bring him.

But could she?

She'd have to think about that.

She finished her sentence: "Michael's the one I got along with best out of the brothers."

"Why?"

"Oh, he was the youngest, and he's shy," Gert said. "Marc's other brothers are very outgoing. It took Michael a while to know how to talk to girls. When he went to college and started bringing girlfriends to family gatherings, I always paid a lot of attention to them, to make them feel less nervous."

"That's nice of you."

"Well, he's a nice guy. Sensitive. Knows more than two poems."

Todd laughed.

"This was our senior formal," Gert said. "Marc and I felt weird, because we were doing adult things but we didn't feel like adults yet. We felt like we were playing dress-up in our parents' closet. We got hotel rooms downtown after the formal and had a party in one of them. It was probably the biggest thing we'd ever paid for with our own money and not our parents'."

"I don't feel like an adult," Todd said.

"Me, neither," Gert said. "I don't know when I will."

"I think you will when you buy a house," Todd said. "I think that must be where it starts."

"Oh," Gert said. "We did. This condo's ours. Well, I'm still paying off the mortgage."

"Oh," Todd said. He sounded uncomfortable. But she had to be honest now. What was one more thing?

"I did feel a little older when we finally bought it," she admitted. "I said to myself, 'We're buying a condo. I guess this is it. We must be grown up now.'"

Todd said, "What about when you got engaged?"

Gert said, "That wasn't so hard. Getting engaged was just like making a promise to always be with my best friend."

Todd looked at her for a second, then back at the album. "Hey, this photo's funny."

"That's Marc's best friend, Craig. They did all kinds of pranks together."

They turned pages together now, slowly.

"You really do have a lot of memories with him," Todd said.

"Well," Gert said, "we *were* together for eight years." She looked at him. "Are you okay?"

"Yeah," he said. "I guess I'm a little…jealous. I know it's stupid."

"Nothing's stupid."

"If all your experiences added up to the way you are now, then it's good."

"Thank you." She looked at him.

"Are *you* okay?" he asked.

She nodded.

"You sure?"

"Yes," she said. She sucked her lower lip.

"What did you like best about him?"

"You really want to know?"

He looked her in the eye. "Yes."

She took a deep breath. "He always took care of me and everyone else," she said. "He constantly did things for his friends, helped them move and lent them books and saw their plays and improv sets. He was the person who, when something was wrong and you were afraid to be a burden but you vaguely mentioned it, he sprang into action no matter what." She took a breath. "He prided himself on his loyalty to friends. And he was so close to his family. He had simple tastes, but he knew how to splurge when he wanted to make people happy. He had these idiosyncrasies, I'm not going to get into them, but they were just the kind of things that attract you to someone and you can't forget." She closed her eyes and thought of the way his nose crinkled when he laughed. "He was always making these goals, lists of things he wanted to accomplish by the end of each month, and he always did. And every year before Christmas, he put together this long newsletter for all his friends. It went on about everything that was happening in our lives: Our job changes, what members of his family were doing, which projects he was pursuing at work, but he'd always throw in a few funny comments, too. One year he included a bar graph of how much my musical tastes had improved since meeting him. And he always made sure to put a line at the end of the letter about how much everyone meant to him and how he was glad Christmas came around once a year because it was a good excuse to remind everyone how much he cared about them. He sent this to like fifty people each Christmas. And then he'd be busy for the entire next week because each and every person on that list would write us back practically a book on what was going on in *their* lives. Marc would respond to everything they wrote." She slowed down. She'd been talking quickly. "To be the other half of someone like that, to be the person supporting him…he was just someone I would have been thrilled to *know*. And I got to *marry* him."

Todd looked at her for a second, then leaned toward her and hugged her.

"I promised myself I wouldn't cry tonight," she said, closing her eyes.

"I wouldn't expect you to act any other way."

That night, lying in bed, Gert decided that one of the hardest things about losing someone was trying to explain just how much that person meant. How could you possibly summarize everything in a person's life? Who could possibly understand the little things, or have the patience to hear them?

But Todd had listened.

She had been wondering before whether you could have room for more than one person in your heart. She still wasn't sure.

And Todd still seemed a little uneasy, regardless of what he said. Whether he'd hang in there for the long run, she didn't know. They hadn't set a date for when he'd see her next. Everything was still in flux.

But she thought that someone who really cared about her would want to know as much as possible about the other person. If she could share her love, then that might open up some room.

# Chapter

## 9

Tuesday would be Marc's birthday.

Gert planned to do what she'd done the previous year. Early in the morning, she'd take Greyhound up to Boston and catch a cab to where he was buried. It was a five-hour bus ride, and she'd get in around eleven.

She hoped she could meet up with Marc's parents there. She would call them beforehand to arrange it.

As she looked up Greyhound schedules on Marc's computer, she thought about Todd, about the dinner they'd had at her house. Todd was so different from Marc. He was earnest rather than driven. He was sweet rather than cocky. He was *easy* to have feelings for. But was that bad?

But Todd could be intense, too. His love for his job, and the way he talked about the beauty of the scenery he passed, killed her.

Maybe there was nothing wrong with having a quieter kind of love, she thought. It was different than the intense kind. Not worse. Just different.

★ ★ ★

Craig Evans was behind the worst things Marc had done in college.

Craig was the reason that he and Marc had decorated the door of their dormroom with street signs from outside. When they'd gotten a letter from the housing dean telling them to knock it off, they'd hung it on the wall inside their room, along with the rest of the street signs.

Craig was the reason that Marc had helped form a college cover band called Crusty Oatmeal Spoon.

Craig was the reason that Marc mailed faux admissions office letters to everyone on their freshman floor saying that their records had been lost and they would have to retake the SATs.

These things didn't end when Marc met Gert—they only calmed down a little.

Craig liked Gert a lot. Marc had dated one girl before Gert, and Craig had said that Gert was a big improvement.

When Gert approached the crepe place in the East Village, which was cleverly named The Crepe Place, Craig was sitting in the window and broke into a wide smile when he spotted her. He was in town for an economics conference. Gert saw that he still looked about eighteen years old—no facial hair, just ruddy cheeks. His mop of blond hair always reminded her of a teenage Ricky Schroeder more than the all-grown-up *Rick* Schroeder. Marc had actually gotten people to call Craig "The Ricker" in college.

When Gert entered the restaurant, Craig had already made his way to the door. "Hey," he said, hugging her tightly. She felt a sharp stab of sadness, thinking Marc should be there, too.

"How are you?" Gert asked as they made their way past a few square tables, each painted a different color. "Congratulations again!"

Craig had met his fiancée while teaching. The girl had been a senior in his class, but they hadn't started dating until after the semester ended—a fact that Craig was always quick to point out.

"There's so much I want to ask you," Gert said, draping her coat over the back of her chair.

"Me first," Craig said. But before he could start, a waitress appeared and took their beverage orders. Craig said, "So how's Henry, and how are your friends…."

"My brother's fine, friends are fine…."

"And your parents?" Craig asked.

Gert smiled. "They're fine. They've given up on convincing me to move back to L.A."

Craig moved his straw around his water glass. "Not going to give up on New York just yet?"

"Well, everyone says not to make major changes the first year after a death," Gert said. "It's a year and a half now, but it's still too soon, and I'm trying to stick it out. I don't want to move home and sit in my parents' house dwelling on my misery."

"Yeah," Craig said. "You can stay in New York…"

"…and sit *here* and dwell on my misery," Gert finished, and they both laughed. "I'm just not ready to leave just yet."

"You're brave," Craig said.

Gert shook her head. "People always say that," she said. "And it feels like they must be talking about some other person, because I don't *feel* brave. I just go on."

Craig looked surprised. The waitress brought them their orange juice. It looked pulpy. Gert watched the bits of orange settle to the bottom.

"Have you talked to Marc's parents?" Craig asked.

Gert took a sip and shook her head. "They don't talk to me."

"What?" Craig seemed surprised. "Why not?"

She shrugged. "I haven't seen them since last year. It's almost as if I'm barely related to them now."

"But they're your relatives."

"They might not be. With Marc gone, they have no official connection to me."

"Wow," Craig said. "I never even thought of that." He didn't seem to know what to say.

"No one does," Gert said. "It's not something that should ever happen. They didn't even call me on Christmas. I sent them a card." She stared into her juice. "I think sooner or later we're just going to be like people who were never related in the first place."

Craig looked surprised. The waitress returned for their orders. Gert asked for a "Nutella delight," which was described on the menu as a "Thick crepe filled with fruit and chopped peanuts, drizzled with chocolate/hazelnut topping." It sounded like something that should be in a museum.

"I'm going to try to see them next week, though," Gert said. "I'm going to visit Marc's grave."

"For his birthday," Craig said, remembering.

"Yes."

Craig smiled. "Do you remember the time that he turned twenty-one and we all took him skydiving?"

"*You* guys went," Gert said. "I didn't want him to go."

Craig shrugged. "You have to feel your oats, or get them out of your system, or whatever."

Gert watched the shadow of the ceiling fan spinning on the table. "So," she said, "the Ricker's finally getting married."

"Oh, don't call me that," Craig said.

"Ricker," Gert said. *"Riiickyyyy Schrooooeder."*

"You're doing Marc's dirty work."

"He'd want it that way," Gert needled.

Craig said, "You know, at the beginning of this past semester, I was telling one of my classes about how Marc had gotten everyone at school to call me Ricky Schroeder, and one girl said, 'Who's Ricky Schroeder?'"

"Oh, no," Gert said. "How could she not know? He was on *NYPD Blue.*"

"I guess she didn't watch," Craig said. "And she's too young for the other stuff."

Gert shook her head. "We're getting old."

"I know. That's been dawning on me lately."

"Me, too," she said. "When Marc was alive, I never thought

about it. But now, I think about it all the time. I think when you go through change at the same rate as someone else, you don't notice it as much. Now I'm getting older, but socially, I'm back at the same level as twenty-one-year-olds who just got out of college and are starting to date in the real world. And I'm twenty-nine."

"I can't even imagine how hard that must be," Craig said. "You didn't just lose Marc. You lost all your plans for the future."

Gert nodded. "My whole way of thinking," she said. "I just assumed our future would proceed logically. I never thought about anything stopping it."

"Who does?"

"My support group was talking about that the other day."

"Do you still go every week?"

"Yes," Gert said. "It helps."

The waitress delivered their crepes. They looked like droopy beached whales. Gert began carving.

"Have you made friends in the group?" Craig asked.

"Yes and no," Gert said. "I like them all, but I haven't made enough of an effort to get to know them outside of the group. There was this girl my age, Chase, who I got along great with. But all of a sudden she stopped coming."

"Why?"

"I'm not sure. Some people just aren't ready to mourn in a group."

Gert pushed the pieces of crepe around her plate to soak up the chocolate. It seemed foolhardy to squander such a rich river.

"So," Gert asked, "do you like Lana's family?"

"I do," Craig said. "She's an only child, so there's a lot of pressure on me to be good to her. Luckily her parents don't know about my sordid past."

"Grand Theft Street Sign, the fake letters from the dean…"

"Exactly," Craig said. "I think you're the only girl who knows about that. But I've told Lana about some of the stuff Marc and

I used to get into. And I think Adam told her the rest. Oh, did I tell you, Adam's engaged?"

"Little Adam?" Gert said. "Little, *little* Adam? He was so shy during college."

"He had such a crush on you," Craig said, looking at her.

"No, he didn't."

"Come on," Craig said. "You must have known. He was the worst of all of us. A lot of us were jealous of Marc, but Adam had such a thing for you. He tried to hide it, but he always acted funny when you were in the room. You didn't notice?"

Gert said, "You're exaggerating." She looked at her plate.

"Maybe you really didn't notice."

Gert shrugged.

"You must realize when guys like you," Craig said. "It's hard for us not to."

She felt funny. She kept her eyes on the plate.

"I'll bet a lot of guys ask you out now."

"I don't know that many guys," Gert said.

"But you go out sometimes, right?"

"Well," Gert said, "Hallie and Erika dragged me to a few bars…." She didn't feel ready to tell Craig the whole truth. "There was one guy I started talking to." She moved around a piece of crepe. "I couldn't care about anyone the way I loved Marc, and I think about Marc all the time, but I did have dinner with this guy. And I actually told him about Marc the other night."

"Wow," Craig said. "You're dating someone."

"Not dating," Gert said. "Just getting to know someone."

"I knew you would find someone…" Craig said.

Gert didn't say anything.

"Did Hallie and Erika meet anyone when they dragged you out?" Craig asked.

"No," Gert said. "Hallie and Erika look for specific things, and they beat themselves up when they can't find them. They get really frustrated."

"It takes a long time to get where you want to be," Craig said. "You probably didn't know this, either, but guys like Adam and me spent most of college complaining that all the girls on campus were stuck up. Of course, that's what we thought of anyone who didn't respond to our inept, lame pickup attempts."

Gert laughed.

"It only takes one person to change your perspective," Craig said. "I'm so happy now. I wish Marc could have met Lana. He'd have really liked her."

"I'm sure he would have."

"She's pretty, kind and down-to-earth. Like you."

Gert felt embarrassed again.

"He would have been my best man," Craig said.

"I know," Gert said.

Craig was quiet, looking out the window. "The other day," he said, "I thought about this bet Marc and I made in college."

"Which one?"

"This was the one about celebrities," Craig said. "Junior year, we were looking at this Web site about which celebrities were dead and alive. Each of us picked ten celebrities we thought were going to die soon. We decided that any time one of his celebrities died, I would give him ten dollars, and if someone from my list died, he'd give *me* ten bucks. After college, when someone from either of our lists died, we sent each other the money through the mail. But a few weeks ago, someone on Marc's list died, and I thought for a second how I owe Marc the money, but he's not there to get it. And more of the celebrities are going to go in the future, five years from now, ten, fifteen…and every time, I'll think of how they're outliving Marc. I never thought he'd be the one…"

He didn't finish. He was staring into space, Gert heard traffic passing.

Finally Craig said, "So, what's this guy's name?"

"Which guy?"

"The one you're *not* dating."

Gert smiled. "Todd."

"Oh."

"Do you think it's wrong that I've been seeing him?" Gert asked.

"So you admit you're seeing him."

"Just getting to know him."

Craig shook his head. "There's nothing wrong with it," he said. "Marc would want you to be happy."

"Don't people say that to make themselves feel better, though?" Gert asked. "We were talking about this in my group. If guys didn't want their wives to date someone else while they were alive, why would they want them to do it after they died?"

"Because," Craig said, "they love you. Marc knows who you are. Let me ask you a question: have you put his things away?"

"No."

"Do you think about him all the time? Do you remember every date you went on?"

Gert said. "God, yes."

"Do you remember all the crazy stuff that happened in college?"

Gert laughed. "How could I forget?"

"Do you *want* to forget?"

"No. Never."

"So he's there," Craig said. "You're holding on to his memories."

Gert looked at a fleet of cabs passing out the window. "It was so nice out when I went outside this morning," she said, "and I was thinking that this was one of those Saturdays that Marc would have woken up and wanted to drive to the steakhouse. And he's not here to enjoy it."

Craig grinned. "He would drive three hours to get to that stupid steakhouse!"

"I know."

Craig looked out the window. "I miss him, too."

On the subway back to Queens, Gert leaned against the seat. She felt tired but she also felt unburdened. She had talked to

Craig for another hour after the meal. She had felt so light after that. Like she had expressed feelings she couldn't to anyone else.

Why didn't she feel half this good after talking to Hallie and Erika? Not even half as good? It wasn't just because Craig knew Marc; Hallie had known Marc, too.

She could say it had to do with their bitterness and jealousy. But Gert had to admit there was more to it.

It had to do with her, too.

Gert had always made more of an effort to talk to guys. She had always felt more inspired or motivated by them. They cut through the bull. They had better senses of humor. They didn't get offended by little things. They had similar tastes to hers.

And maybe, Gert thought to herself, it was easier to enjoy someone's company when they potentially could be attracted to you.

During college, Gert didn't have that many female friends. She often preferred to hang out with Marc's friends. She liked being the only girl in a group of guys. It was interesting that way, challenging. Girls were boring.

She'd been lying to Craig when she'd said she didn't realize some of Marc's friends had been attracted to her. She *had* known. She always could tell, although she never said anything to Marc. It wasn't that she wanted them to want her, but she did feel a little bit more of a charge hanging out with men. She could be herself with them.

She didn't pass judgment. She was the type to let boys be boys.

But then, wasn't it that attitude that had led to Marc's death?

That day that Marc wanted to skydive when he had turned twenty-one, Gert hadn't wanted him to go. She didn't understand it at all. If he loved her so much, she said, why would he take that kind of risk?

But she didn't stop him.

"You don't want me to go?" he'd asked her the day before, looking puppy-eyed. He reminded her he'd wanted to go skydiving for many years, long before he'd met her. And it was just one time, he said. Just once.

She knew that if she stopped him, he'd still have the urge to do it someday. Maybe it would even come at a worse time. He had to get it out of his system.

"I just don't understand it, is all," she said.

"It's just something I need to do," he said.

When he finally arrived home that night, he took Gert out with his friends to celebrate at the local wings place. They laughed, gorged themselves on chicken and pitchers of beer, and told tales of death-defying feats. Gert said nothing of how she had sat home and worried all day. She smiled at them, never revealing her daylong agony.

Why not?

Because she was the cool girl, the one who got along with the guys. The one who flitted around during Marc's Super Bowl parties making sure the sandwiches were replaced, laughing at playing the subservient better half.

She always got his friends' references. She always took and returned their teasing. She appreciated their canon.

The morning of the accident, Marc had a doctor's appointment. It was Friday. He had a cold that—it had become apparent the previous night—wasn't a cold. It was the flu. The worst he'd had in years. He ached. He shivered. He had a fever. He tossed in bed. He asked if there was something he could take.

Gert told him she'd drive him to their doctor on the Upper West Side. Marc said she shouldn't go into work late. He could drive himself. "I'm a big boy," he said.

Gert told him he looked terrible. He said, sweetly, "I'll look better by the time you get home."

She shrugged, made eggs and coffee for him, and left for work.

Gert didn't know that he'd swigged over-the-counter cold medicine, and it probably hadn't mattered, anyway. He was drowsy from not sleeping the night before. He'd drifted coming off the bridge, gone into the opposite lane and been hit on the driver's side. The driver of the other car was okay, but Marc had spun out of control. He'd probably been knocked unconscious almost instantly, the police said.

Why hadn't she *insisted* on driving him? Why hadn't she simply put her foot down?

Because she wasn't a nag. She was always the girl who let the guys be.

But maybe if she'd loved him more, she would have nagged.

She knew what she should have done. She should have gone into the kitchen, called Missy's voicemail, left a message saying she'd be in late, returned to their room and told Marc he didn't have a choice. She'd drive him to the doctor. That would be all there was to it. She fantasized sometimes about having done this, and how he'd still be here.

She felt the hard subway seat against her back. The people across from her were sleeping, their heads together.

Gert thought of Marc's mother. That was why Marc's mother was angry at her. Marc's mother blamed her. And why shouldn't she? Marc's overbearing mother would never have let Marc drive himself. She would have forced him to let her take him.

If this had been decades earlier, Gert might have been a housewife and would have been home all day to drive him. It wouldn't have been an issue.

But most women worked these days. And Gert wasn't like Marc's mother.

There had been a tension between Mrs. Healy and Gert before that, a subtle one. Mrs. Healy was nice enough at gatherings. But Gert knew Mrs. Healy wouldn't have thought anyone was good enough for Marc. The little things seemed to make it worse. When the two of them had moved in together without getting married, Marc's mother had had a big fight with him about it. Mrs. Healy was just hard.

Inside, Gert knew the accident wasn't her fault. She knew. But she couldn't help but think that she should have trained all her attention on Marc that morning.

She'd given up easily. She was too calm, too matter-of-fact.

She'd never struggled much. Everything had always worked out for her.

The subway lifted a bit. Looking out the window, Gert saw that they were passing a round basilica, then an old stapler factory. She wondered why she tortured herself with such thoughts. Why did she always think about what she hadn't done, who she hadn't been?

Because now she had time for it. All the time in the world.

There was all the time in the world now—plenty of time for self-analysis, for self-doubts, for regrets. Being part of a couple meant you fit somewhere, that your cracks and erosions were hidden to the rest of the world. When you suddenly had that ripped apart, the hidden blemishes were exposed like cross-sections of a log.

Gert had her insecurities and imperfections. Marc had had his flaws, too. But their quirks had been covered by each other. Now she was naked, vulnerable to doubts and stabs of insecurity, the kind that people who were alone probably endured every day.

She'd had a pretty easy life. So she could be easygoing with others. Maybe it had all been too easy. College, Marc and his money, the maid service....

Should Gert now become stronger? Set her foot down about things more? Be less permissive? Push harder to improve herself? Maybe if she was more in control of things and pushed more, like Mrs. Healy always did, she could prevent tragedies in the future.

But it didn't matter, did it?

It really didn't matter if she changed. She could do everything right in her life, and the unexpected could still happen.

That had been her biggest, and worst, revelation of all.

Before Marc's death, Gert had pretty much believed that you got the life you deserved. If you worked hard and were a decent person, things fell into place. She'd earned good grades in high school, worked hard at summer jobs, gotten into a decent college, met a great guy and gotten married. Wasn't that the way it was supposed to go? Wasn't that a routine chain of events?

She'd never thought of herself as "lucky"—she had simply done what she was supposed to, and it had worked out like it should. Simple. She wasn't a person who passed judgment or was picky about men. She was kind and nonjudgmental and hardworking. Most people she knew who had worked hard had gotten the same. Well, not every single time, of course—but most of the time, you got what you deserved.

Hallie was right: Gert *had* partially blamed single women for being single. Women like Hallie and Erika had simply made bad choices. They were too selective, or they'd dated the wrong people, or done the wrong things. Gert's life had made sense.

But a year and a half ago, she'd gotten a jolt. It wasn't that simple.

Her therapist had told her that some day, she'd have to face the question of who she had been before the accident, and who she was after it.

Before the accident, she'd been a good person. She knew that. Naive—yes, and complacent—probably. But that didn't mean she was unkind. She was caring, she didn't stereotype people, and she listened to them. Those were admirable things.

But now she knew that being a nice person was about the least you could do. And that rewards were not guaranteed.

It was late in her life, she knew, for her to face this realization. She hadn't even thought it through until right then, although it had nagged at her before.

In some ways, though, she didn't think she really had had to learn such things. What good did it do her? She would gladly relinquish the new knowledge for the chance to run back under the veil of innocence and not have to think about it again.

"Dead" was such a hard word. Sometimes she had to consider it over and over—dead, dead, dead—twisting it, turning it, the way people did with some phrases, the idea that someone so vibrant and full of life had completely ceased to be. Someone who took charge of everything, who had to have the best and nothing less, would be denied so many wonderful experiences in life. Gert couldn't help thinking of it over and over—Dead, dead, dead. Gone. Completely. Over. Marc's body had just stopped working.

Sometimes she tried to imagine the terror he'd felt during the split second when he realized he was going to crash. What had he thought of? That he was about to die? That he might never see her again? That he wouldn't get to do any of the things he'd dreamed of?

Marc's father had asked the police a hundred times if someone had cut Marc off on the road. Everyone wanted to believe something different. Mr. Healy wanted to believe another driver was at fault. Mrs. Healy wanted to believe Gert hadn't taken as good care of him as she should have. Gert didn't want to believe he was gone.

There would never be a bright side. There would never be some new information or occurrence that would make this okay. That was another thing Gert had had to learn. In the past, she had always found silver linings: Miss the bus, you can walk and get exercise. Rains on your family picnic, play board games with the kids inside. But for this, there were no silver linings. Just crude realizations.

Gert wanted to shake herself out of this, to think about her next date with Todd, or spring, or something else. She sometimes descended into this pit where she had to think the worst thoughts ever. She didn't want to be naive, or be caught by surprise again. She had to face facts. Life could be random. It could be miserable.

She felt so much older than twenty-nine. She thought about Todd. Could she ever talk to him about feelings like these? Did someone like Todd need to think about what she was thinking about?

Maybe Todd *didn't* need to. He had been patient with her, but he was still in a different world. He didn't need to analyze tragedy. Maybe her pain really made her too different from people her age. Maybe it would make her unreachable.

Walking off the train, she saw the sunlight bounce off the railing under the elevated overhang, and it surprised her for a second.

Maybe I'm being ridiculous, Gert thought. Yes, she had become more aware of the potential for disaster in her life. She'd been complacent before, and she still had much to learn. But there was no reason that she had to dwell on the potential for hidden tragedy all the time. She didn't have to be guarded for the rest of her life just because of something that had happened when she was twenty-seven.

Still, it could have held off a little longer. She could have enjoyed a longer honeymoon.

But she would have gotten that jolt, that reminder of the lurking random unkindnesses of the world, days later anyway. Four days after Marc's accident, she had felt the world burst open when everyone else had. She had only smashed into reality a few days ahead of schedule.

# Chapter

## 10

Gert was thankful for Hallie and Erika the next day, because they were going to walk around Manhattan asking for men's phone numbers, and she'd tag along, trying to enjoy the harmless fun. It would take her mind off of—well, her mind.

It was a sunny Sunday. They met for brunch first. Gert decided she needed a drink. Mimosas sounded good to her. She'd drink a few and watch Hallie and Erika undertake their boy hunt.

The brunch place was on 72nd Street. Both Hallie and Erika looked good that day. Hallie had gotten her light brown hair cut. It was short and straight. Erika's dirty-blond hair was in a black bandanna. Gert thought that Hallie was pretty, even if she wasn't glamorous like Erika. Anyway, glamour could be off-putting.

"So in case Eden doesn't work out," Erika said, sitting across from Gert and Hallie, "and we don't find anyone today, on Friday I saw this guy who might just be perfect for me."

"Great," Hallie said.

Gert was hopeful for her. "Where'd you meet him?"

"Welllll…I didn't actually *meet* him," Erika said.

*Uh-oh,* Gert thought.

"My company's been designing these facebooks for a law firm," Erika said. "I was going over them to check for smudges and stuff, and this guy was in there, Tom Rossover. Have you ever seen someone, and just knew right away that the two of you would click?"

*No,* Gert thought. *Not from a photo in a facebook.*

"All I have to figure out is how to meet him," Erika said.

Gert could see Hallie's mind working.

Hallie snapped her fingers and said, "Got it. We'll hang out outside his firm one day. When he comes out, you can go up to him and say, 'I know you.' You and Tom will go through all your colleges and careers, which helps him get to know things about you, but then all the sudden you can snap and say, 'Now I know. You're in the facebook my firm is designing.'"

"That's brilliant," Erika said.

Even Gert had to admit it was good.

Erika smiled. "Who's up for flower juice?"

"Flower juice" was the house specialty, a blend of four fruit juices and two mysterious flowers. The girls suspected the juices to be banana, orange, tangerine and grapefruit, although they weren't sure about the flowers. The waitress had heard their guesses but refused to confirm or deny. Erika said the juice had medicinal properties. Hallie said it prevented dandruff. Gert thought that she'd like to bring Todd to try it one day.

That was the good thing about new relationships, Gert thought—you got to introduce the things you loved to the person you loved, bring them into your world. It would be the great thing about having kids someday, too.

When the waitress returned with the heavenly nectar, Erika said, "Can you imagine if guys knew the lengths we went to to get their attention? They think *they* make the effort."

"Brett Stoddard knows," Hallie said.

"Oh, how was your date with him last night?" Gert asked.

Hallie grinned. "He recited the Shelley poem!"

"He did?"

"Yeah, and you know what?" Hallie said. "I knew what he was doing, and I *still* felt seduced by him. I couldn't help it. He asked me a thousand questions about myself. He asked me what I brought for show-and-tell when I was in *kindergarten.*"

"What did you bring?" Gert asked.

"A box of 64 Crayolas," Hallie said. "And he asked me my favorite cheese."

"What's your favorite cheese?" Gert asked.

"Jarlsberg," Hallie said. Gert wondered why she didn't know these things about Hallie. She realized she'd never asked. It all went back to the fact that she tried harder with men. Maybe *she* should ask more questions of Hallie.

"The point is," Hallie added, sounding impatient, "I've never met a guy who focused on me so much. He's amazing."

"Did you ask anything about *him?*" Gert asked.

"I tried, but mostly he kept the questions on *me,*" she said. "And he kept staring at me like I was the most fascinating person ever."

"He's a player, all right," Erika said, folding her napkin.

"Maybe he's not playing," Gert said.

"Oh, he totally is," Hallie said. "It's all an act. Do you think he really cares about what I brought for show-and-tell or what my favorite cheese is? He wants me to *need* him. And it's hard to resist. I mean, he's such fun to be with."

Erika shook her head, then reached for a Sweet'N Low for her coffee. "It's the guys you really like that make it impossible to do the dating rules," she said.

"Damn straight," Hallie said. "That's what's known as the Rule of Rules. Whichever dating rules you're following, it's going to be nearly impossible to follow them for the people you like, and easy to follow them for ones you don't—which makes them have the reverse effect you intend."

She sipped her flower juice, then put down the mug pointedly. "Eventually you have to learn to control yourself," she said. "When you've got the experience and maturity to do that, *that's* when you finally move ahead." She slapped the table. "And by gum, this is that time."

Walking from the Eighth Avenue subway stop down to 42nd Street, Gert noticed a baby bawling, and a couple peering into their carriage. Erika seemed to be noticing, too.

"Look at them," Erika said. "Letting their baby howl like that. Saying, 'Look at us. We're a cute happy couple and now we have a cute happy baby. We're just cute happy people.'"

Gert felt concerned. She recognized another rule—or more, a syndrome—that Hallie and Erika had never verbalized: *Single-itis.* A disease characterized by bitterness and craziness after several years without a fulfilling relationship. The symptoms were vocalizing awful dating rules, hating them and simultaneously following them, being bitter about all members of the opposite sex and resenting anyone in a decent relationship.

Gert remembered Erika saying, that night at the sleepover, how it wasn't healthy to be without a boyfriend for that long. When Todd touched her, no matter what they were doing, it was something that she'd missed for a year and a half, and she hadn't realized how much she needed that. She wondered how Hallie and Erika had survived so long without regular intimacy. She had trouble relating to their level of bitterness and jealousy, but on an intellectual level, she somewhat understood it.

Right now, she tried to guess what Erika was thinking. *Do those people with the carriage know what it's like to be the rest of us? Do they ever have any problems? Do they think I'm single because of something I did wrong?*

Gert thought that Hallie and Erika couldn't help being angry, but Gert didn't know how much longer she could have patience with their games. She had a feeling that unless she could find a way to become closer to them, there would be some sort of blowup.

On 42nd Street, there were artists drawing caricatures and homeless guys holding signs saying clever things like "I admit it. I need \$\$\$ for booze." The biggest attraction seemed to be the Asians with their beautiful spray-painted moonscapes, the latest trend in sidewalk art that had suddenly appeared the summer before and snagged tourists' hearts. Gert didn't know who the first person to do this was, or why it had suddenly replaced writing kids' names in Chinese letters in popularity.

The three women settled into a spot near the economic development office. They leaned against the marble wall of a slanted building. Its face sloped backward slightly at a 110-degree angle and shined despite a thin coating of accumulated dirt.

"Now," Hallie said, "the code for if you see a cute guy will be, 'Hubba hubba.'"

"What?" Gert asked.

"Erika," Hallie said, "will you explain to Gert the origin of 'Hubba hubba'?"

"My pleasure," Erika said. She gazed toward the sky, which was getting grayer. "Well," she said, "way back when I used to work in Rye Playland at the admissions gate, a co-worker of mine would always say 'Hubba, hubba' when she saw a cute guy coming up to the ticket line. We'd all look to see who she was talking about, and then we'd see if our judgment matched hers. So to carry on the tradition today, we will use 'Hubba hubba' as our alert."

"Thank you, Erika," Hallie said. "Let the scouting begin."

Gert looked for possibly single men in the Times Square crowd. On a Sunday, there were more likely to be tourists than residents on their way to work. But tourists were fair game. Hallie had once told Gert that she wouldn't mind meeting someone from far away. Midwestern guy from the plains? Perfect. She could move out there and milk cows with the man she loved. Heck, maybe she was just looking for a reason to leave.

"Hubba hubba," Hallie said.

Gert saw the man in question. He looked to be in his twenties, but he was unfortunately with his parents. Hallie stood up on her tiptoes, watching him, waiting for him to peel off from them for a second—maybe toward Virgin Records, which she thought might well be appropriate—but in the end, he didn't.

"Hubba hubba," Erika said.

"Where?" Hallie nearly got whiplash.

"Brown pants, brown shirt."

They looked to the left.

Gert saw who they were talking about. He was even wearing a brown cap.

"I think he's a UPS worker," Erika said.

"At least he's color coordinated," Hallie said.

Gert leaned against the building, tired. She craned her neck to look at its top. Sometimes it hurt to do that.

"Hubba hubba," Erika said.

Gert turned her head. "Where?"

"Black pants. Blue jacket."

The three of them looked down the block.

"That girl's with him," Hallie said.

"Are you sure?"

"She just had her hand in his back pocket."

"Maybe she wanted gum."

They could leave and see a movie, Gert thought. Or go up to the Met. It was a nice day for it, and she hadn't been there in ages. She'd last gone six years ago, when Nancy had visited.

"Hubba hubba," Hallie said.

"Where?" Erika asked.

"Blue jeans. Red shirt."

The gentleman in question had thinning hair, but he was cute, and he looked the right age. He was walking swiftly toward them, carrying a tennis racquet. Gert had played tennis a lot in high school. She hadn't done it much after getting married. She was thinking about taking it up again now.

When he neared them, Hallie said, "Excuse me, sir."

"I'm in a hurry," the guy said.

"This will only take a moment," Hallie said, turning to follow him. "We were wondering if you're single."

The guy looked back and laughed. "I'm not married. But I live with someone."

"Oh, thanks," Hallie said.

"Wait," Erika yelled. "Are you thinking of breaking up with her?"

The guy turned again, smiled, and shook his head.

Hallie turned and looked at her. *"Are you thinking of breaking up with her?!"*

"You're too defeatist," Erika said, taking a cigarette out of her purse and leaning against the wall. "There are a ton of guys in New York who keep living with someone just because it's too expensive for them to get their own place. People in this city postpone breaking up for months because rents are too high. But they're dying for an incentive to leave. If you wait until they decide to do it on their own, they'll go to a bar, meet a new girl in two and a half minutes, and be off the market again. So your only chance is to catch them when they're still safely in one place, and verrrry unhappy."

"Point taken," Hallie agreed.

They leaned against the wall. A few minutes passed without any sightings.

"Hubba hubba," Erika said.

"Where?"

"Yankee cap. Blue jacket."

The man was across the street. He waited for the light to change, then walked toward them.

"Paul!" Gert said in delight.

"Gertie!" Paul said. "How are you?"

He reached her and they hugged. It was the guy Gert had dated in college before Marc—the one who had glad-handed all the profs and deans. They hadn't dated long, but they still had said hello when they passed each other on campus, and now, when they occasionally crossed paths in New York. Gert was glad she hadn't gotten involved with Paul. He seemed kind of phony, a bit of a social climber. But still okay.

"How are you?" Paul asked again, looking vaguely at her friends.

"I'm fine," Gert said. "This is Hallie and Erika."

"Nice to meet you," Paul said, shaking their hands. "You both live here?"

"Yes," Hallie said, smiling at him.

"Are you registered to vote?"

"Uh," Hallie said, "I'm registered at my parents' house."

"You should register *here,*" Paul said. "Gert's registered, right?"

"Yes," Gert said. "In Queens."

Paul looked at Hallie and Erika. "Do you two know that the Board of Ed. elections are coming up?"

"No...."

"They are," Paul said. "And we've also got the statewide assembly primaries, and all of this has an impact on your life. I know you may not have kids yet, so you don't think the Board of Ed. matters to you, but if you wait until you have kids to get involved and make changes, those changes won't go into effect until your kids are nearly ready to leave the system."

"But..."

"The second thing is, whether you use the schools or not, all of us pay school taxes with our property tax dollars," Paul said. "You guys are taxpayers and you should take every advantage of your right to vote."

"I don't pay property taxes," Hallie said, trying to look past him. "I'm a renter."

"Oh, but renters do pay property taxes," Paul said, moving his head so that he was still in line with her face. "I hear that all the time from people your age."

"How old are *you?*"

"That's where you're wrong. Part of your rent does go to municipal taxes. That's why rents in New York are so high: Municipal taxes. Look me in the eye and tell me you hear what I'm saying."

Hallie and Erika both stared at him.

"I hear you," Hallie said flatly.

"You've got to use your right to vote," Paul repeated. He laughed. "Sometimes people spend more energy thinking of excuses why they *haven't* registered than it would take to actually go register."

He stared at them.

"Promise me that you'll at least register in time for the primaries," he said.

"O-kay," Hallie said.

"Great," Paul said, shaking their hands. "So I've done one good thing today. Gert, is your number the same?"

"Yes. It's listed."

"Good. Let's do lunch soon, when we're not so busy. I'm on my way to a meeting, Local Council of District Carpenters. Very important union. Good to see you all."

"Good to see *you*."

He took off.

A second later, Gert said, "Oh, my God, I'm sorry. I forgot to ask Paul if he's single."

"Don't worry about it," Hallie said.

"Don't," Erika said.

They looked both ways up and down the block.

"Hubba hubba."


"Where have you been all day?"

Cat slid in the door at eight o'clock as they were watching *Butch Cassidy and the Sundance Kid,* which was somewhere in the ten-to-twenty range in the canon.

"My parents were in town," Cat said.

"I know that," Hallie said, barely masking her annoyance. "You were supposed to meet us after lunch."

"They wanted to take me shopping." Bags hung from her arms like ornaments from a Christmas tree.

"Well," Erika said, looking over the first page of her notebook, "we're not sharing any of our men."

"I'll come next time, I promise," Cat said before she disappeared into her room.

"Nice to have Mommy and Daddy do everything for you," Erika said.

"As if we'd turn down the help," Gert said. She threw a popcorn kernel in the air and caught it in her mouth.

"I wouldn't," Hallie said. "I'd take anyone's help."

"What are we going to do with all the phone numbers?" Erika asked. "Are we really going to invite all the men to a 'Stud Party'?"

"Yes," Hallie said. She kicked off her shoes. "If only one hot guy starts dating us from it, it'll have been worth it."

"Maybe they'll fight over us," Erika said.

"We know they're good-looking, and we know they're single," Hallie said. "This is the best thing ever."

Gert looked up. "What would be the next step?" she asked. "Let's say you go on a date out of this. Would you be the one to pay?"

"I don't know," Hallie said. "See? This is why women never attempt this. What if a guy I picked up today started dating me. Would I pay *every* time? Would I be expected to make the first move physically, too? I should write a letter about this to a women's magazine."

Cat came out of the kitchen with a bag and mouthful of Chee•tos. "You sooood," she said.

"I've never made the first move, physically," Hallie said. "I don't think I could do it. In order for men to give us the level of attention that we deserve, they've got to be pursuing us and in love with us, because anything less won't hold their attention. Guys just naturally get distracted more easily. There's too many women for them to be distracted by. I'm sorry, but a relationship will never work if the woman is the one doing the chasing."

"Then the gender roles can't fully switch," Gert said, wiping butter off her fingers.

"Right," Hallie said. "If I ever did ask one of these guys on a date, I'd still leave it up to them to call afterwards. It has to snap back into its normal mode or it'll never work. Why do you think Erika ends up stalking from afar most of the time?"

*"Shhhh!"* Erika said, pointing the remote control at the TV and turning up the volume. "I like this part!"

It was the "Raindrops Keep Fallin' on My Head" scene. Paul Newman and Katharine Ross were riding a bicycle.

"This movie is not what I thought it would be," Hallie said.

"When they made it, they were debating whether to make it a comedy," Gert said.

"Oh," Hallie said.

"Movies you've heard about for years sometimes are completely different when you actually see them," Gert said.

"Usually worse," Erika said.

"When Marc had me watch *Midnight Cowboy,* I thought it was going to be an adventure movie," Gert said. "But it's not."

Hallie seemed annoyed at what was on the screen. "It's a bank robbery movie, and they're doing wheelies," she said. "It doesn't work."

Gert remembered when Marc had her watch it one rainy afternoon sophomore year, downstairs in the living room of the house he lived in. Various other guys drifted through the house and stopped to watch, and by the end, there were five guys standing behind the couch, transfixed. Gert had felt good about this, for some reason. Maybe it was that Marc was the trendsetter in the house. But he'd taken her out to dinner after the movie, showing that he wanted to be with her alone—not with his guy friends.

Gert reached for more popcorn. Her mind drifted to Marc's family. They hadn't returned the two messages she'd left about meeting up with them Tuesday. Maybe they'd just been busy. She'd try once more.

It also had been a few days since she'd seen Todd, but she'd talked to him on the phone. They had a dinner date set for Wednesday, the day after she would get back from visiting Marc. If things got uncomfortable with his parents, at least she could tell Todd about it. He'd sounded a bit strange on the phone, maybe still getting used to the idea of dating a widow. But no matter what happened, at least she'd see him Wednesday.

She didn't consider the possibility that this might change.

"Before we finish our happy celebration of the Manhunt," Erika said. "We must take a new visit…to Challa's Corner!"

Gert's stomach dropped. She'd hoped the pursuit of Dr. Eden had helped her forget. She didn't know why Erika had to bring up something that continually upset her, when they all had been relaxing. Maybe Erika had to keep confronting herself with the reality of it, just like Gert had to keep thinking about Marc being gone.

"I thought you were taking a break from it," Hallie said, making Gert glad she wasn't the only one concerned.

"I haven't checked in three days," Erika said. "I swear I'm cutting down. I just can't quit cold turkey. Next time I'll wait four days."

They trooped into Hallie's bedroom. Gert was reluctant to leave the couch, but was happy to flop onto the big bed. Hallie turned on the computer and Erika sat in the chair. Challa's blue screen came on, but no one was expecting what would pop up next.

Amid the usual graphics, there was a giant message that said:

WE'RE PREGNANT AGAIN!!!! Click *here*.

Erika looked as if she was in a daze.

Gert couldn't help staring at the screen. She was thinking: They're my age. The two of them met five years after Marc and I did. And they're already on their second kid.

Erika clicked for the message board, her hands shaking a bit.

"Congratulations, guys!!! Love, Annie."

"Best of luck."

Erika looked appalled but kept her eyes on the screen.

Finally she threw her hands up and moved backward.

"It's a train wreck," she said. "I keep waiting for them to break up, and I see more and more steps in his life. First he's married. Then he's got a kid. Soon he'll have *two* kids. How long do I have to wait until the divorce? Aren't fifty percent of marriages supposed to end that way? Am I supposed to wait until he's forty-nine for him to finally realize we should be together?"

"Erika…" Hallie said.

Erika's face was turning red. She shook her head. "If he saw me again, I know he'd want me. A woman who had two kids can't measure up. She's probably stretched and fatlike right now."

"*Er.*"

"Just let me do this one thing." Erika began typing.

"You said you weren't going to write any more messages," Hallie said.

"Just one more."

She typed: YOUR CHILD HAS COME FROM THE IN-CUBUS. WATCH FOR CLOVEN HOOVES.

She blasted it into cyberspace.

Hallie reached over to shut down the computer.

"Mark my words," Erika said, looking at them both. "She's ruining his life. His desire for everything is completely lost. He was talented. He was going to go to grad school for architecture. What happened to that? He should be designing buildings instead of working at a job that has nothing to do with art. He needs someone who'll complement him and awaken his passions, not someone who lets him be so…settled. This Web log is evidence of a great big nothing. It's time to remind him what creativity and passion are. The kind that *we* had."

Gert didn't think Erika was getting any better, three-day blog hiatus notwithstanding.

# Chapter

## 11

The wind was blowing Tuesday morning, the day Gert was going to see Marc's grave. The weather was perfect for Boston: cloudy. A mess. It would probably take longer than usual to get there. There were rumors of snow. It hadn't materialized, but dirt and leaf bits whirled through the air.

Marc's family had not returned her third call. Were they avoiding her, or just consumed by Michael's upcoming wedding? She had her cell phone with her in case they called back. She imagined Mrs. Healy getting the messages, but Mrs. Healy wouldn't be the one to return them. If anyone would, Mr. Healy would.

She wondered again if she should take Todd to Michael's wedding. She would feel better having him there. But it might also be an affront. It might be like telling Marc's family goodbye. She wasn't ready to do that.

Still, if they were going to make her feel uncomfortable, shouldn't she move on as well? Or at least take steps in that direction?

★ ★ ★

Gert had taken along the *Economist* to read on the bus. It was one of Marc's two-year subscriptions she hadn't canceled. But she ended up putting her head against the window to sleep. The sky was overcast, and the back of the bus was dark. She slept through most of the five-hour trip.

It was lightly drizzling when they got in around noon. Gert groggily headed through South Station, but stopped at one of the kiosks to buy a donut—strawberry frosted with yellow sprinkles.

When she stepped outside, the wind hit her in the face right away.

She brushed the hair out of her eyes and headed across the street. Red tape streamed off striped orange barricades. There was always construction going on across the street from South Station. She made her way around the plazas and office buildings toward the subway.

A few drops of drizzle stung her. Saplings in a plaza swayed ominously. The weather was mocking her. It was Marc's weather. It had always felt this way when they'd gone up to Boston to visit his relatives—frozen, stinging. Marc had always walked her through it, pulling her into a warm restaurant, a cozy tavern, his parents' living room. But today, there was no one to guide her through the bitter cold—only the cold itself.

Gert had to take the red subway to the green subway to an MBTA commuter train to a taxi to the gravesite.

The cemetery was two hundred years old—at least, the part right behind the church was. Two hundred years ago, someone had erected a little white church on a few acres of property, and a small circle of graves followed. For 170 years, no one new was buried there. In the 1970s, new owners bought the property and began expanding the cemetery far back.

Gert opened the front gate slowly. The graves went back in rows like teeth. On one side, knotted trees gnarled around a metal fence. Abutting it was a backyard with a swingset, and Gert wondered if those kids got ribbed at school for living next to the cemetery, or whether the house was the site each year of the coolest Halloween party around.

Gert walked past the thirty-five original graves. They were brown instead of gray, and the most legible one said a woman had "Dy'd—1823."

She heard the swingset creaking. Gert headed back to the newer rows. Before she came to Marc's grave, she stopped at one that she'd noticed last year. It belonged to a kid who had died on Sept. 11, 2001. He wasn't really a kid—he was in his early twenties—but Gert was starting to think of anyone who was more than a few years younger than she as a kid.

She stood in front of the kid's grave.

"Hi, Colin," she thought. "Remember me? I said hello last year." She had kept meaning to look on the Internet to find a victim profile on Colin from the *New York Times*. Gert really couldn't be sure that Colin had died as a result of the attacks, but she assumed.

Colin's grave always reminded her that she'd been lucky to have gotten to spend eight years with Marc. Gert thought about what it would have been like to lose him when they were both twenty-two. They had known so little about relationships when they'd met. They had had to learn so many steps together. But they were also supposed to grow old together. They were supposed to be there through every step of life.

In the row behind Colin's grave was Marc's. He'd been buried next to an uncle who'd died young, in 1985. The uncle was only twenty-nine at the time, and had had leukemia. He would be in his forties today. He'd died young, and he'd still be young today.

As Gert knelt down, she saw someone coming through the cemetery gates at the far end. It looked like a woman with curly hair, and Gert first thought it might be Marc's mother, but it was just a stranger.

Gert sat Indian-style on the ground.

Marc's grave said:

Marc Howell Healy
1974—2001
Beloved son, husband, uncle, brother
Forever in our hearts

Gert wondered what the protocol was; whether, if they'd had a kid together, "husband" and "father" would come before son. Were there rules on that, or was it decided by the family? She didn't know. She'd been in such a bad state after the accident that she'd paid little attention when Marc's father had taken care of everything.

She smelled the damp, rich soil. A thatch of grass rustled in front of the grave.

"Hi," Gert said.

That was all she needed to say. Sometimes, when they said hi to each other, it meant everything. Sometimes he'd look at her and say it while they were watching TV, just to remind her how happy he was that she was there.

"I don't know what to say, because I really don't know if you're watching me," she said. "Maybe you're with me all the time."

She pictured him leaning against the grave, looking at her and smiling.

"I need to talk to you," she said. "You know I love you. I *always* love you."

She told him about work and Craig, and about the little blond-haired girl across the street being old enough to walk. Then she sat there for a while, listening and thinking. She heard birds chirping behind her. She thought about the first time she'd gone to a cemetery, when her mother had brought her to *her* mother's grave. Her mother had said to the grave, "Mom, this is my daughter, Gert. We named her after you." Gert had been surprised to hear her mother call someone "Mom." Her mother *was* Mom. How could she call someone else Mom?

A car that needed a new muffler motored past.

"So young," a voice said behind her.

Gert jumped a little. The old woman behind her had a round, motherly face. She was wearing a raincoat and a hood, with just her face showing, and somehow that made Gert think of a nun. She was carrying purple flowers.

Gert wiped herself off, but didn't get up. "It was a car crash," Gert said.

"You were married to him?" The woman had a Boston accent.

"Yes."

"My son," the woman said, waving her hand at a few rows over.

"Did it happen recently?"

The woman shook her head. "Twelve years ago today," she said. She didn't say anything else.

"Marc died a year and a half ago," Gert said.

"You're not from Boston," the woman said.

"No," she said. "New York. And L.A."

The woman said, "I'm sorry."

"I'm sorry for *your* loss, too."

The woman looked at the ground. "My husband doesn't come here anymore. His health isn't what it was. I don't even remind him his son is gone."

Gert nodded.

"You can't forget," the woman said. She gave Gert a brave smile. "I live around here, so I'll put flowers on your husband's grave when I come up."

"Please do," Gert said.

The woman nodded her head, then turned around and walked away.

Gert watched her trudge toward the far end of the cemetery, toward her son's grave again.

Gert thought that if this had been a movie, the woman would have offered her some worldly advice that suddenly snapped everything into perspective. But instead, all she'd done was remind Gert that the pain doesn't go away.

Lachlan answered the door. Lach was one of Marc's nephews. He was thirteen. Gert was amazed at how tall Lach was now, but more, how mature he looked. She'd last seen him a year ago, on Marc's last birthday, but he hadn't had partially shaved hair and an earring then. He could be any teenager hanging out with his friends at the mall, or in a music video.

"Hi, Aunt Gert!" Lach said. His voice was changing, too.

The first time she'd met him, he'd been four, dressed up for church.

"Hey! Are your grandparents here?" Gert asked. "I tried calling."

"They've been out all day," Lach said. "At the cemetery."

"Oh. I didn't see them."

"They were going to go to lunch first and to do wedding stuff. Do you want to wait in here?"

"Nah." She realized how sad she must look, and she gave Lachlan a smile. "I'm going to see you at the wedding."

"Oh, good!" he said. "You're coming? I'll see you."

"You tell them I said hi, all right?"

"Yeah. I will."

Before she could step down, Lach opened the screen door and gave her a quick kiss. "Bye, Aunt Gert."

She walked back down to the corner and called the taxi service on her cell phone.

She checked again for messages. There weren't any.

She called her voicemail at home. Nothing.

Why wouldn't the Healys call her back? Wasn't that cruel?

She could call them when she got home. She would call and call until she got them, rather than leaving a message. She wasn't going to let this go. She didn't want to end their relationship with them chickening out.

It would really make Michael's wedding uncomfortable if they weren't talking. She'd rather talk to them now, know what she was facing. Even if they weren't going to have a relationship, she didn't like ending it on bad terms. And ignoring her on Marc's birthday was bad terms.

Waiting for the Greyhound, she made one last quick check of her messages. Still nothing. She thought about how Marc had left a message on her cell phone the day before he'd died. She'd been at lunch and hadn't answered. He left her the address where they were going to meet his business associates after work. She'd listened to it and saved it. After he died, she had been listening to messages again and was startled to hear his voice, so lively, as if nothing was wrong. She'd left that message and resaved it. She realized it was the only recording she had of his voice, except for maybe a few seconds on the wedding video. She was amazed that you could be with someone for eight years and never think to tape their voice. She had photos, but few recordings. How could she not have tapes of him?

Eventually she'd borrowed someone's speakerphone, dialed into her cell phone voicemail and played his message over the speakerphone so she could tape it on Marc's stereo. She didn't know what she'd do with the tape, but it was his last message and she felt a need to keep it.

By the time she got home that night, there was a message on Gert's home voicemail from Mr. Healy. He said that he was sorry, that they hadn't gotten her messages until late. She had trouble believing it, but maybe they were just old people who didn't bother with things like answering machines. She didn't want to believe they would just snub her.

"We'll see you at Michael's wedding," Mr. Healy said. "You know you can call us if you ever need to talk."

His voice wasn't very emotional, Gert thought. He sounded perfunctory. He sounded like he really didn't care whether she called. And even if they hadn't gotten messages from her, they should still have reached out to her on Marc's birthday anyway. Was it so much to ask to be treated like a family member by in-laws? Did you have to be a blood relative to be considered worthy of loving someone?

There was a second message on her voicemail—from Todd.

There had been a time not long ago when she'd never had a two-hour period during which she didn't think of Marc, and today, she'd had one in which she hadn't been thinking about Todd. Hearing his voice was reassuring.

He said that he'd hoped the trip had gone well and that he'd see her the next day. She felt better.

She thought of calling him back, but it was late. He'd sounded tired in his message. He was at a hotel in Buffalo after a late-night run. He had told her his schedule was starting to get crazy again.

She didn't realize that this was about to cause a problem.

# Chapter

## 12

Gert must have been a party to at least three conversations during college about how studies had shown that women's menstrual cycles converged when they lived together. She'd gotten a little tired of that conversation.

But now, she was beginning to wonder if friends' bosses' cycles converged, too. Because she, Hallie and Erika were all dealing with insane bosses that week.

Hallie had gotten hollered at for forgetting to order food for a business meeting. Erika hadn't noticed that in a facebook she had designed, a guy's name had been spelled "Thodore." Missy was stomping around the office, waiting to snap about something.

Gert kept her mouth shut. She didn't want to give her an excuse to yell at her.

Finally, Missy dumped a batch of surveys on her desk for her to analyze.

"I need these done by tomorrow morning," Missy said. "First thing."

Gert had been depressed that day already. Todd had called before lunch and postponed their date until the following day because of work. Now the surveys meant staying until at least eight. After Todd had canceled, Gert had planned to just head home after work, sink into the couch and watch mindless TV.

"Don't look at me like that," Missy said.

Gert hadn't been looking at her like anything. She turned her head away so that Missy wouldn't see her face. She didn't want to cry.

Missy stood there a second, then went back to her office. Gert heard the door slam.

Was this what always being loyal and working hard got her? Even when Missy wasn't angry at Gert, she never thanked her or told her she'd done a good job.

Gert took a deep breath and stared out at the buildings of the city.

Missy stomped back over to Gert's desk. Gert tensed up again.

"I'll be back by three," Missy snapped. "Make sure you get through half the pile."

Then she left.

Gert waited until the elevator doors had been closed for a few minutes. She got up, strode briskly through the hall and went into the bathroom. She shut the stall door and sat on the toilet. She tried to breathe so she wouldn't cry.

*Missy means nothing,* she told herself. *It's not personal.*

Gert needed to be reminded that she was a good person, that her hard work mattered. That *she* mattered.

The bathroom door opened.

"Who's in theaahh?" a voice said.

"Dawn," Gert said, "go away."

Dawn giggled and closed the door.

Gert calmed herself down, went back to her desk and called Todd's cell phone. She got his voicemail.

"Missy's on the warpath," she said. "I could use some cheering up."

When she hung up, she felt a little better. She rubbed her eyes, did a few surveys, and thought she'd steal forty-five minutes for lunch.

★ ★ ★

She sat in the back corner of the gourmet pizza place, the one that charged four dollars a slice. The slice she had chosen for that day had black olives, extra cheese and fresh mushrooms. She was a fan of any place that used fresh mushrooms. Neither she nor Marc could ever tolerate those rubbery canned ones. Mush*ruins,* he had called them.

From the back corner, she had a prime view of the other people in the pizzeria. Three businessmen were lunching near the door with female colleagues who were dressed much more nicely. A young woman was sitting across from a man, fiddling with her Palm Pilot as he talked to her. Next to the refrigerator full of bottled fruit juices, a heavyset guy in a gray suit was diagramming something on a napkin for two younger guys.

Gert touched her cell phone, making sure it was on.

She became conscious of the fact that everyone else in the pizzeria was with a group. Some were talking and laughing, some were businesslike, but they were all with someone.

She felt like she was hogging a table. There were people standing near the counter, looking for a place to sit. A guy and a girl up front were staring at her as they talked.

She suddenly didn't want to be there. She ate quickly and got up to leave.

Maybe if she stopped thinking about Todd, he'd call.

She kept on going through the surveys. They had proposed names for products and asked people to rate them on a scale of one to five. All of the names for medicines seemed to have an "X" and end in "N."

Gert thought of a few new ones. She jotted them down on a clean piece of paper, then turned the letters into bubble letters, with shadows.

By three, Missy hadn't returned. Gert had gotten through half of the surveys. Still, every once in a while, her mind would drift for a few minutes, and she'd have to snap herself back.

Todd hadn't returned her call. He had never waited this long to call her back before.

She moved through more surveys. She thought of more names for products. Most of these probably had been computer generated, she thought. Still, it might be fun to suggest some.

*That's what I should be doing,* she thought. *Creating. Pitching. Not tabulating.*

An hour passed, then two. She straightened out her pile.

Todd should have been able to tell from her voice how upset she was, right?

She decided she'd gotten too dependent on him. Why had she done that?

She checked her voicemail at home. There was one message, but it turned out to be an automated voice trying to sell her a vacation. They seemed to be replacing telemarketers.

She really wanted to hear Todd's voice.

At six, she left. Missy had come and gone. Gert had an hour's worth of surveys to finish, but she took them home with her. She couldn't stand sitting at her desk for a minute more. Her back was starting to hurt.

It was dark outside. As she made her way through the crowds to the subway, everyone was hurrying—probably to dinner dates and their significant others, their foot rubs and warm baths.

It wasn't until eight-thirty, when Gert was recovering in front of a TV full of bad sitcoms, that Todd called.

"What's up?" he said.

"Oh," Gert said. "I had a lousy day—"

"Good. It's hard to hear you. We're about to go through a tunnel."

He sounded emotionless. When he could talk again, he said work was crazy and he had to get off quickly.

Gert felt fear creeping into her voice. She calmed herself and spoke evenly.

"I'll still see you tomorrow, right?" she said.

"Right," Todd said. "I'll see you."

He didn't sound excited. But he probably couldn't talk anyway.

"See you," he said again. Then he hung up.

She sat there, stunned. She realized they hadn't decided on a time. But he could still call her tomorrow with one. Still, she thought of calling him back to ask, just so she'd feel better.

She couldn't let herself.

She remembered what Hallie had said.

When the women were the ones doing the chasing, there was a problem.

That night, Gert lay in bed and stared at the ceiling. Something about the conversation had unnerved her. Todd had said he'd had to go twice. He hadn't sounded excited about seeing her. He didn't seem concerned at all that she'd had a lousy day. A few weeks earlier, he'd swept her off to dinner when she'd had a lousy day.

But she was probably imagining it. Why should she be unnerved by a short conversation? He was at work, for God's sake. They were still meeting tomorrow. She'd realize when she saw him how silly she was being.

Her lids shut, and she was too tired to think about it anymore.

In the morning, Missy popped in and out and seemed too preoccupied to say anything to Gert. Gert had nothing to do, so she kept occupied on her computer in order to look busy. She checked the Onion, Modern Humorist, and her e-mail. Hallie had forwarded something entitled, "Why tool boxes are like men."

In the afternoon, Todd called and broke the date.

He said he'd finally gotten back home a few hours earlier. He'd tried to fall asleep, but couldn't. He had lain in bed for hours. Now he had to start work again at midnight. He knew he needed to get some sleep first, so he'd be alert for the trip.

He didn't sound disappointed.

She certainly felt disappointed. She had to see him to make sure things were okay with them.

"You can come to my house to sleep," she said.

Right away, she got a sinking feeling that she shouldn't have offered, especially when he was quiet for a second.

"Oh, I could," Todd said. "It's just, it's easier for me to leave from here. I don't want to cause you any trouble."

*It's no trouble,* she thought.

"Okay," she said. She thought for a second, and added, "I have work to do tonight, anyway."

"That's good," Todd said. He still didn't seem concerned. "Maybe we can see each other Saturday. Can we try for then?"

*Try?* She hadn't seen him in almost a week.

"Oh, sure," Gert said.

She closed her eyes. This was slipping away from her.

He said, "Okay. We'll talk then," and got off.

He didn't say he was sorry for canceling at the last minute.

Maybe he wasn't sorry.


In college, on the ceiling of Gert and Hallie's dormroom, Hallie had stuck glow-in-the-dark stars. At first, Gert had found this strange, but she had come to like staring at them at night to fall asleep. She would look up and wonder what she'd do for a living someday, where she'd live, whom she'd marry. She would stare at them until they turned into white bursting supernovas.

Gert rolled onto her side.

Saturday. Saturday. They'd meet up Saturday.

Had Todd said, "We'll *try* to do it Saturday" or "We'll *definitely* do it Saturday"?

She knew he hadn't said "definitely."

He was losing interest, maybe. Had she let him jump in too quickly?

Maybe Hallie and Erika were right. She should have played harder to get. She should have played games.

The rules Hallie and Erika had clung to hadn't been invented in a vacuum. Other people talked about "rules," even though it was usually with great disdain—but there had to be some truth to them. You couldn't give a guy too much too soon— that was just a fact. They'd get bored. Why had Gert thought she'd be immune? Was she so great that these maxims would never have to apply to her?

What had gone wrong? Was it the confession about Marc? Or something else?

She tried to remember how she'd looked on her last date with Todd, what she'd been wearing and what she had said.

She should have been paying more attention to Todd, she thought. She had never really thought about how *he* might be viewing their relationship. And *was* it a relationship? It had been a little more than a month—but it was a good month.

She hadn't ever doubted for a minute that it was the start of something bigger.

*I'm spoiled,* she told herself. *You have to do work to keep a guy interested. You can't get lazy.*

She tried to replay her conversation with him of just a few hours ago. She almost wished she'd taped it; then she realized how irrational that was.

She rolled over and gazed at the clock radio. It was eleven. Eight hours until she'd have to get up again. She didn't think she'd fall asleep.

*You were lucky,* she told herself. *Meeting someone like Todd isn't easy. You were very, very lucky.*

There weren't a lot of guys who would have asked to see pictures of her husband and their wedding. There weren't many who would confuse Heckle and Jeckle with Jekyll and Hyde and laugh about it. There weren't many who would try to convince her that New Jersey was beautiful.

*I love him,* she thought.

Okay, so she wasn't *in* love with him, and it wasn't exactly the same way she'd loved Marc. But she knew she did love him, in some way, and it was definitely evolving. What was the likelihood she could feel that way about someone else?

She couldn't ever go back to those bars with Hallie and Erika, even if she'd only been once or twice. She couldn't become inured, accepting crumbs because she thought that was as good as it got. She couldn't pursue barfly party boys who oiled themselves up, tucked their shirts into belted pants and used "dude" as every part of speech.

And how could she go through telling the next guy that she was a twenty-nine-year-old widow? Or thirty? Or thirty-one?

*You're getting carried away,* she thought. *If Todd didn't want to see me, he wouldn't have even mentioned Saturday, right?*

Maybe he wanted to break up that day. Oh God. That was why he had kept postponing. He needed to give her the "We have to slow down" speech. And he was dreading it.

But he hadn't said anything negative about their relationship. Just that he was tired from work. Wasn't she overanalyzing? Being paranoid?

Still, there was one truth. No matter how close they'd gotten, no matter how happy she'd felt about him, there was absolutely no guarantee that he wouldn't break it off. He wasn't her fiancé. He wasn't her husband. He hadn't introduced her to his parents, or met hers. They hadn't stated any commitment. They'd casually mentioned going to his friend Howard's wedding that summer, and at some point they were supposed to take that train trip to the chocolate festival. But was that a guarantee?

*This is too hard,* she thought.

*I've done this already. I've been married.* Why was this uncertainty, this dating process, thrust upon her again?

Hallie had tried to tell her. Dating wasn't fun. It was work. Animals didn't do it. The modus operandi should be this: Find someone, grab them, dive down into your rabbit hole and don't come out.

In the absence of a guarantee, you had only faith. Faith that the other person felt the same way, that if you perceived the relationship progressing, the other person did, too. Faith that if it was meant to be, it *would* be.

Was that enough?

Gert pulled her blanket over herself and shivered.

Maybe Todd had met someone else on one of his train trips. He was cute, enthusiastic, and honest. He was away a lot. The other girls out there probably didn't have problems, were more carefree. Maybe Gert's past weirded him out too much. Maybe he'd simply felt his enthusiasm waning.

She needed another chance.

*I should have met him later,* she thought. *After I'd had more experience dating, like Hallie and Erika. Then I would have been better at it.*

She hadn't even done one thing to show Todd how much she'd liked him. He'd done plenty of things for her. He'd sent her a silly card at work two weeks ago that had an orangutan on the front. When she'd opened it, it had said, "I value our primate time together." She hadn't sent him a monkey card in return.

But hadn't she often told him he was a great guy? She had. And she'd let him sleep over. Obviously she liked him.

So what had she done wrong?

If only she was as confident as she'd been a month ago. Hallie was right about the Rule of Rules: The times you needed to follow the rules most were the times you couldn't. If Todd hadn't called her after they'd met at the bar, she would have never thought about it. Now she cared, and she had to stop herself from calling *him*.

She was two steps away from phoning him and begging him to lay it on the line, to tell her where they stood.

And that was the surest way to freak him out.

He wasn't ready for that. He wasn't her boyfriend. He was just a guy she'd met at a bar.

Did she have "I'm just calling to say I miss you" status with him?

Not at eleven-thirty at night.

She remembered the morning she'd kissed Marc for the last time. She'd told him she loved him. She always did. They'd had a good morning before he'd died, but there was always more she wished she'd said.

And now she wanted to say things to Todd, and she was stopping herself.

What if he was in a train wreck tonight? Wasn't it better just to let the chips fall where they may? Wasn't Todd against games, anyway?

No, no, no. She couldn't call him. He was a young guy. She was used to committed relationships. He wasn't. He'd be scared off.

She had to talk to someone, though. A friend.

She considered her options. Hallie might just confirm that Gert had made mistakes and tell her to follow the rules next time. She didn't want to hear about it right now.

There was Nancy in L.A. Nancy would be perfect—she never judged Gert on anything. She would talk her through it. But it was late to call someone with a husband and kids.

Oh, wait—it was eight-thirty L.A. time. Perfect.

Nancy's phone rang. And rang. They must be putting the kids to bed, or out eating at Johnny Rockets, Gert thought. The kids loved it when the wait staff climbed on the counter and danced to fifties tunes.

Gert rolled over and put the phone on her stomach. She stared at the lit-up numbers. Might as well try Hallie anyway.

She dialed and waited. The phone rang six times.

Gert remembered that Hallie often turned the ringer off at night. She hated it when people did that. It was like saying: *Have your emergencies during business hours, or don't bother us.*

She usually didn't call her parents until Sunday night, but this merited a call.

She dialed and let it ring. Her mom picked it up.

"Hi, Mom," Gert said, her voice quavering.

"Are you all right? Where are you?" she asked.

"I'm fine," Gert said. She tried to keep her voice even. Moms could detect upset in seconds flat. "I sort of…I'm being silly, probably…but Todd hasn't been talking to me much in the last few days, and he says his job's been busy, but I'm worried he's losing interest."

"It's Gert," Gert heard her mom say to her dad. "Well," her mother said, "remember, it hasn't been very long that you two have been dating."

"I know."

The last time Gert had been home, for Christmas, her mom had told her that she was sure she would fall in love again. But as soon as Gert had started dating Todd, her mom had shifted to don't-get-hurt mode.

"Maybe he *is* tired from work," Gert's mom said. "I'm sure he's not even realizing how he comes across."

"Maybe," Gert said. "But Marc would have realized."

"It's hard to replace someone who was so special."

"I'm not trying to replace him."

"That's not what I meant. I'm sorry. That was the wrong word. I just mean that Todd is going to have to learn. He's young, isn't he? He hasn't been in a real long-term relationship before."

"What if he doesn't *want* to be in one?"

"From what you've told me, he likes you a lot," Gert's mom said. "And you're strong. You know that?"

"I don't feel strong," Gert said.

"You are. Remember that no matter what happens, you're a wonderful person and you will always find lots of people who'll love you."

Now Gert wanted to cry. That sounded like something you told your spinster aunt who was never going to get married.

"When are you coming to see us again?" her mom asked.

"I don't know," Gert said. "Around Easter?"

"Come out and stay with us," she said. "We'll go on vacation somewhere. Henry, too. That'll give you something special to look forward to no matter what happens."

"I like that," Gert said. "Can we do that?"

"Sure."

Gert felt a tiny bit better when she hung up.

But there were still seven hours to kill before work.

She set her clock radio for the next day. She changed the station so she wouldn't have to hear Crappy the Clown when she woke up. She didn't think she could deal with Crappy tomorrow.

The clock radio went off at seven-thirty.

"Oh man, what I could do to her," said a deep voice. "You've got a great body, you know that? Mmmm….yeees. Turn around. Do you ever wear a thong? Gary, who's outside? Lesbians? Oh my God! This is…what is this? Oh, we have to go to a commercial."

It was Howard Stern. Gert got up and turned him off.

Standing in front of the clock radio, staring at the hazy red numbers as her eyes came into focus, she figured she'd get a disgusting breakfast to wake herself up. Maybe coffee and a chocolate croissant. She saw guys at work eating like that every morning, and didn't know how they avoided turning into blimps. Well, not all of them avoided it. Hallie had always said it was better to eat junk food in the morning, so you had the day to burn it off. Hallie was very nutrition-conscious.

Gert got to work at 8:30 a.m., and Missy was already in the elevator. She looked tired, but she was wearing a peppy blue suit.

"Well, you're in early!" Missy said, brightening.

Gert was surprised to be greeted so enthusiastically, but maybe she'd have a decent day after all. "I couldn't sleep," Gert said.

"Man problems," Missy said.

Gert said, "How did you know?"

"I didn't. I was talking about *me*." Missy paused. "Once we get settled, let's go back downstairs for some coffee."

★ ★ ★

Heading to her desk, Gert remembered when she'd gotten the call at work about Marc. Missy had been wonderful. She'd gotten Gert downstairs, put her in a cab, handed the driver $100 and told him not to stop until he got her to the hospital.

"Gert?" Missy said as they walked back to the elevator.

"Yeah."

"I know I haven't been the greatest person to be around the last few months."

Gert decided to let the silence hang there a little. Then she said, "You've been fine." She didn't think she'd been convincing.

Missy shrugged. "I know you have your own problems besides getting the brunt of my shit," she said. "I've been taking things out on you, and it's not fair." She wasn't looking at Gert. Gert didn't want to look at her, either.

"It's okay," Gert said finally, to break the silence.

Missy said, "Just because I'm your boss, it doesn't mean you have to kiss my ass. I'd feel better if you said, 'Missy, you treated me like shit and I don't deserve it.'"

Gert ignored her and looked at the floor. It was white and full of footprints.

"Say it," Missy said.

"Missy, you treated me like shit and I don't deserve it."

"You're fired," Missy said. "Ha, ha, ha. Let's get some joe."

In the diner, Missy took off her suit jacket and sat down. She was wearing a sleeveless dress. Gert could tell she was at the gym all the time. No wonder the mailroom guy liked her so much. She was toned.

"Whatever's going on in your life, you can tell me about it," Missy said. She fussed with her silverware, wiping it off with her napkin. "I owe you that," she said. "Besides, I'll admit, I'm pretty low on female friends right now. And the guy I'm with most…well, talking isn't his strong suit."

Gert laughed. Having talked to the mailroom guy once or twice, she was sure that was true.

"So what's up?" Missy said. "Tell me. You said you had man problems…"

Gert looked at her face distorted in the metal carafe of cream. The waitress arrived and they ordered coffee.

"Well," Gert said, "some friends took me to a bar last month. I met a guy there."

Missy smiled. "Good…"

"He's from southern Virginia…" Gert said. "He's twenty-six."

"Younger man…good…."

"He's very sweet."

Gert told Missy all about Todd. When she finished, Missy said, "He sounds wonderful."

"He is."

"Maybe he *is* just working hard," Missy said.

"He might be," Gert said. "But how do I know?"

Missy smiled at her, then turned her attention to her newly delivered coffee cup. "Well," she said, "here's what you do. Keep yourself busy constantly until you're supposed to see him. That's tomorrow night, right?"

"Yes. Saturday."

"I'm sure he'll see you Saturday. You don't want him to know how crazy this is making you. You really have to avoid thinking about it."

"How?"

"You go to the gym, right?"

"Yeah…sometimes."

"Go today. Run, step, lift weights, anything to make you feel better about yourself. What else can you do?"

"Go to the movies? Visit friends?"

"Oh my God! Of course, go to the movies. Buy your friends some drinks. And make sure you wear the cutest clothes you can find. For yourself, not for men. Try to look sexy. Don't wait until you're forced."

"Okay."

"And when you're out, don't think about Todd, and don't answer your cell phone. Your instincts were right. No matter what, do not call him."

When it was time to pay the check, Missy looked through her wallet for some cash. Suddenly she said, "Do you want to see a picture of Derek?"

Gert nodded. Missy produced a snapshot of a guy who was young and fit, with a carefully groomed mustache and bulging arms.

"He'd never be the type to invite me on a train ride," Missy said. "He'd never tell me he looks forward to having kids someday. But who gives a fig?"

Gert didn't say anything.

Missy took back her photo of Derek, then looked at it herself. "Don't ever decide against taking something that makes you happy," Missy said. Gert wondered if Missy was just trying to convince *herself.* "If I were still living with Dennis, I'd be miserable all the time."

"When did you two meet?"

"Me and Dennis? Or me and Derek?"

"Dennis."

"Oh, in high school," Missy said. "There were a lot of guys after me. Dennis was average-looking, but I'm telling you, he worshiped me. After a while you decide, if someone's going to treat you like a queen, why fight it? We had a few good years. It doesn't last forever. The more you realize you can have in life, the more you want."

Gert knew she wasn't the same type of person as Missy. She definitely would choose Dennis over the mailroom guy.

"Anyway, now Dennis is obsessed," Missy said. "I'm sure he took that FedEx from your desk. He knows I'm not coming back, regardless of what happens with Derek. As soon as you left that message for him, he knew he'd make me crazy by swiping it. He always calls Derek's house to see if I'm there, and then he hangs up. We have Caller ID, so I know. He doesn't even bother to hide his number."

Gert thought that was too bad.

Missy yawned and rubbed her eyes. "He's going to have to get over it," she said. "Even if I didn't have Derek, I could never go back to Dennis. I've come too far."

At four, Missy let Gert leave work early. Gert was pleased to be able to use the gym with the room nearly empty. Unfortunately it wasn't completely empty. The Annoying Gym Guy who worked there was hovering around her side of the room, near the windows. All the treadmills faced the windows. The windows, in turn, faced a luxury hotel across the street. But the hotel's windows were black and couldn't be seen through.

Gert stared at the clouds reflecting in the hotel, put on her headphones, and started walking to a U2 CD.

Gert thought briefly about Todd. Then she thought that she shouldn't think about Todd. Then she thought about the fact that she should run for thirty minutes and not think about Todd. She'd get just as toned as Missy. Then everyone would want her. Especially Todd. Wait, she wasn't supposed to be thinking about Todd. She wasn't doing this for Todd. She was doing it for herself.

What a load of pig offal that was.

She pushed the buttons to increase her miles per hour to 3.5, then 4. Then 4.5. She was sprinting now.

This felt good.

Yes, it would all work out. She'd be beautiful, funny, and fit. There were plenty of people to meet out there, and if not, she'd revel in her aloneness for a little while longer. Was being alone really so bad?

She didn't see the Annoying Gym Guy anymore. Perhaps he'd retreated back to his little office by the free weights instead of bugging her. Good.

A faster song came on. Gert pressed the treadmill to get up to 5. She watched a piece of paper fly through the air outside. She watched a plane soaring in the distance. It seemed really low. She kept her eye on it until it disappeared.

She closed her eyes for a second and felt her muscles work-ing. She really *was* doing this for herself. She should go three times a week. She always said she was going to get on a sched-ule, but hadn't.

She hurried a little more and was running briskly. She pushed the machine to 6.0. Nothing bothered her. She was in the Olympics, twenty yards from the finish line.

She started to get winded. She pushed herself for a few minutes more, then pressed the down arrow to return to a walk.

The machine didn't slow.

It had happened before when she pressed it too fast. She pushed again.

It stayed at 6.0.

She waited a couple of seconds, then pressed again.

It was still at six miles an hour, and she had to keep running quickly.

She looked around. The room was empty. The mirrored wall in the back, by the free weights, showed only bars and pulleys. The Annoying Gym Guy definitely must have gone into his little office.

She was getting tired. She pressed the down arrow again, but nothing happened. She felt sweat on her back, and on her forehead.

She couldn't jump off. It was moving too quickly.

She looked around again. She couldn't believe it. She had ac-tually become a cliché. You weren't supposed to literally get stuck on a treadmill.

Maybe she was being punished for something. For all the things she had taken for granted, for the fact that she had never joined a gym until now.

She collected her wits and pushed again. Maybe she'd been doing it wrong.

Nothing.

She sensed someone near the back of the room. It was the Annoying Gym Guy, but he was too far back for him to hear her. And the noise coming from her machine would drown her out.

She irrationally wondered if he'd rigged the machine to get back at her for being snippy to him. That would be a good way to get back at someone—fix the treadmill so it'd get stuck. There could be a movie, like *Speed,* where you had to keep going six miles per hour because if you slowed down, the treadmill would explode.

The sweat was dripping down her back, under her shirt, now. She panted heavily.

She felt panicked.

*Calm down,* she told herself. *The gym will fill up soon. Someone will know what to do.*

Her cell phone was on the sill in front of her. It was too far to reach.

A new guy came into the gym. He was skinny and hairy in a sleeveless top, which hairy guys shouldn't wear, and he sat down on one of those giant blue rubber balls on the floor. They reminded Gert of the animal things you used to hop on in preschool. She wasn't sure what they were called. Or what they were for, exactly.

The guy wasn't close enough to hear her, either. She pressed the button once more. Still stuck.

The Annoying Gym Guy was coming to the middle of the room. He was wearing his oversize glasses and a fluorescent netted shirt.

She managed to turn her head. "Excuse me, sir?"

He didn't seem to hear.

"Sir?"

The Gym Guy jogged over. "Yes, ma'am?"

"I can't get this to slow down. I'm stuck."

The guy said, "Just push it."

*Brilliant,* Gert thought.

The guy reached out and pushed it himself, but it didn't change.

"It's stuck," he said.

*Thanks.*

He shook his head and tried again. "This has never happened before," he said.

The hairy guy on the blue ball hopped over. "Is she stuck?" he asked.

"Looks that way," the Gym Guy said.

The hairy guy hopped on the ball and stared at her.

A girl entered the gym, thin and blond, and noticed something was wrong. She came over to watch.

Not only was Gert embarrassed, but she had to keep running six miles an hour.

"Can't you unplug it?" the blond girl asked.

"It would stop too quickly," the Gym Guy said. He moved forward and said to Gert, "Okay. Here's what I'll do."

Someone else was coming into the gym. Gert hoped it was someone sane, but it was a buff fellow who veered toward the free weights.

"You see the treadmill next to you?" the Gym Guy said. "I'm going to drag it back a little, then get it up to 6.0. When it's ready, you can jump sideways onto it and keep running at the same pace."

The Gym Guy and the hairy guy shimmied between the two treadmills and pulled back the one that was parallel to Gert's.

The Gym Guy turned it on and got it up to 6.0. Gert watched it while she ran. She was ready to collapse.

"Okay," the Gym Guy said. "We're spotting you. When I say jump, jump!"

Gert kept running, though. What if she slipped and fell off? Still, she had to make that leap.

She focused on the parallel treadmill. She watched it so much that she slipped for a second. She balanced herself and kept running. She prepared to jump sideways.

She hesitated for a second. Then she jumped.

Landing on the new treadmill, she righted herself and began running.

"Yeah," the blond girl said, and people clapped.

"When you get off, come see me," the Gym Guy said, and then he walked to his office.

After Gert eased the speed down, she went back to the guy's office.

His office was small, with flyers pinned up about fitness tips and anatomical diagrams. There was a metal desk with piles of papers and a few framed photos. One was of a stately, but pretty, woman with a teenage boy next to her. Another was just a boy.

"Did you ever take the orientation class?" the guy asked, sitting at his desk.

"No," Gert said, looking at the ground.

"You're supposed to take it right after you join."

"I know," she said.

The man stared at her.

She looked up.

"I guess I never wanted to acknowledge that I joined a gym," she said.

He didn't seem to understand.

"I didn't want to believe that this is my life…. I always thought going to the gym was for people with low self-esteem."

He still looked puzzled.

"My husband died a year and a half ago," Gert said. "My college friend, she goes to the gym…a different one…she suggested I start going. But I resented being here."

"The gym is supposed to make you feel better, not worse," the guy said.

"I know," Gert stammered. "It usually does." She tried to think of a polite way to leave. She just wanted him to understand so he wasn't insulted by her snippiness.

"My wife died five years ago," the guy said suddenly.

Gert stopped.

The guy motioned to the picture on his desk, the one of the older woman. They were quiet, looking at the picture.

"I'm remarried now," the guy added.

Gert saw there was a different photo by the wall.

"I'm sorry about your loss," Gert said.

"It's all right," the guy said.

But Gert knew it wasn't really all right. He was lying to himself, like everyone else.

She forced herself to smile, though. He had his pain. Why had she been thinking only of herself?

"Well, I'll take the intro class," Gert said.

"You should," the man said, nodding. "It'll help you."

She left. She got the feeling that even though she wasn't staying to talk more, he understood.

Warm water splattered against Gert's back. It pummeled her neck, tickled her spine, streamed down her buttocks. She turned toward the shower faucet and let it rail against her face.

Before Marc had died, showers had been a chore to endure on a cold morning. Then, after Marc's death, she just couldn't bear them in the winter anymore. It was just so cold and dark out in the morning that she didn't feel like getting in. She didn't need to get up and torture herself. The only benefit to showering in the morning rather than at night was that her hair looked better right after a shower and blow-dry. And who cared about that now? Was anyone she saw during the day really going to complain if her hair didn't look perfect?

But at night, her showers began to take on a new significance. She stayed in for a half hour, let the room steam up, breathed the moisture, felt the warm water beat against her skin. It reached parts of her that had been untouched by human hands for some time.

Nighttime showers were a treat. She turned around, letting the water massage her shoulders. It felt like the most wonderful thing in the world.

She thought of Todd again. Her stomach sank. Now she had

two men to miss. Was this supposed to help? Dating only led to more heartbreak.

She wasn't supposed to think about Todd. Not until he called.

She got out and dried herself off. She found a short skirt. She hadn't worn it in a while. She put it on to look good, as Missy had recommended. As she left the condo, she did feel kind of sexy. But she wanted to look that way for Todd. She needed another chance.

Gert and Hallie were splitting a fried onion at an Irish pub. When Gert had been little, she'd thought they were healthy—after all, they were onions. Now she knew they were maybe two thousand calories, but for some reason, even Hallie joined her in this trespass against good nutrition. It was a special occasion, after all. It was a night to not talk about Todd.

Instead Gert asked about Brett Stoddard.

"I saw him for the third time yesterday," Hallie said, "and we sat on my bed and he looked around and he asked about everything I've ever been interested in, and I don't remember a time when I wanted to take someone's clothes off so badly." Gert thought of Marc burrowing through her closet. "And I had to sit there and tell him I didn't want the responsibility of starting to sleep with him. I said I liked how uncomplicated things were and that I wanted to focus more on getting to know each other. And what I know is, it's killing me! He's incredible."

"He knows how to get your attention," Gert said.

"Exactly," Hallie said. "The third date is usually the time he bags women, and I could see why. Poor things! If I really believed he was a poet and a cook and a philosopher, I'd be in love with him by now. When I told him I couldn't sleep with him, he said he understood. Then I watched him leave and I felt crazed. And I spent the next day worrying he'd never call again. But he already has."

"So it's working," Gert said. She got a sinking feeling again that she'd been too easy with Todd.

"Yes! But how long can I hold out?" Hallie said. "All I can think about now is having sex with him. This is *not* how it's supposed to be."

Gert smiled. She looked behind Hallie at all the shamrocks around the pub. If you donated a dollar to muscular dystrophy, you could sign one. "You only said you weren't going to sleep with him," Gert said. "You can do other things with him, right?"

"We'll do them," Hallie said. "But it won't be enough for me. I'm just a sucker, aren't I? Are all women just suckers? There's some new book on the market now telling men how to seduce us. Why do they need a book to tell them how to treat us? And why does it work so easily?"

"Women aren't suckers," Gert said, shaking her head and spearing the mustard cup with an onion shard. "We just have feelings."

"I know," Hallie said. "You know what he said on the phone today? He said, 'You're the first girl in a long time where I don't think it's entirely physical.' And I'm trying not to let myself get emotional over him. But it's all related!"

"Maybe you should just go with your feelings," Gert said.

"No." Hallie shook her head. "I'd end up just like every girl who dates him—dumped. For once, I'm going to stick it out. I'm not going to let some silly female emotional feelings—and, okay, some physical feelings—ruin this. He'll be the best boyfriend around."

Gert was doubtful. But she didn't think she was one to talk right now.

"You told me not to mention Todd…" Hallie said.

"Let's don't."

"But you're worried," Hallie said. "I can tell."

Gert was.

"With one phone call, I can find out what Brett knows," Hallie said.

Gert *had* started to feel crazed. But could Hallie really help her? If she was going to see Todd tomorrow, maybe she should just hold out.

"There's nothing I can do anyway," Gert said. "You said it yourself. When women are the ones doing the chasing, it's never going to work. Todd either wants to keep seeing me, or he doesn't."

"But you should at least know what you're up against."

"Why would it help?"

"Because," Hallie said, "then you'll know if there's anything you can do to get Todd back. If Todd's just bored, you can act indifferent next time he calls, and show him you're not putting pressure on him. And if he does have another girlfriend, then you're going to have to be seductive and beat her out."

Gert thought about it. Maybe for once, Hallie's manipulation would help her.

Gert watched a couple stroll past the front window, laughing. Gert wondered if Todd really *did* live with a girl. Or maybe he had a girlfriend where the train went. Right now, he might be strolling the cold streets of Binghamton, holding her hand and telling her about the sprinkles at Busch Gardens. And the girl would have no idea about Gert.

Todd was a great guy. Had he really had only one major relationship by twenty-six? That didn't seem right.

Maybe he had a girlfriend at every whistlestop.

Yet again, Gert felt naive. Always, naive.

"You know," Hallie said, "Todd told us these things about Brett, but what if he knows so much because that's what *he* does? Todd knew a lot about Brett's 'three dates and out' rule, about how he acts sincere and then dumps girls…. What if all along, Todd's been telling you about *himself*?"

Gert nearly dropped her piece of onion.

That was it, wasn't it?

Todd *had* asked her lots of questions about herself, especially the night that she had finally told him about Marc. Maybe he'd said all that to try to get into her pants again. A seduction book would tell him to act exactly the way he had acted. And now, for him, the chase was over.

But Todd didn't seem like that.

How could she know?

"He didn't dump me after the first time that he…uh… spent the night," Gert said.

"I know," Hallie said. "But it doesn't hurt to know as much as you can. You still haven't met this guy, Doug, he rooms with. Have you ever talked to him on the phone?"

"I never call Todd's home number. He uses his cell."

Hallie looked at her.

Gert felt stupid.

"You don't have an address, I suppose," Hallie said.

"I do, somewhere. He sent me a card at work."

Hallie brightened. "We could go to his place, knock on the door and see if a girl answers," she said. "Then we'll leave."

"What if a guy answers? He'll tell Todd we were checking up on him."

"Doug's never met you, right? He won't know who you are. Or we can just say we're delivering something. Then we'll try to peer inside the apartment."

Gert didn't know if this would work. It sounded like something Erika would suggest.

But she wanted to know. Now.

It was nuts, but it would make her feel *less* nuts to do it.

"What could we be delivering?" Gert asked.

"Flowers."

"That's pushy," Gert said. "Todd will get them when he gets home and he'll feel pressured."

"How about a bottle of wine?" Hallie asked.

"He doesn't drink."

"But *you* do."

"Still pushy."

"Oh! I know. We'll do a survey."

"At eight o'clock at night?"

Hallie thought.

"I've got it!" she said, snapping her fingers. "We'll say we're thinking of moving into the building and we're knocking on doors to see what the units are like. Doug, or whoever lives there, will have to invite us in."

"To look at his unit?"

"It's brilliant!" Hallie said. "Credit, please. We can still go see a movie after."

Like clockwork, Erika appeared as they were polishing off the last crescents of the beer-battered onion. Gert wasn't surprised that Erika showed up. She wondered if the girl had any other friends. Then Gert reminded herself that in New York, she didn't have many, either. She hadn't noticed when she was with Marc. They had socialized with neighbors and married couples and his associates, but she'd never really become good friends with them. Some of the women at the support group were nice. There was a retreat planned for the summer. She would go. She'd become better friends with them. Still, she wanted Chase to come back. Maybe she could make a better effort to find out what had happened to her.

"I'm sorry I'm late," Erika said, sitting down. Her eyes were red, and her eyeliner was wet.

"Were you looking at Challa's Web site again?" Hallie asked.

Erika nodded. She bit her lip. "I still can't believe they're having another baby. Why can't I ever feel okay? Why can't I ever call up the Web log and find something that actually makes me feel like I did the *right* thing by breaking up with him? Then I wouldn't feel so bad. How come Challa can't write, 'Dear Web log. Today Ben beat me. Also, he smells like bad cheese.'"

"Maybe the whole thing's fake," Hallie said. "Maybe he *does* beat her, and she only keeps the Web log to put a sunny face on things. Maybe it's like her fake fantasy life that she…"

"Bullshit!" Erika said. "Stop trying to comfort me. You're about as comforting as Plexiglas."

"Well, you can help me comfort Gert," Hallie said.

"Comfort her about what?"

Hallie explained her plan.

Erika smiled. "Now you're talking," she said. "Don't worry. You're in good hands. We're experts at this."

Gert had a sinking feeling. Still, she now felt as irrational as Hallie and Erika often did. She wanted to *know.*

Todd's building was on Washington Street in the West Village, not far from the Hudson River. Gert had never been that far west in the Village before. It was near 12th Avenue. It was quiet and seemed good for families, with little row homes and an elementary school.

Todd's building was old. It was pink with white trim, settled between two shorter brownstones. The three women walked into the foyer, and Gert noticed that they had those copper mailboxes with antique intercoms. She was sure Todd was delighted by this. Todd loved old things.

*Damn,* she thought. *I like him.*

Why did she have to start thinking about him now that he was about to dump her?

The elevator, too, was a classic. It required one to push the doors open and closed. Inside, the metal arrow pointed to the little numbers representing floors. Gert knew Todd probably loved this, too.

Ugh.

They stepped out into the hall. It was quiet. There were long opaque windows at both ends. They ambled down to apartment 4D.

Hallie knocked.

There was no answer.

Gert was glad, in a way. They'd go see a movie, she would go home, and there would be a message from Todd affirming their date for Saturday. Everything would be fine.

"Hold on," Hallie whispered.

They heard footsteps. Gert tensed up. She almost didn't want to know. She wished she hadn't come here.

What if Todd was actually home? What if half the time he pretended he was away when he was simply shacking up?

The door opened. A tall guy with messed-up hair and half-closed eyes stood there in a red sweatsuit. As soon as he saw Erika, he straightened up.

"Sorry to bother you," Hallie said. "We're looking to rent an apartment here, and we're meeting with the landlord tomorrow. We were hoping to look at some of the apartments first. Would you mind if we took a look around?"

The roommate shrugged. "I guess not," he said. "It's kind of a mess, but…"

"That's okay. We're just curious."

They entered slowly. The living room was dark yellow and pasty, with an orange couch that looked like it had been there for decades.

"That was here when we moved in," Doug said.

"How lucky for you," Erika said.

On a wall was a framed poster of a half-naked woman. She was wearing black leather pants. Gert hoped it was Doug's and not Todd's.

"Yours?" Hallie asked him.

Doug nodded. "It's a cover from a record," he said. "I'm not obsessed with naked women or anything." He looked at Erika. "I mean, depending on who."

"Can we see your room for a sec?" Hallie asked.

He led them toward it. The four of them peered in. It was sloppy, with books and clothes everywhere, but the CDs were in a tower that stretched to the ceiling.

*How very like a guy,* Gert thought. *The room's a mess, but the CDs are perfect.* Doug's mattress and box spring were on the floor, under dark drapes.

"I'm not into heavy decorating," Doug said. "I just sleep here."

"Do you have another bedroom?" Hallie asked innocently.

"Oh, yeah, my roommate's," Doug said. "But he's never here."

"Why not?"

"He works ridiculous hours," Doug said, heading into the living room. "And when he's around, he's at his girlfriend's all the time."

"*All* the time?" Erika asked. "Wow, they must keep really busy."

"I guess," Doug said. He stopped in front of Todd's door.

Erika said, "They must go at it like rabbits."

Doug laughed. "I suppose." Gert looked down.

"I'll bet they really wake the neighbors," Erika said.

"All right!" Gert said.

Doug opened Todd's door.

Gert tensed up again.

The three of them peered in.

There were no pictures of girls on the wall.

Gert let herself breathe.

The room was small, with a single bed that was not made up. The shelves were neat enough. There was a laundry basket full of clothes. Todd had a framed poster of a DeLorean on one wall. It looked like it had been there for a while. The glass was dusty.

She thought she might ask Todd about it. But of course, she couldn't.

"Does your roommate *like* his girlfriend?" Hallie asked, standing in the doorway. Gert was annoyed. As far as she was concerned, the investigation had gone far enough.

"I assume," Doug said, shrugging. "He's always over there." He smiled again.

"What's her name?" Erika asked.

She tensed up again. What if he said another girl's name?

"I think it's…Gert, or Gertie," Doug said. He shrugged apologetically. "Kind of old-fashioned."

Erika played with a blue pamphlet she picked up on the radiator. It was called, "The War and the Second International."

"Well, Doug," Hallie said, shaking his hand, "you've been a real help."

"Hey, you know my name," Doug said.

"You said your name," Hallie said.

"We're sure you said your name," Erika said.

"You distinctly said your name," Hallie said. "Or I saw it on the mailbox."

"Okay," Doug said. "Well, when you guys move in, come knock on my door. *Me cosa es su cosa, comprendi vous?*"

"Uh," Hallie said. "Thanks."

"Yeah." Doug grinned.

"And thank your roommate for us, too," Erika said. "Tell him to keep on giving it to this Gert woman."

"Let's go," Gert said.

Walking out of the elevator downstairs, Hallie said, "Well, now we know the truth. Todd doesn't tell his roommate about his secret girlfriend in Binghamton."

"Oh, stop," Gert said.

"No, seriously. Don't you feel better now?" Hallie put her arm around her.

Gert was a bit relieved. There had been some benefit to manipulation…well, maybe. If Todd ever introduced her to Doug, though, she'd have some explaining to do. "I guess I do feel better," Gert said. "But he still might break up with me tomorrow. He's away and he doesn't care."

"Well, we'll see the movie, and you'll forget all about it for tonight." Hallie kept her arm around her, and Erika patted her other shoulder, and for a minute, she was part of a team.

The theater was moderately crowded. They had decided on a mindless adventure film that had just opened. Even if it cost seventeen dollars for the movie, popcorn and soda, it was just the therapy Gert needed.

But Gert felt cold in her short skirt. Hallie gave her her coat to drape over her knees.

The movie was over by eleven.

"It had its moments," Hallie said as they descended toward the back exit.

"The one guy looked like Ben," Erika said. "That bugged me."

The crowd slowly squeezed out the back door. Gert accidentally stepped on the back of a woman's shoe. The woman gave Gert a nasty look.

The guy she was with turned around to Gert. "You just stepped on her shoe," he said angrily.

"Don't tell us problems," Erika said. "Give us solutions."

"Excuse me!" the guy said. "What did you say? And why is it *your* business, bitch?"

Gert looked away. They were all going through the door. The guy was tall and heavy, with a chain around his neck. He looked at Erika, waiting.

"You know she didn't mean to step on her shoe," Erika said. "And there are bigger tragedies than having your shoe accidentally stepped on. Just move along, asshole."

The guy's eyes narrowed. His girlfriend hung on his arm and chomped on her gum.

"What did you say, bitch?" the guy said again, stopping. They were out back now, by the Dumpsters. Other people were moving down the alley.

"You shouldn't call women bitches just because they speak their mind," Erika said. "See this girl you're with? Do you think she's a bitch? And don't look away, sweetie." Erika looked at the girl. Gert just wanted to get out of there. "Why do you date a guy who calls women bitches? Do you think that's right, or don't you have a mind of your own?"

"You better—" the girl started, looking at the guy.

"You better shut your mouth right now," the guy said, getting closer to Erika. "Or I'll show you how to mind your business."

"We apologize," Gert said. Her legs felt cold, and she felt vulnerable in high heels.

"Good; now I think *you* should apologize," Erika said. "My friend's husband died a year and a half ago, and she's been through a lot."

"Oh really?" the guy asked. "Is that why she's dressed like a slut to go to the movies?"

Gert looked down at her waist. She wanted to cry. She pushed her skirt over her legs.

"Well, you're dressed like a pimp!" Erika said. "And your girlfriend—"

Hallie grabbed Erika's arm. "Let's go," Hallie said, and she and Gert pulled her away.

"It bothers you that a woman talked back!" Erika called behind her. "You thought you could mouth off for no reason."

Once Erika, Gert and Hallie got far enough away, Erika looked back. *"Pimp!"* she yelled. Then they all ran down to the subway.

"You're stupid!" Hallie said, panting as they went through the turnstile. "You could have gotten us killed! What if we see them in the middle of the night somewhere?"

"We won't," Erika said.

"How do you know?" Hallie said. "I don't feel safe anymore. What if we bump into him in the street?"

"That's what he *wants* us to think," Erika said.

"What if he'd tried to hurt us?" Gert added. "What if he'd had a knife? Did you want to die being right?"

Erika said, "He shouldn't go through life thinking women are bitches if we don't do exactly what he wants."

It was only later, when they were recouping with coffee at a diner near Hallie's apartment, that Erika admitted that she wasn't sure what had gotten into her.

"I think I'm losing it," she said. She put her head in her hands. "I just couldn't let it go. When he said 'bitch,' something in me snapped. I'm just tired of everyone being an asshole."

Hallie shook her head. "I always think the world is this wonderful place," she said. "And then I remember how you have to always be careful. We could have gotten hurt back there, easily. I don't like being so cynical, but something like this sends you back to the beginning. I should start taking tae kwon do again."

"I think martial arts just give you a false sense of security," Gert said. "If someone's stronger than you, they're stronger than you. Ever tried to wrestle a guy? It doesn't matter if they're short or scrawny or quiet. They pin you in two seconds flat."

"When have you wrestled a guy?" Erika asked her.

Gert thought. Her brother. And Marc. A guy on her floor freshman year when most people were home on break. It hadn't gotten far, in that case. But it was fun.

"Self-defense teaches you to act only as a last resort," Hallie said, looking at Erika. "*Some* of us could use that training."

Gert pushed her skirt down again. She still felt cold and ashamed. She thought that the world wasn't set up to get through without someone to protect you. That guy would never have said anything to her if Todd had been there.

Where *was* Todd, anyway? She wanted Todd. She needed Todd. Why deny it?

Slumping over on the subway going home, trying not to think too hard, Gert hoped there would be a message from him on her voicemail when she got there. She had given him enough time. At least she hadn't sat home all night waiting for him to call.

But there was no message.

# Chapter

13

Saturday morning, the phone still hadn't rung. She was grateful for the widows' support group. It would go until almost lunchtime, and by that time, Todd probably would have left a message about dinner.

When Gert left the condo, bright sunlight was making sharp tree-shaped shadows on the sidewalk. She stepped carefully around them, thinking that if she were a kid, she would take fat pieces of chalk and trace them.

She wended her way to the corner, around planters and street signs, and that was when she saw him. It was his brown hair. And his haircut.

Marc.

He was just a few feet ahead of her....

The guy turned around.

It wasn't Marc, of course. Gert's heart dropped.

She had seen look-alikes before, on the way to the supermarket or to work, and they'd caused an instant jolt that scrambled her brain. It could be the haircut, or the eyes, or the curve of their mouth. Whenever she saw them, her heart lifted for a second, then plummeted.

It wasn't as if she thought Marc was alive. It was just that she'd gotten that little surge she always used to get upon seeing him. Only now, it simply reminded her that it couldn't possibly be him. It never would be.

The community center was quiet, its horizontal shades pulled low. There was a huge kids' calendar on the wall, made out of construction paper, and on top of it, it said, "March goes in like a lion and goes out like a lamb." Gert thought it was supposed to be March *comes* in like a lion. But the more she looked at it, the less sure she was. She'd learned that in elementary school, and now she couldn't remember. A sure sign of old age.

Chairs were squeaking into place. Gert sat down. She remembered how foreign she'd felt the first day she came to the group. Support groups had always been for other people, not her. They had been something to joke about. "The first step," Marc's friends had said, "is admitting you have the problem." Support groups had been things to make fun of on *Saturday Night Live.* Support groups had been things for people on the news or movies of the week. Support groups were for the people her mother helped through whatever fund-raiser her busybody friends were running and enlisting her in. Support groups were for Victims. Gert had never been a Victim. It was far better to be the one who helped than the one who needed the help.

As much as the group helped her, as much as she got along with the women, she'd never lie and say she wanted to be there. It was not about having fun. It was about surviving. And what was surviving? Solely the act of not giving up.

The only real living she'd done lately was with Todd. And now that might be gone, too. There was still much surviving to be done.

★ ★ ★

Gert adjusted her pocketbook securely below her chair—even in a safe space you could never be too careful, so she wound its loop around one of the chair legs. She caught some movement out of the corner of her eye.

Chase was coming into the room.

Gert sat up and waved to her. Chase smiled and sat down next to her.

"Where've you been?" Gert asked. "I've been wondering if you're okay."

"I'm okay," Chase said. "It's just—"

"Ladies," Brenda said. "It's time to begin."

"I'll tell you later," Chase whispered.

It was a tough session, full of tears. Michele said that weekend was her wedding anniversary. That spurred talk about anniversaries and birthdays. Brenda said that for her husband's birthday, she'd celebrated by baking his favorite kind of layer cake, lighting a candle, and eating it alone. Everyone said they would have joined her if she'd told them. But Brenda said she *wanted* to be alone. And she wasn't really alone, she said, because she felt like her husband was in the room. She said that when she finished singing happy birthday to him, one of the candles went out. Gert, although chiding herself for her cynicism, wondered why Brenda had left her window open in the middle of March.

Chase just sat there, quiet. Gert wished she would talk. Maybe if Gert said something, it would get Chase to open up.

"I saw a look-alike the other day," Arden said.

"I did, too," Gert said. "Actually, this morning, on the way here."

Arden shook her head. "Does yours live on your street?"

"I don't think so," Gert said. "This one was new."

"Mine lives near me, and I've seen him a dozen times," Arden said. "And *still,* I always think it's Steve for a second."

Gert thought that the idea that time would heal things was

crap. Other things might happen in your life to compete for your attention, to take your mind off your loss for longer periods, but the pain would still be there, surging up at unexpected moments. An anniversary, birthday, or cruise brochure would make it spike.

Toward the end of the session, Chase finally spoke. "Something funny happened this week," she said.

Gert looked up.

"I think the last time I came here, I said I was still crying a lot," Chase said.

"We remember," Michele said.

"Even the littlest thing would start me off."

"I've been there," Leslie said.

"Well," Chase said, "last week, instead of crying uncontrollably, I started laughing uncontrollably, and it was over the dumbest thing. I don't think I've laughed that hard in ages."

"What happened?"

Gert noticed her hesitate a little. Gert thought Chase probably was the type who alternated between scared and strong. Gert saw that in herself, sometimes.

"I was looking at one of those widow support groups on the Internet," Chase said. "This one had a list of dumb things people say to widows."

"Oh, God," said Michele. "Those are terrible."

"Some of them were worse than anything I've heard before," she said. "Things like, 'At least you got the insurance money' and 'What are you going to do with his car?' So I was reading down the list, and this one woman said that she had been talking with friends at a party, and they brought up the fact that her husband had died a year ago doing construction. And a guy who was standing in the group said, 'Shit happens.'"

Chase laughed and rubbed her eyes. A few other women laughed.

"I know it wasn't funny," Chase said. "It's just, it was so much worse than any of the things I've heard, so it caught me off guard somehow and it made me laugh. And then I just let myself keep laughing."

"That's *good,*" Brenda encouraged.

"I'm not saying I won't still cry all of a sudden," Chase said, "but it was the first time in a long time that I had a good laugh."

Everyone started clapping.

When the meeting started to break up, Gert didn't want to lose another opportunity. "How are you?" she asked Chase again.

Chase picked up her pocketbook, but didn't get up to leave. "I'm fine," Chase said. Then she smiled shyly and looked at the ground. "Well, not really fine. I'm just used to saying that. You know how it is. Every day, there's some new thing to deal with."

"I know," Gert said.

Chase didn't seem to know what to say. So Gert said, "We should get lunch sometime. It might be neat to talk about it."

"Really?" Chase said. She seemed pleased. "I'd like that."

Gert figured she could ask Chase then where she'd been for six weeks. She looked through her purse for a business card, but she realized she'd given the only one she'd kept there to Todd. *Jeez,* she thought. *I'd better get used to giving my number to people.* Marc had been the real networker. She wrote her number on the blank sheet in the back of her appointment book that said "birthdays" but never got used. She ripped it out. "Do you want to do it during the week?" Gert asked. "Or on the weekend? Where do you live?"

"Park Slope," Chase said, "but I'm thinking of moving. It's too big for just me, and this friend from college is moving to New York and I think she wants to live with me. But she's a partying type, so I know she'll drag me out to bars. I'm not sure I'm ready for that."

Gert smiled. "We'll have to talk about that," she said. "I happen to have some experience in this particular topic."

# Chapter

## 14

It could end up being one of the most important nights of Gert's life.

Gert didn't think she was exaggerating. Didn't all encounters with the opposite sex during your twenties have a potential impact on the rest of your life?

Todd was coming at six to take her out. He'd left a message that morning saying he'd pick her up at her condo. They'd already decided to go out for Greek food in her neighborhood. During the call he'd sounded fine but harried. She didn't know if there was a breakup speech coming or not.

She had to make sure she'd look good for him.

Hallie had told her to wear boots. "They're witchy, but sexy," she'd said. "They always work for Erika." Gert didn't have sexy boots, and she wasn't about to run out and buy some. But she had a blouse that fit her tightly, without looking slutty. She didn't think Todd had seen it. And she would wear the cute skirt from the night at the movies, even if it had made her feel bad. She thought about the fact that she was trying to seduce someone a year and a half after her husband had died, and she had to look away from the mirror.

*Stop it,* she thought. *Stop it. Your life will never change if you think like this.*

She cared about Todd, regardless of her feelings about anyone else. She didn't want to lose him.

She finished getting dressed. She put makeup on. Todd had to want her intensely the moment he saw her.

Looking in the mirror again, she thought she had overdone it and she wiped some of the makeup off. Todd hadn't seemed to be into makeup. But after she wiped it off, she thought she should put some of it back on.

Her nose was running. She went into the bathroom to wipe her nose and wash her face. Then she reapplied some of the makeup.

Finally, at five, she was satisfied.

But what if it was for naught? Was she getting dolled up for a guy who wasn't interested? What if Todd stood there, looking at her in her skirt, and broke up with her?

She tried not to feel as vulnerable as she looked.

Gert decided to put on a game show. She sat on the couch to watch. She remembered the Saturday nights her parents had gone out when she was little, how she and Henry had sat on the couch all night with the baby-sitter watching TV, even though there was never anything on because the networks expected everyone intelligent to be out on a Saturday. They always had to settle for *Solid Gold* and the *Tim Conway Show.*

Gert wondered if Todd remembered those shows.

She looked at the clock—5:40. She didn't want to move, lest she muss herself. It didn't take much.

She stared at the TV again, keeping perfectly still. She thought of women in the fifties who sat home waiting for the phone to ring. How desperate she was. How unliberated.

*So what?* she thought. *You have to compromise if you want to get something important.*

On the game show, the host said to the contestant, "It says here that you're the youngest of six children."

"Yes," the contestant said.

"What was that like?"

"By the time I got hand-me-downs, they were back in style."

The laugh track roared. The doorbell rang. Gert gulped. She got up, smoothed her skirt, and took baby steps to the buzzer.

Todd looked surprised when he came in. He lit up when he saw her. "Wow!" he said. He gave her a hug. "I don't know how I got through these last few days without seeing you."

She held him tightly. He said into her ear, "I missed you. I have something for you."

He had one hand behind his back.

*I've been acting crazy,* she thought. *Maybe he would have been happy to see me any way I looked.* But she decided the effort was worth it. Maybe she had needed to remind herself to not take him for granted.

"It's chocolate," Todd said, pulling away and presenting a black box with a big bow. "Straight from Binghamton."

"Didn't know Binghamton was a chocolate town."

"They have this wonderful candy store on Water Street," Todd said, closing his eyes. "Some days, the smell wafts through the entire town."

"It sounds great," Gert said, snatching the box.

"It is. I'll take you sometime."

Gert sat on the couch with him to open the package. There were black and white truffles inside, and one that was white with red stripes. She picked out that one and offered it to him. He shook his head and motioned for her to eat it.

She popped it into her mouth. It had peppermint inside.

"Mmmm," she said, closing her eyes.

"Good?"

"Oh, yeahhhh." Her mouth was full of truffle. She chewed and swallowed. "How was the hotel?"

"Same as always," he said. "Mostly I slept. I missed you, though. I was dreaming about you."

"Really?" she said. "What was I doing?"

"Can't remember." He was honest, as always. "Do you still want to go out? It might be nice to stay in. We could order takeout and have some wine. Well, you'll have the wine. Unless you had your heart set on Greek."

She shook her head. It flattered her that he wanted to stay in now. "You can decide," she said. "You've been working hard."

"You're the one who waited for me." He stood up and took her hand. "Let's stay here. I'll go downstairs and pick up some cherry ginger ale for me and wine for you." He pulled her up, off the couch.

"We still have the bottle you brought last time."

"We do? Good."

Around two in the morning, she woke up.

He was sleeping next to her. His wavy hair was a mess, and his face was relaxed, almost smiling. *He must be dreaming,* she thought. She liked this. One of his hands was on the sheet, near his mouth, a bit babylike.

It was so cute.

Earlier, she had confessed about how worried she'd been when he'd broken the dates. Todd said he'd been frustrated that he couldn't see her those times. He'd been angry with himself, he said. Gert thought that that might have been why he'd sounded short with her.

Still, she knew Todd hadn't fully understood how he'd come across. He seemed pretty clueless about the way it had seemed to her.

But she wasn't going to push it. Maybe he just wasn't experienced enough to know. He'd have to learn.

Then again, what if he was just covering up? Instead of thinking that things were back to the way they were a week ago, maybe Gert should still be on guard. Maybe she should stay suspicious, keep worrying about how she looked and everything she said.

She just had an instinct that Todd wasn't the type to hide things. She'd always had good instincts about people. All her life. But how could she ever really know for sure? How could you know about any guy? Could she even have been one hundred percent sure about Marc?

She watched Todd move his arm to his side in his sleep. He looked so peaceful, yet handsome. She wasn't sure that she could go five days without seeing him again.

But it would be up to him, wouldn't it?

*It's always up to them,* Gert thought. Guys complained that women had the upper hand, but women seemed only to have the upper hand about maybe whether to have sex. All the decisions getting to that point seemed to be men's, she thought.

She wanted to know if Todd would stick around. What made something a relationship, exactly? The fact that they weren't dating anyone else? The daily phone conversations? Sleeping over?

She needed something more concrete than a candy box.

She didn't want to think about it anymore. She just wished Todd would say something. She didn't want to be the one to bring it up.

She thought again of Michael's wedding. What a mess that would be if she brought Todd.

But maybe she should.

Then again, she didn't even know if Todd would still be with her by then.

She needed a sign.

Gert stirred uneasily. She heard the clock radio humming. She wanted to go back to sleep. But she wasn't tired.

She couldn't stare at Todd anymore, nor at the clock radio. She got up. The Internet was always there for times like these.

She tiptoed through the hall into Marc's trophy room. She kept the light off and shut the door gently behind her. The moon was out, and it cast a glow over his desk.

Gert looked at the houses across the way, especially the one with the unlit Christmas lights. She imagined the little blond-haired girl upstairs sleeping, snug under the covers. Everyone should be doing that right now.

Gert yawned and waited for the Internet to load. The bright screen lit up the whole room. She stared at the browser field. Often in the past, when she was lonely, she'd thought that there must be something out there in cyberspace to assuage her loneliness—but usually, there wasn't. Cyberspace was overrated, she thought. She was reminded of the Bruce Springsteen song "Fifty-seven Channels and Nothing On," only in this case, it was fifty-seven million Web sites and nothing worthwhile.

Well, there was one thing: discussion sites for widows. They had proven helpful in the months after Marc had died. It was useful to read how other people found ways to tackle the same challenges she did.

Nowadays, she occasionally logged in and answered posts from other widows. That way, at least one good thing was coming out of what had happened to her. After Marc had died, there had been times when she wondered what the point of her going on was. Did the world really need one more miserable person tromping through it for fifty years? But if she could help other people, there was still a point.

The site generally had a lot of people popping in and out. They came a few weeks after their loved one died, posted a ton of messages—"This happened to me, did this happen to you?" "Is it normal to feel this way?" "When will I start feeling better?"—and then moved on.

Gert scrolled down for messages that didn't have replies.

A girl named Kora31 had titled her message "First-time poster."

Hi everyone. I'm new to the board. My husband Dave died two months ago and I'm at the end of my rope. I just go through the motions at work and I smile when I really want to cry. The long and short

of it is that my doctor wants to put me on antide-
pressants. The thing is, I don't feel like I have a men-
tal problem. I SHOULD feel miserable about Dave.
I don't think I should be taking drugs to feel better.
I was wondering if anyone else has faced this.
Thanks.

Gert replied:

When I was depressed, my doctor asked me if I
wanted to be on something, too. Everyone's feelings are different. Are you able to get through the
normal activities of the day? If you wear all black
and show up for work four hours late, it might be a
problem. My NON-expert opinion is that if you feel
like you can't get through your regular activities,
you might want to consider medication. Not to
change how you feel—just to get through the day
without being miserable. But whether you NEED it,
I'm not sure. And OF COURSE it's perfectly logical
to miss Dave!

Gert hesitated for a second before writing Dave's name, then
chided herself. She had heard so many friends hesitate before saying Marc's name. They would go as far as to rework entire sentences so that they lacked a subject. They'd say things to her like,
"Wasn't that the time when…your room got painted?" rather
than "Wasn't that the time Marc painted your room?" That was
the one thing Gert liked about Hallie—Hallie had never flinched
when talking about Marc, or uncomfortable topics in general.

Gert read on. There was an unanswered message that was
from two hours ago. It read:

MY GOD, IF ONE MORE PERSON TELLS ME I'M
LUCKY THAT I'M STILL YOUNG AND HAVE MY
WHOLE LIFE AHEAD OF ME, I AM GOING TO

*SCREAM.* I WANTED MY WHOLE LIFE AHEAD OF
ME TO BE WITH SAM!!

Gert had heard that one, too. She wrote back that she sometimes thought about what Marc would have been like at different ages, how he would have been as a father, a boss, a
forty-year-old, the coach of his son's Little League team. Marc
would have gone on to do so many wonderful things. There
was so much ahead of him. Gert would always miss him as she
went through each stage.

Another post simply awed her. It said:

Lots of people find one person, and they love that
person for the rest of their lives. Why does everyone expect my feelings to suddenly change just because he's gone?

Gert wanted to print that one out. But she hadn't replaced
the ink cartridge in the printer in ages.

The last post that Gert responded to was just one of the sad
messages that someone had typed for a loved one's anniversary.
It said:

Dear Chris, it's been a year since you were taken
from me and I miss you every single day. For every
person who was touched by you, there are five
more who would have been touched if you had
been allowed to grow old. Those people will never
know their loss.

Gert responded, "Chris sounds like a great person. You're
right—it is all of our loss." Sometimes people needed to hear
that they weren't mourning someone alone.

There were posts about stupid comments and posts about
finances and posts about what to do with a late husband's be-

longings, but nothing about dating again. She sat in Marc's gray office chair and swiveled a little.

Then she remembered Colin, the kid whose grave was near Marc's.

She typed his name into a search engine and came up with fourteen entries.

The top one was an obituary from his hometown newspaper. The article mentioned that Colin had had a Web page.

Gert typed in the address. The site materialized on her screen. At the top, it said, "This site was last updated: Aug. 30, 2001."

It had pictures of trips Colin had taken, of family members, and of college. There was a calendar of silly days like National Pug Day, and a list of "Colin's links."

Gert clicked the first link. It went to Colin's résumé. At the top of the résumé was the name of the trading firm he'd been at. At the bottom, it said, "Other interests. Fluent in French and Spanish. Play tuba."

*Tuba?* Gert thought. *My God, every person who died, they had such interesting things about them. Things we'll never know. Each young person did, indeed, have five people whose lives would have been touched by them for every one who already was.*

Gert clicked Back on the browser to return to the main page. At the bottom it said, *"Sign my guestbook."*

Gert clicked it.

There were scattered messages to Colin that had been left over the years. There were two posts on Sept. 11, 2001.

"Hey, Col. You got out of there—right?"

"COLIN!! COLIN!! What's going on there, man? Talk to me!"

The Sept. 12 posts were more fearful.

"Colin—your sister says your family hasn't heard from you. I know you're ok and will turn up, but I want to tell you I love you."

"Col—Mary says she heard you worked there. I know your first priority isn't this site, but please just post something here to let us know you're ok."

"Col—You're in our hearts and prayers."

Then, there was Sept. 13.

"C—I haven't told you in a while how much we miss you at school. The paper isn't the same without you this year. I'm sorry I waited 'til now—I kept meaning to tell you."

Gert clicked a link to the college newspaper and put Colin's name into the search field. She found twelve columns he'd written during his junior and senior years. One paragraph started with "When I have kids…" It was something he'd casually thrown in, not knowing, of course, that he'd die two years later. Who suspects that? If you're young and in good health, you assume you'll live forever.

Another link on the homepage said "Mary," and it went to a girl's site—apparently Colin's girlfriend. Mary's site was normal and up-to-date. She had gone on with her life. But in the corner, in a purple box, it said: "Colin Daniel McKinney 1979-2001. I will never forget you, honey."

Gert stared at that for a while.

She ended up spending a half hour following all of Colin's links. She followed link to link to link to link. She assumed eventually she'd link all the way to someone she knew, but she didn't.

Even after she was done looking at the links, she felt that she only understood one-fiftieth of Colin's personality. He had had so many quirks, so many connections. The world had really lost someone special. After another half hour, she was frazzled. She looked at the time and was surprised by how late it was. Gert stared blankly at the screen until the screen saver came on, reminding her to go back to bed.

# Chapter

## 15

Gert felt like being alone with Todd that night, but she had already agreed to the double date with Hallie and Brett Stoddard. She hoped they could eat their sushi quickly and get home. Erika and Dr. Eden had planned to come, too, but Eden had been called to the hospital at the last minute. Erika was going to pick him up after his shift and take him out anyway. She said that if he was exhausted, he'd be more vulnerable. And she could seduce him with words and wine.

Gert was relieved she'd have to deal with only one manipulative couple tonight and not two. Still, she had an obligation to go along with it. It was because of Hallie that she'd met Todd in the first place.

As she waited outside the restaurant with Hallie, facing the street, Gert told her how things had worked out over the weekend with Todd, how he'd come over and they'd eaten in instead of going out for Greek food. Hallie smiled and said she was glad. Gert thought she seemed sincere. Maybe because Hallie was dating someone now, she didn't have to be jealous.

Hallie looked especially good that night, Gert thought. Her

light brown hair was back in a barrette. Dating someone you liked made you more attractive. And Hallie needed to be—the dinner was a rare fourth date with Brett Stoddard.

"There they are!" Hallie said.

Brett and Todd were approaching from across the street. Gert had never met Brett before. He struck her as attractive, even though he was a bit plain-looking. He had floppy pale hair that reminded her of straw, a hangjaw smile and high blond eyebrows. He was wearing a denim jacket and had nice lips.

Todd introduced Brett to Gert, then took Gert's hand and led her through the vestibule into the restaurant. There were small cardboard posters for Broadway shows there, and a pocket full of take-out menus. Inside, fish bubbled in an aquarium filled with fluorescent stones and coral. Some kind of purple light beamed through it. The place was packed with young people.

The waiter took them to a corner table with green place mats. Todd and Brett sat directly across from Gert and Hallie. Sitting down, Gert felt strange. She'd never actually been on a bona fide "double date" before. Who did such a thing anymore? You couldn't really flirt with someone if you had your best friend sitting next to you. Unless you were weird. Gert had seen fifties movies with one couple making out in the front of a car and another in the back. She had never been one for public displays of affection. Private displays of affection were much nicer.

Gert caught Todd looking at her. She smiled, and he winked back at her. She felt better. They'd get through this, help Hallie and Brett become closer, and then they could be alone.

The waiter left a porcelain pitcher of warm tea on the table, and Gert poured for everyone.

"So," Brett said. He looked up and smiled at Hallie. "Who else here besides me knows how to use chopsticks?"

"I don't," Todd said.

Hallie waved her hand. "I do!"

"I became an expert when I lived in China," Brett said.

"You're kidding," Hallie said. "You never told me you lived in China."

"For six months after college, I taught English there."

"Wow," Hallie said. "You can speak Chinese?"

"I can speak English," Brett said.

"That's all it takes, I guess," Todd said cheerfully, and Gert appreciated that he was trying to keep the flow going.

When the waitress came, they ordered a sushi platter for four. Gert thought of the long strips of salmon, sweet eel and pasty avocado, and started to get hungry.

"I haven't had sushi in weeks," Hallie said, rubbing her hands together. "And I love it."

Brett suddenly focused on her. "You should have told me," he said. "I would have taken you. There's this amazing place in midtown. We're going." He reached out and took her hand.

Gert could feel the seduction radiating outward. The guy was good.

"So, Brett," Gert said. "You and Todd were college room-mates, right?"

"Sophomore year we were in a quad," Brett said. "It was me and this guy Dan Weinisch and Todd and this guy Paul."

"Dan and Paul were business majors," Todd said.

"Yep, and Todd and I were the history and English geeks," Brett said. "Whenever Dan and Paul had to take a liberal arts course, I did all their homework. But some of it was poetry, so that was fun."

Something seemed off about this. Gert caught Todd's eye but didn't smile, because Brett would have seen. She just doubted that Brett loved doing other people's homework, even poetry, and it didn't seem like something to brag about anyway.

"Where are Dan and the other guy now?" Gert said as the waitress brought their little salads and peanut sauce.

Brett and Todd looked at each other and laughed. "Paul's a broker and has no life," Brett said, "and Dan, I don't think he works. All he does is try to schtup every girl he meets." He looked at Hallie. "I hate it when guys treat women like that."

Hallie smiled at him.

Todd, more diplomatic, said, "Dan just got a little out of control senior year. He was shy for the first three years and then he worked as a lifeguard for one summer and came back and decided he had to make up for everything he missed."

"It's kind of pathetic," Brett said. "Not to mention unfair to women." He looked straight at Hallie. "Weinisch acts all sweet and shy, focuses on them, gets them in bed and then he never calls them again. It's disgusting."

"I'm glad *you're* not like that," Hallie said to him, and she took his hand again. Gert felt Hallie kick her under the table.

Brett seemed to be enjoying the attention. Or maybe the tension; Gert noticed that they were staring at each other an awful lot, and she wondered if the fact that they hadn't actually had sex yet was making them both hot and bothered.

The waiter came out with their platter of rice rolls and dumplings. When Hallie moved some morsels onto her plate, Brett looked at her and said, "My, you *are* hungry, aren't you?"

Hallie smiled and ate.

"We're going to that place in midtown. That's it," Brett said. "Case closed." He reached for the plum wine and poured her a full glass.

Hallie was smart, Gert thought. She was just letting him work his charm.

"When I was in Japan…" Brett started.

"I thought you taught in China," Hallie said.

"I did. But I went to Japan the following year. Anyway, they had this place that had every kind of food you can imagine in sushi. They had, like, plum rolls and peach rolls and broccoli rolls and onions and eggs."

"That sounds good," Hallie said.

"I can cook it for you," Brett said. "I've cooked sushi." Gert wondered how many girls he'd fed this to. The line, not the sushi.

Gert watched Brett as they ate. She noticed that he would look at Hallie once in a while and smile. Hallie was lapping it up. Why shouldn't she?

When they finished the platter, Todd announced he had to

get to bed early because he had a busy day tomorrow, and he and Gert got out of there as soon as they could. Brett had told enough stories about how many things he knew how to do and how he would do them for Hallie. He was a superman for her favorite things.

As the subway shot out of the ground, leaving Manhattan's skyscrapers behind, Gert said to Todd, "It was nice to finally meet Brett."

Todd smiled at her uncertainly, then broke out in laughter. "How uncomfortable was that?"

Gert burst out laughing, too. "I don't know," she said. "I'm trying to figure out the best part. Brett pouring her more plum wine after every single sip she took…"

"Or telling Hallie how much he hates when guys treat women badly," Todd said. "Brett was like Dan Weinisch's idol back in school."

Gert rested her head on his shoulder. It felt so good to be with someone who didn't play games, someone honest. Todd put his arm around her. She smelled his freshly laundered shirt.

"Do you think it was okay to introduce them?" she asked.

"Do *you* think she'll be okay?" Todd asked.

"I was more worried about Brett," Gert said. "Hallie knew what she was getting into."

Todd smiled. She could feel his shaven chin move. "You know what?" he said. "I think Brett really likes Hallie."

"How can you tell? You said he treats every girl like that."

"Well, most of them," Todd said. "Every girl's a different challenge. But she has him working overtime. So maybe he'll learn something, for once."

Gert closed her eyes. *What are you learning?* she thought. *Are we in a relationship, or what? Say something.*

When she opened her eyes, she took in the darkness of the subway tunnel outside the window.

When they got to her living room, they went immediately to the couch and kissed more frantically than they ever had.

Marc had always been passionate with her. Todd was a little more tender. When Marc was kissing her, he'd often acted as if he was protecting her from every horrible thing in the world. Sometimes he'd been so intense it had made her shiver. But this time, so was Todd. Gert felt so relieved to be away from the jealousy and resentment of the rest of the world, to be with one caring person who was so straightforward and earnest and passionate. She squeezed him so tightly she thought she would never stop....

He backed off, lifting his head. "Are you okay?" he asked.

She sat up. "I'm sorry...."

"I was just surprised," he said.

"I didn't mean it...."

"No," he said, smiling. "I liked it."

# Chapter

## 16

After Todd had left to go to work in the morning, Gert checked her e-mail to see if Hallie had written about her date. There was, indeed, a message from Hallie. It was entitled "News."

Gert clicked on it.

It said:

G,

When Erika got home with Eden last night there was a message on her voice mail. Her father had a mild heart attack. They expect him to recover but it mt make her feel good if u dropped her a line. She feels kind of lonely. She's up with her family. H.

Gert wrote back:

How awful!! I expected an update on your date, and now this! What's her cell number?

Gert deleted some junk e-mail. Before she got off, she clicked "new mail" again. Hallie was obviously online. She wrote:

917-555-3172. Btw, she said Eden was so drunk he wouldn't have been able to do anything but sleep, and she put him in a cab. Anyhow, I had the greatest time with Brett. Details later. But NO, we didn't... We have a fifth date set up for next week!! Maybe he's not going to be a game player anymore. I might get to see the real Brett Stoddard. What do you think?

Gert wrote back:

I hope you can find out if there *is* a real B.S.!

Three days later, Erika returned to New York. Hallie had asked Gert to meet the two of them for margaritas and tortilla chips after work. Hallie's fingers crept through the basket looking for ungreasy chips, as if there were such things.

"It was so draining," Erika said. "I had to prop my mom up, then she had to prop me up, and then I had to prop her up."

"But your dad'll be okay?" Gert asked. Her father had high cholesterol, so she knew what it was like to be worried about fathers and their hearts.

"Yes, thank God," Erika said. "They say he'll come out in a few days as good as new."

Hallie broke a chip in half and put the other half back. Then, after a few seconds, she ate the other half anyway.

"It was so hard," Erika said, pulling the bowl closer to her. "My sisters and my cousins were there and they all had their boyfriends and husbands helping them out. And the guys comforted them every step of the way. All I could think about was how much Ben loved my dad. And my dad *loved* Ben. I actually came close to calling Ben. I knew he would be concerned."

Hallie shook her head. "It's hard to get through anything alone these days."

"No shit," Erika said. "Everyone kept asking me why I didn't have a boyfriend, like I really needed the reminder. They constantly say things to me about Ben, too. My little sister kept saying, 'I miss Ben. He was cute.' Like I needed her to tell me."

Gert watched Hallie pull the bowl of chips back toward her. At this rate, they should just get two bowls, she thought.

"But I hung out with my cousin Jim and his new girlfriend," Erika said. "She's like the coolest person. You know how sometimes you meet someone and hit it off right away, and you get along better with them than people you've known all your life? I only wish that would happen with a *guy.* It hasn't happened to me since Ben."

Hallie shook her head. "I don't think it's *ever* happened to me."

"You've never met someone who you thought was your soul mate?" Erika asked.

"I don't know," Hallie said. "What *is* a soul mate, anyway?"

"It's what I said," Erika said. "You meet someone, and you just click. You have the same ideas about life. You don't even have to finish your sentences, because the person already knows what you mean."

Hallie turned to Gert. "Do you think Todd's your soul mate?"

Gert said, "I don't know. It's nice if you can be with your soul mate. But you don't always necessarily want to end up with your soul mate. Sometimes, besides the similarities, you need differences to make things work. That's how you learn."

"What about Marc?" Hallie asked. "Was he your soul mate?"

"I don't know if he was entirely, either," Gert said. "He was a great guy. There were things I loved about him, and things I just thought were cute. I don't know if I could say he was *perfect* for me. Or that I would have wanted him to be."

Hallie shook her head and looked at her plate. "Maybe we've all lowered our standards."

"Well, we said we're not even sure exactly what soul mate means," Gert said.

"Which proves," Erika said, "that none of us have met ours. Because we'd know."

"Soul mate isn't necessarily the standard you want," Gert said, looking at her.

"Because we can't find it?"

"Maybe," Gert said. "I'm not sure. I think souls can grow together, too."

# Chapter 17

Chase was smiling.

They had agreed to meet for lunch at a trendy café that was midway between both of their jobs. Chase wanted to buy Gert the prix fixe lunch, which included the house specialty, crumbled duck soup. This place had been a favorite of Chase's and her husband's before he died. She liked to eat there, but not alone.

When Gert came in, the eatery was alive with chatter and clanking plates.

"Raspberry crème brûlée with shaved chocolate," Chase said, holding up the sturdy one-page menu. "Need I say more?"

"Chocolate!" Gert said, sitting down. "But I don't know if I'll have room after the duck soup, grilled shrimp appetizer, salmon steak and salad."

"When you see the raspberry crème brûlée, you'll have room," Chase said. Then suddenly, she looked sad.

"What?" Gert said.

"What what?"

"You looked sad for a second."

"Oh, nothing," Chase said. "Well, you probably understand.

I had a flashback. Right after he met me, John said the way to a woman's heart was crème brûlée."

"It doesn't hurt."

Chase unrolled her napkin in her lap. "So who's this guy you're seeing."

"His name's Todd," she said. "He's great."

Chase smiled warmly. It felt strange to Gert to sense support from a friend that wasn't the least bit tinged with jealousy.

"Maybe there's hope," Chase said. "I can't imagine seeing someone. I know it might happen eventually. It just seems really distant right now."

"I couldn't imagine it, either," Gert said. "But then it happened. I think it has to be the right kind of person. Even more than the timing."

"Maybe."

"It has to be someone who is very, very, very patient."

"You're lucky you found someone who cares enough to *be* that patient," Chase said.

"I know," Gert said. She really did know.

"Do you still have Marc's things around?" Chase asked. "I don't mean to pry."

"Don't worry about it," Gert said. "I do have some of Marc's stuff around. Todd deals with it, just like I deal with it."

Chase said, "John's photos are all over my house. I can't take them down."

"Isn't that hard?" Gert said. "Seeing their picture, and knowing they'll never get to grow old? I'm going to be an old lady some day, and I'll still have a photo of Marc at our Fourth of July picnic, looking twenty-seven and full of his future."

Chase smiled knowingly.

The waitress came by and took their orders. She seemed to be absentminded, humming some foreign song. This made Gert laugh, and Chase laughed, too. In a minute, the waitress returned and doled mesclun salads onto their plates. She was still humming. Maybe they were just getting closer to spring.

"Do you go to the support group every single week?" Chase asked.

"I try," Gert said. "Why don't you go?"

"I don't know," Chase said, looking at her plate. "Every week, I *intend* to go. Then Saturday morning comes, I'm tired, it's not a work day, and I say to myself, 'There's enough stuff I feel miserable about. Why do one more thing?' So I just don't."

"Well, you *shouldn't* make yourself go if it makes you feel miserable," Gert said.

"Being there makes me feel *better*, once I get there," Chase said. "It's the dragging myself there that's hard. I do see a therapist once a week, though. It helps some."

"I did that for the first six months," Gert said. "I go on the online support groups now, sometimes."

"I like those!" Chase said. "Last week, I got on after work, and I felt absolutely horrible, and I wrote, 'If one more person says, "You've still got your whole life ahead of you," I'll scream!'"

"Oh my God!" Gert said. "I think I answered that post!"

Chase laughed. "There were three others like it that same day. None of us is really that different."

Gert shook her head. "There was something I was thinking of posting there, but I haven't."

"What?"

"Well," Gert said, forking some mesclun, "I want to post about dating again." She always had trouble picking up leafy things with her fork. "No one really writes about that there. And I've felt so guilty. I do care a lot about Todd. But I can't stop having this little ball inside of me of tightly wound feelings for Marc. And it doesn't go away. Half of me wonders whether, thirty years from now, it will still be there just as strong, bouncing around inside of me. And the other half is scared that it *won't.*"

"Are you afraid of being happy?"

"Maybe I'm afraid of being *too* happy without Marc."

"Not that I'll be any different," Chase said, "because I won't, but I *do* know that you shouldn't feel guilty. Thirty years from now…you'll just have to feel how you feel."

"I'm scared of a time when I won't feel anything for Marc," Gert said, "and yet, I'm scared that if I always have strong feelings for him, I won't be able to put a hundred percent of my energy into Todd or whoever I end up with."

"We just might not recover fully," Chase said. "I don't think we should kid ourselves. These were our first loves. We met them practically when we were kids, didn't we?"

"Yeah," Gert said.

"John's bound up with my move into adulthood. Relationships were so new to me at the time. And when you get hit with your first one—wow. When you're older, and you're starting over, it's not as new. There's all this stuff that came before."

"That's right," Gert said. "When you're younger, they get your whole heart. And now I'm supposed to ask for mine back."

The waitress collected their plates, which now contained soggy leftover stems. Crumbled duck soup was on deck.

"Starting over with dating is hard," Chase said. "So is having to start over with friendships, though."

"Tell me about it," Gert said.

"I don't think that college friend who was going to move in with me is still going to," Chase said. "Part of me is glad."

"What about friends at work?"

"Everyone at my job is like fifty-five," Chase said, shaking her head.

"I know the feeling," Gert said.

"You want to hear something funny?" Chase asked.

"I'd *love* to hear something funny."

Chase smiled. "I was trying on clothes in The Gap the other day," she said, "and I came out of the door to my dressing room at the same time as this girl across from me was coming out. She was our age, and was fat and had freckles, and she was laughing, just completely cracking up, and she had this big pile of clothes in her arms. And she said to me, like she had known me forever, 'Oh my God! I always try on clothes and nothing fits, and today everything's fitting and I don't know what to do about it.' And she just *cracked up,* and her clothes were falling off her arms, onto the floor, and it was so funny."

"That *is* funny," Gert said.

"I laughed, because it was funny. And she laughed, too. It was so easy. She seemed nice, and funny, and I thought, *We could be friends. This is a person who I'd like to be friends with.* Then she left."

"You didn't say anything else to her?"

"What was I supposed to say? 'Uh, excuse me, will you be my new friend?'"

Gert laughed. "'Yeah, can I get your phone number?'"

"'Miss, would you like to have dinner and a movie sometime?'"

They laughed.

"How do you pick up a friend?" Chase asked.

Gert shook her head. "Nothing is easy anymore," she said. She smiled and raised her water glass. "To new friendships."

"To new friendships," Chase said.

The waitress brought out the crumbled duck soup, and Gert was pleased to find big hunks of duck. She thought of something, spooning for a chunk.

"Have you been to a sleepover lately?" Gert asked Chase.

"You mean, the kind people have when they're twelve?"

"Exactly," Gert said. "But with adults."

Chase laughed. "Sounds like fun, but no."

"Hallie and Erika are having this weird sort of party in a few weeks." She told her about the "Stud Party," to which they'd invited the men whose numbers they'd gotten in midtown. "And after the party's over we're having a sleepover to compare notes. It'd be nice to have another slumberer along."

"That sounds great," Chase said. Gert thought it would be a much better party if Chase were there.

# Chapter

18

Gert stirred restlessly. She and Todd had had dinner together at the condo. She hadn't been that hungry because of her lunch with Chase, but Todd had gotten back from work late, famished and pooped. Gert had told him about her lunch, and he had craved the duck soup, so they'd had to find something similar—and settled on barbecued wings from Kentucky Fried Chicken.

As they'd eaten, she'd thought that this definitely seemed like a relationship. But he still hadn't said anything to indicate it.

During dinner, Todd had told her that Chase already seemed nicer than Hallie and Erika. She'd smiled. She wondered if it was simply pointless to hang on to her friendship with Hallie and Erika. She'd been really trying. Maybe she'd just outgrown them.

Yet, something kept her from giving up completely. She didn't want to ditch Hallie just because she'd met a guy. She'd done that once before. If Todd left, Gert knew Hallie would still be there. Hallie always had been. Hallie had always liked Marc, too, even if she was jealous. How many other people would always be there?

★ ★ ★

Todd stirred in bed. He was on his back, asleep.

The phone rang.

Gert opened her eyes fully and looked at the clock radio. It was 1:18 a.m.

Her heart stopped. Good news never came at that hour.

Maybe it was just Hallie, having gotten back from a night of bar-hopping. She hoped so. She'd had enough scary calls in her life.

She picked up the phone.

"Gert?"

It *was* Hallie. Good.

In bed, Todd shifted but didn't wake.

"You have to get dressed," Hallie said.

"Why?"

"I need your help. I have to pick up Erika from the police station."

"What? It's…" She sat up and cradled the phone. "What happened?"

"I don't know, exactly. She's in Connecticut. They charged her with harassment. I know it's late, but we don't want to drive up there with just us. We could really use your help."

"Who's we?" Gert asked.

"Cat and me. She has a car. Her parents made her keep it as a condition of moving to New York. They planned a terror escape route for her."

Gert rubbed her eyes and looked at Todd. He was waking up. She said, "I'll help you." What else could she say?

"Can you be outside your building by two?"

Words she'd never wanted to hear.

Todd opened his eyes and looked up at her. "Who was that?" he asked, squinting in the dim moonlight.

"Hallie," Gert said. "Erika's been arrested for stalking or something."

He sat up. "And you're going somewhere?"

"Yeah. Hallie wants me to go to the police station with her."

Todd said, "I'll go with you. You can't take the subway alone at this hour."

"We're driving."

"What? Where?"

"Connecticut."

"Who has a car?"

"Cat, Hallie's roommate. Her parents bought her one."

"Nice."

"I hope Hallie has the bail money," Gert said, getting up to find a pair of jeans.

Todd pulled on his pants. "How much is it?" he asked.

"I didn't ask. What do you think Erika did?"

Todd said, "What do *you* think?"

"I'm pretty sure her ex-boyfriend lives in Connecticut. Maybe she went to his house."

"Wow," Todd said. "Didn't you just have dinner with Erika a few days ago?"

"I did," Gert said. "Maybe she went back up afterward. She's been in a bad state."

Standing at the bottom of the driveway, they were both silent, staring across the street and waiting for Hallie and Cat to arrive. It was freezing out. Todd rubbed his hands together.

Gert looked at the white town houses and thought about the little blond girl again. She hoped that the girl was warm under the covers, dreaming.

"When they pick us up, we should stop for coffee," Todd said.

"I could run upstairs and make some."

"Nah. I guess once we get going it'll be fine. The car has heat, right?"

"If what I know of Cat is true, her parents probably had it insulated with wool."

Gert noticed that Todd kept looking across the street.

"A big family lives there," Gert said. "They always leave their Christmas lights up until spring."

"That's lazy," Todd said.

"Maybe they don't want the holidays to be over."

Todd thought about this. "That's true," he said. "Who can blame them?"

An engine sounded. Both of their heads turned. A Ford Contour was making its way up the street. Gert thought that if this wasn't Cat and Hallie, she'd be pretty scared.

The car came to a stop in front of them. Cat was at the wheel. Gert was surprised she could see over the dashboard.

Looking at Hallie up front, Gert felt a momentary twinge of sympathy. Despite her flaws, Hallie was still willing to help her friend in the middle of the night.

Hallie got out and opened the back door, letting Todd slide in. She closed it and said to Gert, "You're bringing him?"

"He was here," Gert said. "I can't just send him home."

Hallie sniffed, "Well, I guess there's room," and went back inside.

Climbing into the back seat, Gert suddenly felt a bit of sickness run through her. She hadn't been in a car much since the accident. She stared at the dashboard.

She'd let the junkyard keep Marc's car. Who really needed a car in the city, anyway? Why had they bought one in the first place?

She looked around for her seat belt. Cars were death traps. She knew that now. It didn't matter how many safe car trips she'd been on in her life. If you weren't careful every second, something could get you.

"Put your seat belts on," Gert said.

"Mine's on," Hallie said. Todd reluctantly put his on.

Cat leaned back and handed Todd a cup of Dunkin' Donuts coffee. Then she passed back a box with three doughnuts left in it.

"Oh, man!" Todd said. "Bavarian crème!"

Gert blew into the air just to see her breath.

"They were half price," Cat said. "Six for three bucks."

"Hallie, you ate a doughnut?" Gert said. "I'm shocked!"

"I didn't," Hallie said. "Cat ate all three."

Cat stared ahead innocently.

"Should we go?" Hallie asked.

"'We've got a full tank of gas, half a pack of cigarettes, it's dark, and we're wearing sunglasses,'" Todd said. "'Hit it.'"

No one said anything.

"That's from *The Blues Brothers*," Todd said. "Just trying to lighten the mood."

"Don't," Gert said, taking his hand.

Cat started the car.

"Is The Blues Brothers in the male canon?" Hallie turned around and asked.

"That would fall under '70s *Saturday Night Live*," Gert said, yawning. "We'll add, '70s *Saturday Night Live*, anything related to '70s *Saturday Night Live* and anything relating to the actors from *Saturday Night Live*."

"That would cover the shocking omission of *Animal House*," Todd said.

"A real classic," Gert said.

"How come," Cat said, from up front, "when certain movies are popular with girls, they're called 'chick flicks,' but there's no equivalent for guys?"

"How about 'dick flicks,'" Hallie said.

"Can you put heat on?" Gert shivered. Todd saw this and massaged her knee.

"We have it on in front," Hallie said. "I'll switch it."

Gert leaned back, watching the buildings grow in size, knowing the car was approaching a bridge. She closed her eyes. She could just nod off, but she couldn't fall asleep. She didn't know if Cat was a safe driver. She wouldn't be able to drift off, as she might have in the past.

"So tell us what happened with Erika," Gert said. Todd, who had had his eyes closed, opened them slightly.

"I don't know all the details," Hallie said. "Apparently Erika went up to Ben and Challa's house and Ben wouldn't let her in. She tried to push her way past him and Challa. One of them called the cops."

"I never thought she would go that far," Gert said.

"I didn't, either," Hallie said. "I shouldn't have encouraged her. I just thought the stuff she was doing was funny."

They were quiet for a minute. Gert heard the heat blowing.

"She should see a therapist," Gert said. "I know it's not my business, but…"

"I know," Hallie said. "They'll force her to, I would think."

"If they don't, you should suggest it. She might listen to you."

"I will," Hallie said. "I have to."

"Did she sound hysterical?"

"No," Hallie said. They were passing a group of tall unlit co-ops with flat roofs. "She sounded like a mess," Hallie said, "but also like she was holding it together. She called her family first, but they didn't pick up, and then she decided she doesn't want them to know anyway. She only needs two hundred and fifty dollars bail."

"She didn't have it?"

"They won't take credit cards."

"Are there doughnuts left?" Cat asked from the driver's seat.

"Four doughnuts?" Hallie asked. "Haven't you reached the legal limit?"

"I ate a light dinner," Cat said.

"How long does it take to get to Darien, anyway?" Gert asked.

"It's not *Dar*-ien," Hallie instructed. "It's Dari-*anne.*"

Gert looked out the window. They were all quiet for a while. Not many cars were on the road. There were more delivery vans. When Gert did see a car, she wondered just what emergency had brought these people out in the middle of the night. Compared to other people's emergencies, Hallie and Gert's expedition probably was no big deal.

An eighteen-wheeler came by, honking at them for going too slowly.

"Well, excuse me for going the speed limit," Cat said.

"Don't listen to them, ever," Gert said.

"I know," Cat said.

"You need more coffee?" Hallie asked Cat.

"I'm awake," Cat said, but a yawn swallowed the last syllable.

"Maybe we should turn on the radio and sing to keep ourselves awake," Todd asked.

"Let's not and say we did," Hallie said.

"I was just suggesting…" Todd said.

"It was a good idea anyway," Gert said.

"My friends took a road trip to Virginia once, and we would have all fallen asleep unless we were singing," Todd said.

"I don't quite feel like it," Hallie said, "being that my best friend's been arrested."

"I would actually like to sing," Cat said.

"See?" Todd said.

"Thanks for sharing," Hallie said. "Radio stays off."

Cat hit the power button. Gert was impressed. It was the first time she'd ever seen the girl assert herself.

The song "Don't You Want Somebody to Love" came on, and Cat and Todd sang along to it loudly.

Hallie shook her head.

When they crossed into Westchester, Todd snapped his fingers.

"I got it!"

"What?"

"The other poem that Brett knows," Todd said. "I've been trying to remember who wrote the second poem Brett knows."

"I only remember the Shelley one," Hallie said.

"The other one is by Keats," Todd said. "And it mentions Darien! It goes, 'Silent, upon a peak in Darien…'"

"I told you," Hallie said. "It's Dairy-*anne.*"

"Well, maybe in the Keats poem it's pronounced Dari-*inn,*" Todd said.

"I have to go to the bathroom," Cat said.

"Didn't I ask you if you had to go before we left?" Hallie asked.

Gert thought she'd had the same conversation once with her mother when she was five.

"I didn't have to go then, but I do now," Cat said.

"Maybe there's a rest stop coming up," Hallie said.

"There aren't any rest stops in Connecticut," Cat said.

"I thought that was Rhode Island," Gert said.

"It's some state," Hallie said. "Well, we'll have to be on the lookout."

"Too bad you're not guys," Todd said. "It's easier for us to go to the bathroom on road trips."

"You mean because you can just whiz wherever?" Hallie said, turning around. "Girls can do that, too."

"How?" Todd challenged.

"Well," Hallie said, "I'm not going to explain to you how girls go to the bathroom. It takes a little more effort, but we can."

"Do you, like, spread your…"

"Stop it!" Cat wailed. "You're making me need to go!"

"So go!"

"I'm not going by the side of the highway."

"Why not?" Todd asked. "Hallie just said it was easy."

"I didn't say it was easy. I said it wasn't impossible. Gert, why'd you bring him?"

*Because I needed to bring someone sane,* Gert thought.

Another semi truck pulled aside them and gave a long honk: *BEEEEEEEEEEEOOOOOWWWWWW….*

Cat floored the car for a second, and it lurched forward.

"Whooooooa, Blossom," Todd said.

"'Whoa, Blossom?'" Hallie said, turning around again to look at Todd. "That was a generation Y reference, not a generation X reference. How old are you?"

"I'm twenty-six," Todd said. "I am fully planted in X, thank you very much. I said 'Whooooaaa, Blossom,' to make *fun* of generation Y."

"Ha!" Hallie looked at him. "*Family Ties* or *Simpsons?*"

"What?"

"You heard me. *Family Ties* or *Simpsons?*"

"*Simpsons.*"

"You chose wrong. That's Gen Y. Gen X's frame of family-show reference is *Family Ties.*"

Gert leaned her head on the side of the car. She was tired, but still wouldn't let herself nod off.

"Do another one," Todd said to Hallie.

"Reagan or Clinton."

"Clinton. Who wouldn't say Clinton?"

"Clinton," Cat said.

"Clinton," Gert said.

"Okay," Hallie said. "So that one wasn't fair. I'll come up with a better one. Madonna or Britney."

"Madonna," Todd said. "See? I'm definitely X."

"Pac-Man or Pokémon?"

"Pac-Man."

"Rugrats or Smurfs?"

"Smurfs."

"Nintendo or Atari?"

Todd paused. "Well, that one isn't really fair, because…"

"You're out," Hallie said, sitting back in her seat, satisfied.

"No I'm not!"

"You're out."

"Gert," Todd said. "Isn't that one not fair…?"

Gert took his hand. "You're out, sweetie," she said. "Nintendo is for kid brothers."

When they eased off I-95 and onto country roads, Gert looked out at the sky. Many more stars were out than at home and it made her miss the suburbs for a minute.

People looked down on the suburbs, but sometimes Gert really missed that way of life. She couldn't go back there now; she'd be too lonely if she was surrounded by all married people and kids. But she had always assumed she'd go back someday, to raise a family.

Gert looked at Todd. He was leaning against the window, gazing drowsily ahead.

"I'm not sure where we go from here," Hallie said.

*That makes two of us,* Gert thought.

"There's a gas station ahead," Cat said.

"I can get directions," Todd offered.

They pulled into a gas station and Todd headed for the brightly lit box in the middle of the island. The store looked like a sitting duck for anyone with a gun in the middle of the night. Gert worried as she watched him disappear into it.

When Todd came back, he had both directions and coffee.

"My hero," Gert whispered to him when he slid back in, and then she gave him a quick kiss on the cheek.

"Okay," Todd said. "Here's where we need to go…." He navigated, like a good conductor.

They passed fancy houses with three stories and ample lawns. Hallie said they should have been golf courses, not front yards.

"No wonder Erika's jealous of Challa," Hallie said.

Gert thought she could understand it, looking around.

"What a life," Hallie said.

The police station was so small it could have been a fast-food joint. On one side of the parking lot, the slanted spaces were filled with police cars, and their lines reflected in bright white.

Hallie led the way into the building. They pushed through the two glass doors that fronted the station's tiny square lobby. The reception window was empty.

Hallie pressed a buzzer.

A woman's leathery face appeared in the window. "Yes?"

"We're here to post bail for Erika Dennison," Gert said.

The woman disappeared without saying anything. A male cop's face appeared. "Who you here for?"

How many people could they possibly have in lock-up at the Darien jail? "Dennison," Gert said.

The cop opened the door. "Downstairs," he said.

As he walked them down, he said, "You know, your friend ought to get some counseling."

"We know," Hallie said.

Another cop came out, and the first one said, "There's something wrong with that girl."

"She's been through a lot lately," Todd said. "Why don't you think about that before jumping to conclusions?"

Gert watched Hallie look at Todd. Hallie looked surprised—even grateful.

They waited by the desk. Soon, Erika came toward them down the hall. Gert had never seen her without makeup, even at sleepovers. Then, Gert noticed something else: Erika was the same height as she was.

Gert had always thought Erika was tall. But now, rattled, tired, in no makeup and no heels, Erika looked small and vulnerable.

Gert thought she looked more attractive this way. She was sure Erika wouldn't agree, but it was true. She didn't look as intimidating.

"Guys, please don't pass judgment," Erika said. "I'll tell you what happened, but please don't pass judgment."

"We won't," Hallie said.

"I don't want *him* to pass judgment," Erika said, pointing her thumb at Todd.

"He won't," Hallie said.

They filled out the paperwork and walked outside.

"I'm hungry," Erika said in the car.

"When did you eat last?" Hallie asked.

"I don't even know," Erika said. "What time is it?"

"I think we passed a diner on the way," Cat said.

"It was a mile back," Todd said.

"Todd's our navigator," Hallie said. She looked at Todd and smiled.

Gert was surprised. She was glad Hallie appreciated Todd. And she was glad she'd come, too. She'd been useful to them for a change.

Gert took Todd's hand. It occurred to her then that of the four women, she was the only one with a boyfriend there. The only one to have someone to help get her through it. She felt sorry for Hallie and Erika—it *was* hard to get through things alone.

"We'll stop at the diner," Hallie declared.

Erika noticed the coffee cups around the car. "How much coffee did you guys drink?" she asked.

"I don't know," Hallie said. "We got coffee at a gas station, and some at a rest stop."

"I used to think Connecticut didn't have rest stops," Erika said.

"I thought so, too," Hallie said. "Isn't there some state that doesn't have rest stops?"

"Vermont might not," Cat said.

"Vermont doesn't have billboards," Todd said.

"Maybe it doesn't have rest stops, either," Hallie said.

"It has rest stops," Todd said. "No billboards."

"How do you know?" Cat asked.

"We could use a billboard to tell us where this diner is," Gert said. But then she saw it.


At the diner, a tired-looking waitress met them at the brown Please Wait to Be Seated sign. There were only three other people in the joint: A man with gray hair and ripped pants—Gert was reminded that somehow, poor people ended up in rich towns, too—and across the aisle from him, a handsome Indian kid of about twenty who was staring at a pretty woman with skinny glasses. Gert wondered if they were on a date, or married, or something else.

The five of them sat at a table and Erika folded her napkin and wiped her eyes. She looked like she was about to start sobbing. "I just…" she said.

"You don't have to explain," Hallie said.

"I want to," Erika said. "I *want* to explain."

Maybe she would, Gert thought. Maybe they would talk about something real, like their feelings. Like friends should.

The waitress returned, and Cat ordered rice pudding. The rest of them just asked for coffee.

"So what happened?" Hallie asked.

Erika wiped her eyes again. "I was on the Web site again."

"I *told* you…" Hallie said.

"I know." She took a gulp of water. "It's gotten to the point where sometimes I don't even feel like I can sleep at night unless I've checked to see if there's anything there. When I remember everything that's happened in my life, everything I've lost, a pain just sears through my body. I need to know what's going on in his life. I can't help it."

Gert looked at the Indian guy and the girl. They were having a pretty intense talk. Maybe one of them wanted to be more than friends, and the other didn't. Dating was hard. She certainly knew that now. It had been fun in college—but the stakes hadn't been so high.

"After my father had the heart attack and I went back to New York, I was on the Internet until 3:00 a.m. every night," Erika said. "I was just looking for something to feel better."

Gert recognized this syndrome.

"I couldn't help but wonder if, even a little bit, Ben missed me," Erika said. "How could he forget all the years we spent together? They were great years. I didn't want to spend the rest of my life wondering about what could have been. I couldn't make the same mistake twice, if there was a chance. I had to at least *see* Ben. I had to *know*.…"

"What did you think would happen?" Hallie asked.

Erika shrugged. "I don't know," she said. She fidgeted with the paper from her straw. "I don't feel right being completely shut out of his life. But I guess there's no proper way for me to be in it."

Gert felt the same way about wanting to be in Marc's family.

"I know all of you think I should just move on," Erika said. She looked at Gert and Todd. "I know you do. But you know what? Ben and I had a bond. I can't help how I feel."

"I know," Gert said.

Erika kept focused on Gert. "The day he finally got his first job, during college recruiting, right before graduation," she said, "we went out and drank champagne. We came back to my room and conked out together. We loved celebrating everything. We couldn't come up with enough things to celebrate. I can't forget that. He has five years of my *history*."

The waitress delivered their coffees, and they added sugar and cream. Todd didn't add anything. He had told Gert once that he drank a lot of black coffee on the train at night. It was something she knew about him. One of the idiosyncrasies she was getting used to. The kind of thing she'd miss if he was gone.

She tried not to think about that.

"When did you get here?" Hallie asked Erika.

"Around ten," she said. "Ben told me to go away, that his family was sleeping. He wouldn't talk to me for even a second. He blocked the door. Like I'm *shit*." She wiped her eyes. Her cheeks were still clammy-looking from her last cry. "And you know what the strange thing is?" she said. "I don't regret what I did tonight. Yes, I got caught, and yes, I'll get counseling, and yes, I can't *do* this stuff anymore. But I couldn't spend the rest of my life wondering. I had to do *some*thing."

When they finally headed back in the wee hours, Gert was the only one awake, besides Cat. Todd was asleep in the middle of the back seat, with his head on Gert's shoulder. Hallie was on his right, leaning against the window, her mouth open a bit. Erika was sleeping up front. Gert still couldn't sleep.

Gert watched Erika sleeping. Erika looked peaceful, innocent, relaxed—for a change. Gert wondered if that's what Ben had thought when he watched Erika sleep, so many years ago.

Gert was reminded of something Chase had said at lunch the other day: When she and Gert had met their boyfriends, they had practically been kids. And so, Gert thought now, were Erika and Ben.

It was true that Erika had been the one to decide to break it off. But how could she have known the right thing to do when she was only twenty-four? How could you be expected to always make all the right decisions for the rest of your life when you were less than a third of the way through it?

Gert felt lucky. She'd known she loved Marc. She couldn't have imagined breaking up with him. But how could she fault anyone for making such a decision? Even if one's early twenties were considered adulthood, with all the craziness in the world, you couldn't tell what might happen. You might change, the other person might change, the world might change. In your twenties, you might be afraid to commit to someone because it was for the rest of your life—but if you broke up, that might turn out to be for the rest of your life, too.

Gert thought of something else.

If this had been forty years ago, they all might have married their college sweethearts right after school. They wouldn't have put it off and deliberated on it, wondering whether to hold out for the perfect love. Erika and Ben might be married now, and Erika would not be living the life of uncertainty she was. Of course, right now she might be in a miserable marriage. Still, the pressure would be on her to make it work. The pressure would *not* be to hold out for the perfect person.

If Chase had married John right after college instead of just being his fiancée for years, she would have lost her husband, rather than someone she wasn't officially related to.

Gert had been sure, a year ago, that no one's pain could be like her own. Not Erika's. Definitely not Hallie's. Just a month and a half ago, Gert had been furious that Erika could remotely compare her situation to Gert's.

But maybe to Erika, her pain *was* just as gripping, Gert thought. Gert wondered if she was doing the same thing she accused others of—making assumptions about how someone else should feel. Besides missing Ben, Erika had to bear the burden of knowing she made a choice she regretted.

*Who am I to decide,* Gert thought, *that Erika doesn't have the right to feel pain?*

★ ★ ★

Erika stirred as they were nearing the big city. Gert watched her open her eyes. She looked scared for a second. Then she gazed around. Gert knew Erika was suddenly remembering everything that had happened tonight. It had to be a painful awakening. Gert had had many of those.

Cat noticed Erika waking up, too. She put the radio on low. It was neither Crappy the Clown nor Howard Stern, but a jazz station. A DJ with a mellow voice was speaking: "It looks like it's going to be cool today, but it's expected to finally warm up later in the week. And after such a rough winter, we could sure use it. But don't get too comfortable, friends. Forecasters say we could actually be in for a rare April snowstorm...."

Erika was looking around.

She turned to face Gert. She wiped her hand across her face.

"What time is it?" she asked, squinting.

"It's five-thirty," Gert said.

Hallie woke up, too. "Sleep," Hallie said to Erika. "It's okay."

Erika wiped her eyes. "I want to say something," she said. Todd stirred. "I want to thank you guys for coming to get me in the middle of the night. I know it was a lot to do. I'd still be back there if it wasn't for you."

"It's okay," Hallie said. "It's what friends are for."

"I didn't mean to be rude to you, Todd," Erika said. "You have a lot of balls to come up here at this time of night."

Todd smiled. "I don't have work today," he said. Gert squeezed his knee.

It was around 6:00 a.m. when they finally coasted back over the bridge into New York City, just as the first tiny windows of the skyscrapers were lighting up.

# Chapter

19

Gert was exhausted at work when she got in. She lay her head on the desk. She thought about how her father's law firm in L.A. actually had a room where tired employees could sleep. It was more like a chamber than a room.

Gert couldn't take a nap anyway. Months ago, she'd scheduled her gynecologist checkup for that day at lunchtime, which meant she didn't have time to waste in the morning.

Gert's gynecologist was an older woman to whom Gert had never really liked talking about her sex life. She always reminded herself that there were probably three thousand people like Gert passing through the door each year. The doctor probably wouldn't say, "You slut!" when Gert answered questions. Although that might make a good *Saturday Night Live* skit: the prudish gynecologist.

Maybe she could work that into one of her PR campaign ideas. She had talked with Missy about those the day before. Gert had been nervous about approaching her, but Missy had understood. Missy's guilt had probably worked in Gert's favor. Gert let it.

In the gynecologist's waiting room, there were two pregnant women Gert's age. One of them saw her looking and smiled at her, and she smiled briefly but averted her gaze. She felt jealous, behind and barren.

She reached for one of the magazines on the center table. Unfortunately, they were all women's and parenting magazines. She immediately became angry upon looking through one. It contained one of those articles implying that women gave up marriage and babies in their twenties in order to "focus on their careers." She was tired of hearing people repeat the same stupid thing, as if there were massive herds of women declining dates with wonderful men or trying not to meet their match so that they could work more. What *did* happen, as far as she saw, was people she knew tried very hard to find love, but if they weren't lucky enough, at least they had jobs to put their energy into. Gert wondered if the writers of these articles wanted women to simply sit at home all day crying to their mothers. Who *wrote* these articles—people who had gotten married at twenty-one and didn't have a clue?

Gert wondered if maybe most of the world was like she had been—needing to believe that anyone who hadn't gotten to a certain stage in their lives had simply made the wrong choices. So then, how would they explain Gert, a woman who had found the right guy—but was now single?

Gert looked up from the magazine. She had actually been like those people. Blaming herself for Marc's death—that had been a logical way to explain why she was alone now. She'd done something wrong, and gotten punished for it. Then the world still made sense.

She felt a stab of selfishness in her stomach. So many of her thoughts of Marc had been self-centered lately—about her facing the world alone, not as much about the fact that he'd never get to enjoy this world with her. She shifted in her seat, feeling a great sadness, wishing he was in that room with her, waiting to find out what sex their baby was.

She again thought of Mrs. Healy. Mrs. Healy was wrong to blame her. She knew Mrs. Healy had her own failings. Probably, she *needed* to blame her. Gert felt better, thinking about this. That's how Mrs. Healy was. Maybe she wouldn't confront Mrs. Healy at the wedding or afterward. Maybe she'd simply feel sorry for her.

Gert suffered through her annual exam. When it ended, her doctor asked her whether she wanted an AIDS test. Gert had to think about it for a second. Every year she had automatically said, "No." It was something she'd assumed she would never have to worry about again in her entire life. Something she'd always been relieved about.

Now it was just one more thing about starting over that was hard.

She thought for a minute.

"No," she said, finally.

When Gert got back to work, Missy was near her desk, filing documents in the metal cabinet. Gert thought it was strange. Missy never did filing herself.

"How was the doctor's?" Missy asked. "Are you okay?"

Gert saw that her face looked just as clammy and tired as Erika's had last night. "It was just a checkup," Gert said. She wished she was in a job where she didn't have to always tell her boss where she was going.

"Oh," Missy said. "One of *those* kinds of checkups?"

"Yes," Gert said.

"Everything in the right place?"

Gert grimaced.

"I don't like them, either." Missy looked at her. "Look, I'm going to be out for a few days."

Gert felt relieved. But she asked, "Are you okay?"

"Yes," she said. "But Derek wants to spend time apart. I

have to look at apartments, get my life together. I shouldn't have pushed him so fast. Moving in together was not a good idea."

Missy kept flipping through the papers in the cabinet, but it didn't look like she was getting anywhere.

"Are you sure you're all right?" Gert asked.

"No," Missy said, keeping her eyes on the papers. "I'm not. Maybe Derek isn't the right person for me, but I liked having him around." She turned to Gert and shook her head. "Dennis kept calling his house and harassing us, which didn't help. I'll kill him if I see him again."

"Don't say that."

"I will. I told Dennis not to come near me. But now Derek doesn't want to deal with me. I tried to make things okay, and I couldn't."

"Then Derek doesn't deserve you."

Missy went back to the papers, but didn't file. "I know that," she said. "I know he doesn't. But I don't *feel* like that. I feel like just another old divorcée."

"Stop it," Gert said, looking at her. She was pretty. "There are a ton of men who'll like you."

"I don't want to *go* through a ton."

"No one does." Gert felt weird trying to comfort Missy. "Hey. My friends are having this, uh, gathering next weekend." Gert explained the Stud Party. "But the guys who come to it will be young."

Missy grinned. "I don't mind…" she said. Then she went to the window to look out at the buildings.

"You know," she said, "neither Dennis nor I is the person we used to be. Sometimes I miss us. When we were young and uncomplicated. But I couldn't go back. Still, sometimes I remember how it felt back then. Maybe I'll feel that way again someday."

"I hope you will," Gert said.

"I know that *you* will," Missy said, turning to her. "Because of the way you are."

"I think I might be on the way," Gert said.

★ ★ ★

That night, Hallie called sounding frazzled.

"What's the matter?" Gert asked, shifting the phone around as she fried herself eggs with Ranch dressing, a dish she and Marc had concocted.

"It's Brett," Hallie said. "He hasn't called in three days!"

"Does he usually?" She turned the gas down.

"He always did," Hallie sobbed. "Even when I thought he wasn't going to, he did. And now, nothing. I played the game too long, and he gave up! He probably thinks I don't like him."

"Well, call him," Gert said.

"I can't call a guy!"

Gert sighed. *"Hallie."* Her eggs were going to get cold.

"What would I say? 'I changed my mind about us sleeping together, so please come over now'?"

"Honesty might be a start…."

"I'm desperate, but not that desperate," Hallie said. "Has Todd said anything?"

Gert said, "Do you want me to ask him?"

"Please, can you?"

Gert called Todd, then ate her eggs, then called Hallie back. "Todd thinks Brett likes having women in love with him," Gert said. "Brett's not sure you even like him."

"I knew it!" Hallie said. "What should I do?"

"Well, you knew how Brett is," Gert said, drying dishes. "You can't help it if he's that way."

"It's not fair," Hallie said. "I thought I'd be different."

They both let that sentence hang in the air, knowing how naive it sounded. Maybe Gert wasn't the only one who was naive. Her most cynical friends were still women—still hopeful at heart.

Gert put a dish on the rack. "Maybe you *should* call him," she said. "You have nothing to lose. Don't tell him you lied in the past, but say you miss him. Then he'll at least know how you feel."

"I don't know," Hallie said. "Maybe I should wait a day. You're coming to the Stud Party, right?"

"As long as I don't have to pursue any studs," Gert said.

"No," Hallie said. "Erika and I need them for ourselves. We just have to make it look like there are more girls there so the guys won't leave. Your boss is coming, right? And that girl, Chase."

"She's coming later."

"As long as she comes. The more, the merrier."

Only a half hour later, when Gert was watching TV, Hallie called back.

"Erika has a new boyfriend!" Hallie said.

"Really?" Gert asked, hooking her finger in the phone cord.

"She said her therapist is making her feel better, and she's been going out to bars alone and meeting guys. She met this older guy who's really into her."

"That's great," Gert said, although she could tell Hallie was a little jealous. Still, Gert had always known Hallie and Erika would do better separately.

"Yeah," Hallie said. "She met him at some bar in the Upper West Side and they spent hours commiserating on their exes." Hallie paused before adding, "She'd just better come to the party. She promised!"

# Chapter

## 20

Hallie's living room was awash in posters: *The Blues Brothers, Reservoir Dogs, The Empire Strikes Back*.

There were already three studs in the room, drinking bottled beers, waiting for more girls to arrive.

"Gert!" Hallie said, hugging her when she came in.

"I don't believe you!" Gert said, looking at the posters.

Hallie said, "I couldn't get *Star Wars*, so I had to go with *Empire*."

"That's fine. But I don't know if guys want women who are *exactly* like them...."

"Why not?" Hallie asked. "You kept telling me about the canon. These posters are perfect."

"The canon is about seeing if you share men's humor, not pretending."

"I'm all about pretending," Hallie said. "Truthfully, there's manipulation in all relationships, isn't there? When you surprise someone with a gift or a vacation or when you whisper sweet nothings, isn't it all designed to get them to like you?"

Gert thought about it. "I guess," she had to concede.

"Anyway, if they like the posters, I'll say they're mine," Hallie said. "If not, I'll say Cat left them when she moved out. It's brilliant."

Cat had left the previous week. Her parents thought the city was changing her too much. They hadn't been too happy to hear about her breaking friends out of jail, or the upcoming "Stud Party."

Cat was only twenty-seven, anyway. She said she might come back when she turned twenty-eight.

"Speaking of manipulation," Hallie said, "I wouldn't mind manipulating a few of the guys here tonight. It might get my mind off Brett."

Gert looked around. "Have you called him?"

"Not yet," Hallie said. "I want to. But I won't yet. He needs to be the one who wants to see me."

"Where's Erika?" Gert asked.

"She's coming," Hallie said. "Boyfriend or no, she's coming."

Studs poured into the room. And they brought friends! Single male friends. "See?" Hallie said to Gert. "There *are* normal single guys out there. But they're not in bars."

"I knew it," Gert said. "Hey, there's Missy."

Missy looked more like a cat than Cat, prancing in in a one-piece, snug-fitting suit. A few heads turned when she came into the room.

"Good!" Hallie said. "She'll keep the studs here."

"She might actually take a few home with her," Gert said.

"That's okay," Hallie said. "I was feeling bad that the ratio was so low. No one's getting lucky tonight."

"Don't be so sure," Gert said. "Stud Number Three and Stud Number Eight just walked out the door together."

"You must be Hallie," Missy said, shaking Hallie's hand. "I've heard a lot about you."

"Me, too," Hallie said. "Good things." Even Gert had to wince and look away when she said that.

"What's everyone drinking?" Missy asked.

"*We're* drinking club soda," Hallie said, "but we're making sure that the guys get drunk."

Missy looked around the room. "Wow, they're cute," she said. "Where did you get them?"

"Times Square," Hallie said.

"And you didn't have to pay? I like your style."

Gert overheard a guy in a corner say to a friend, "Girls just have to accept that men are pigs," so she went over to them. They looked at her as if she was intruding.

"I happened to overhear," Gert said.

"And you're going to argue with me, right?" the guy said. He was average height, with a round face and thinning hair. "Girls aren't any better."

"How so?" Gert demanded, folding her arms.

"Women say they want to find a guy who's nice and has a sense of humor," he said, "but what they really mean is, they want a guy who's nice like Mel Gibson and has a sense of humor like Brad Pitt."

"I've heard guys say that," Gert said, "but that's because they do the same thing, except worse. They go to bars and talk only to women who are extremely beautiful, and then they get turned down because the women they chose are just as superficial as they are. And then they run around saying, 'Girls don't like nice guys.' Why don't you try going up to nice, average women? Then you'll meet women who like nice, average guys. If you pick only the most beautiful women in the bar, you can't turn around and complain that they made the same choice *you* made."

Gert suddenly stopped herself. She realized she was beginning to sound as bitter as Hallie. But she was starting to understand what drove Hallie. How were her friends ever supposed to find a guy who wasn't a jerk when guys *themselves* thought that to get a girl they should act like jerks?

The guy's friends were smiling, seemingly amused.

"So you're claiming women *aren't* judgmental," the guy said.

"*All* women aren't anything," Gert said. "No one is all everything. All women aren't superficial, and all men aren't superficial. Just like all men aren't jerks, and all women aren't jerks. Everyone is different. To make blanket statements about the opposite sex is both bitter and immature."

The guy glowered at her. "Do you have a boyfriend?" he asked.

"As a matter of fact, I do," Gert said.

"Does he look like Brad Pitt?"

"No," Gert said. "And he's a nice guy, too."

"Well, he's ruining it for the rest of us."

"You don't want to try," Gert said. "You say 'Men are pigs' because you want to convince us that all men are like you so that you don't have to do the work of being a decent human being. Someday you'll fall in love—guys like you always do. Then you'll stop being so immature."

The guy rolled his eyes. His friends were still amused.

Hallie had noticed Gert talking to the men and floated over. "Who are your friends?" she asked.

"This guy was just insisting that men are jerks," Gert said.

"Are you a jerk?" Hallie asked him.

"Sure," the guy said.

Hallie looked at his friends. "Are you jerks?"

"No," one of them said.

"See?" Hallie said.

The first guy said, "Well, men are either jerks, or they're liars. I know for a fact that my friends came to this party expecting to have sex."

"That doesn't make you a jerk," Hallie said. "But if you use someone for that and pretend it's otherwise, or if that's the only thing you care about in the world, then that makes you a jerk. And boring, to boot."

"Sometimes we do, and sometimes we don't," the guy said.

"Well, then you're not a full jerk. Congratulations. Now,

grow up. Come on, Gert. There are too many guys at this party for us to be the ones at a disadvantage."

Gert blew them a kiss as she left.

"Where the hell is Erika?" Hallie said. "She better not dis me because of this new guy. She's been promising since she was twenty-four never to be like people who do that."

"You two need drinks," Missy said. She handed them each a cosmo.

"If you liquor us up, you have to promise not to fire Gert if she gets drunk," Hallie said.

"Fire her? She'll get promoted for this idea."

"It was *my* idea," Hallie said.

"Do you freelance?"

Suddenly the door opened. It was Erika, with a man on her arm.

Gert recognized him instantly.

It was Missy's ex-husband, Dennis.

"Uh-oh," Gert said.

"What?" Hallie said.

Missy saw him.

Dennis didn't say anything. He just stood there, surprised.

Missy's eyes narrowed. She stomped toward him.

"Oooh! Stop!" squealed a stud by the wall. He climbed up on a chair.

# Chapter

## 21

They were sitting against the walls of the living room, having cleaned up beer, chips, water and wine. Erika had apologized to Gert for having had to slap her boss. Gert had apologized to Erika for Missy's screaming at Dennis. Erika was in the bathroom cleaning up. Gert and Hallie were dead tired.

"Dennis took really good care of her," Hallie said, running the palm of her hand over the rug. Dennis had taken Erika into Hallie's bedroom and calmed her down. "He seems to really like her."

"We all need people like that," Gert said. "Too bad the studs didn't work out. I suppose the random pickup on the street has the same success rate as anything else."

"Meeting people through friends is the best way," Hallie said.

Now Gert felt guilty. "I'm sorry about Brett."

"I'm probably better off without him," Hallie said. "Why do I end up accepting crumbs, anyway? You know, I was thinking about how when we're young, we look for a guy who's nice and interesting and treats us well. But then we get so jaded that we start giving up basic things. The kinds of things that Todd says to you, and the way Dennis treated Erika before, that's the way it should be. Why do we get so desperate that the Holy Grail is some guy who is half-intelligent, has no visible scars, and is known to seduce women, sleep with them and immediately dump them? Are the Brett Stoddards of the world the best there is?"

"I don't know," Gert said. "If you meet someone great, you know you should stay with them. But if you meet someone who's just semidecent, and you're twenty-nine years old…"

"Exactly," Hallie said. "I used to toss obnoxious men aside without a second thought. Now if I meet one who's single, I'm expected to look for the bright side."

Gert remembered that Chase should be coming in an hour. She looked at the clock.

"It's like the Roosevelt Rule," Hallie said.

"The Roosevelt Rule?"

"'Fear of being alone is worse than being alone itself,'" Hallie said. "When I was nineteen and I didn't have a boyfriend, I never felt bad about it. Because I figured someday I *would*. My friends and I had plenty of fun alone. What ruins the fun is the fear that you'll be that way *forever.*"

Gert knew how scared Hallie was. "You know, you might find someone in the blink of an eye," Gert said. "It could happen tomorrow." But she didn't think she sounded convincing. She didn't like issuing comforting platitudes, but she didn't want Hallie to give up, either.

Hallie stood up and went over to her stereo and fondled the copper Empire State Building on top. "I'm in New York City," she said. "I'm healthy, attractive, and I have a steady job. I should be seeing every play on Broadway. I should be eating at the best restaurants and getting drunk with friends and singing at piano bars. I should be taking road trips across the country and sleeping under the stars. But since those activities are enhanced doubly and triply when you do them with someone you love,

I've put them on hold and instead spent all my time looking for that person. It's just too hard to live in the moment when you know how much better the moment would be if you found someone."

"I know," Gert said, standing up. "I know it's hard."

Hallie shook her head. "No more guy talk," she said. "I'm sick of it. I'm sick of everything being about finding someone." Suddenly she looked as if she was going to cry.

"Are you okay?" Gert asked.

Hallie nodded. "It just seems like everyone leaves me."

"What?" Gert went over to her.

"My roommates, my friends when they have boyfriends…"

Gert walked over and put her hand on her shoulder. "You know," she said, "two weeks ago, I would have said that you were the least bereaved person in the room."

"And now?" Hallie looked at her.

"Now I think that any time there's change, there's loss," Gert said. "Change means loss, loss means loss, finding can sometimes mean loss. I can't judge how you feel, because only you know."

When Erika came back into the room, they ordered pad Thai and dumplings. They decided to sit in the dark and play "truth" before Chase got there—but not limited to dating this time. Hallie said they should just talk about themselves.

"Tell us something different," Hallie said to Gert, sitting on the couch with a small bowl of dumplings in her lap. "Tell us a story. Tell us something that happened when you were little."

"Well," Gert said, "I could tell you about this favorite memory of mine from my childhood, about a restaurant. I've told Todd about it."

"How come you've told Todd and not us?" Hallie asked. "Because we don't have a penis?"

Hallie was right, Gert knew. She still had to make more of an effort with female friends. But she still didn't know if she and Hallie would ever be friends the way they had been in college. They'd both changed too much, and in different ways. Gert still wouldn't give up on her completely, but she felt like she had reached the end of something.

"You guys have to come to therapy with me one day," Erika said. "My therapist suggested I bring my friends sometime anyway. And all we talk about is opening up to people."

"That seems a little odd, but I'll come," Hallie said. "Will you, Gert?"

"I'll take free counseling any day of the week," Gert said.

Erika smiled. "You guys can't come to the next session, though," she said. "I'm bringing Dennis. We're going to talk about how to *properly* get over an ex."

# Chapter

## 22

The lawn outside the church was frozen. So was Gert. It had snowed a few days earlier, and the ground was hard. No one who had planned Michael's wedding had expected it to snow in April.

Gert's gaze moved all over the lawn. There were people in yellows, whites and blues, like it was Easter.

Marc's mother was standing on the steps in front of the church. Her light hair was puffed upon her head, and she was wearing a yellow dress. Gert didn't know how Mrs. Healy would react to seeing her. To comfort herself, she thought about Todd. Sweet Todd, who was waiting for her at the hotel near Boston Harbor.

Gert knew it would be insulting for her to bring Todd to Michael's wedding. But he had insisted on providing moral support, and she was grateful. He'd driven her up to Boston, zipped up her pink dress and told her to have a good time.

Gert moved toward the church steps. Before she could get to Marc's parents, she bumped into Marc's favorite aunt. Aunt Patty had never married, but she loved children, and to her, Gert and Marc were children. "Gertie!" Aunt Patty said, hugging her.

"You look beautiful. Oh, you look as beautiful as you did on your own wedding day." Patty stood back and looked at her. "Honey, how are you?"

"I'm fine, Aunt Patty," Gert said. "But I miss Marc a lot." Already the wedding was making her happy and sad at the same time.

"We all miss him very much," Aunt Patty said. "And I missed you at Thanksgiving. Why weren't you there?" She clasped her hands.

"I don't know," she said. *Because no one invited me.*

"Well, I hope you can make it next time," Aunt Patty said. "Oh, I wish the two of you had had kids. They would have been so cute!" Gert permitted the trespass. "Have you met Michael's fiancée?"

"Not yet," Gert said.

"She's the sweetest girl. An Irish girl, too."

Gert wondered how long people in this country would still worry about where someone's great-grandparents were from. She remembered that Marc's mother had been disappointed that Gert was only a quarter Irish. Big deal.

"Well, I'll see you inside!" Aunt Patty said. "Honey, call me sometime!"

Gert watched her go.

She smoothed her dress and ascended the steps. So many people were talking to Marc's father that Gert didn't feel polite standing there waiting for them to disperse, but she thought it was now or never. Mr. Healy noticed Gert. He looked jolly as ever.

"Gertie!" he said, coming over to her. He gave her a big hug. "It's my old gal Gertie! I'm so glad you could make it. I'm sorry we missed you on Marc's birthday."

"Better planning next time," Gert said.

"Yes," Mr. Healy said. "My old gal Gertie, how are you? How's work? How's Astoria? How are your parents? Is that enough questions? Should I stop now? Should I stop *now*? Should I stop *now*?"

Gert couldn't help but laugh. Right then she found it hard to believe that Mr. Healy had purposely not called her. But avoiding it had probably just been the easiest thing for him to do. After a tragedy, there was a tendency toward easy things. "Fine, fine, fine, fine, fine, fine, fine, good," Gert said.

"I think you put an extra one in there, kiddo," he said. "My gal Gertie, you have to come up and see us next time you're in Boston. Mary, Gert's here."

Mrs. Healy turned her head. "Oh, Gert," she said evenly. "Hello." She looked at her daughter-in-law coolly, then gave her a perfunctory hug.

"Hi," Gert said.

"How are you?" She seemed to be scrutinizing her.

For a second, Gert saw Marc's blue eyes in hers. *Why don't you want to talk to me?* Gert thought.

"I'm fine," Gert said, feeling a lump in her throat. She didn't know how to break through the ice without fighting at Michael's wedding. "I mean, I'm as well as can be expected."

Marc's mother smiled at her again, but didn't say anything. Gert wondered why this woman couldn't just *talk* to her. She remembered something, though. Mrs. Healy never liked emotion. Whenever someone's baby was crying at a family gathering, she had always snapped, "Will someone quiet her down?"

Everyone suddenly started toward the door of the church, as if hearing a dog whistle. Gert was relieved. She could save confrontations for another time. She had to give herself a break. If these people didn't want to try, maybe she shouldn't try anymore, either. But it hurt her. Because she did want to try.

Walking in, she ended up in line with one of Marc's sisters-in-law. Christine had always talked to Gert at family gatherings—girl talk—but she hadn't reached out since the funeral. "Gert!" Christine said. "I've been meaning to call you, but I don't have your number. It was in my old PalmPilot, and I lost it."

"It's listed," Gert said.

"Under what?" Christine said.

"Healy," Gert said. "Same as yours."

"Oh, so you kept Marc's name!"

*Duh,* Gert thought.

They sat together in the third pew. Gert noticed that Christine, who had just had her second baby, still looked round.

Everyone got quiet.

Michael walked down the aisle, looking nervous but handsome. His hair had always been red and wild, but now it had been carefully sheared, the back of his neck shaved and his sideburns short. He looked more like Marc now. Gert's palms got sweaty.

When Michael and his fiancée were up front, they looked at each other the whole time. Michael never seemed scared when the priest asked him if he'd love and honor her. Gert bristled when she heard "till death do us part." No one could have been thinking about that sentence the way she was.

Gert looked around the room. There were couples of all ages holding hands, and one woman in her fifties was playing with the back of her husband's hair. Gert fantasized for a half second that Marc was still alive, and that they were there together.

The newlyweds hugged, and Gert tried to forget everything and just be happy for them.

At the reception, she was seated at a round table. As other people sat down, she tried to figure out which table this was—potpourri, relatives, rejects, old friends. It turned out to be young people—friends of Michael's, former classmates, roommates, playmates. One young couple next to Gert said that they were soon to be married, too. The male half kept running his index finger up and down the length of his fiancée's arm while she talked.

"So," the woman asked Gert. "How do you know Michael?"

Gert was grateful to be acknowledged. "I was married to his brother," Gert said.

"You mean…M…"

"Marc," Gert said. "You can say his name."

The woman smiled. "Well," she said. "You seem to be doing okay with it."

Gert smiled back. "When something like that happens," she said, "you become an expert in smiling when you feel like shit."

A waiter came to fill their glasses and stood between them, saving Gert from saying something worse. She looked away.

"So, who here knows how Michael met his wife?" someone asked.

"She was a bartender in the Rathskeller on campus," Michael's college roommate answered.

"Everyone was after her," a third friend added. "Michael was the shy one. He never hit on her, but on the last day before Christmas break, when everyone was getting ready to go home, he went down there and asked her out."

Gert tried to listen, grateful the whole table was conversing and keeping the attention off her. They were all strangers, and she didn't have anything to add to their discussions about their college antics. She poked at her salad.

"Did you guys see the yearbook?" someone asked.

A guy said, "There was a yearbook poll of the strangest place you had sex, and someone said the Rathskeller."

"It has to be them."

"No it doesn't."

"Yes it does."

"Nuh-uh."

"Yes. She was the only one with a key."

"But Michael's a good Catholic boy."

Gert wished someone was there for her to talk to. Like magic, her cell phone rang.

"Didn't the priest say to turn those off?" someone said.

Gert picked it up. "Hello?"

"All clear?" Todd asked.

"At dinner," Gert said, thrilled to hear his voice.

"Are you doing okay there? I was worried about you."

*"Comme ci, comme ca."*

"What time do you think…?"

"Around seven."

"I'll keep the hot tub warm for you."

Gert smiled. "That sounds so nice." She watched her chattering tablemates.

After she hung up, the guy to her right asked her about herself. He was a college friend of Michael's. He had used the word "dude" a lot but seemed okay. He said he was in his first year of medical school. The stubble and surfer looks were a decoy.

The music started, and he asked her to dance.

*Good,* she thought, getting away from the table. She liked this kid already.

"You're a good dancer," the boy told Gert. He wasn't actually a boy, but she thought of him that way, even though they were only seven years apart. She tried not to feel old.

"I met Marc once," the kid said. "I liked him. He told good jokes."

"He did," Gert said, although "good" was a stretch. They were playing a slow song, and Gert tried to concentrate.

"I can't imagine how you get over something like that."

"You don't ever really get over it." She wondered why this boy found her interesting. She was old, she had been married. Maybe he was attracted to her, or he had a weird widow fixation that he normally didn't get to explore. She decided just to be grateful. She had wondered, in the past, whether being a widow would make her seem old to young people.

A Green Day song came on. Only Michael would have Green Day songs at his wedding.

As they returned to the table, the boy asked Gert if she lived in Boston, and she said New York. The boy seemed less interested after that, and started paying more attention to the other people. But when someone picked up the pink disposable camera from the table, he threw his arm around her and said, "Cheese."

When they were eating the main course, Michael came to the table.

He said "Hi" to the group, then talked to Gert. He bent down and kissed her on the cheek.

"Hi, Michael," Gert said, looking up.

He told her they were going skiing for their honeymoon. He and his wife were big ski buffs.

"And we're going to have a ski-riffic time," Michael added loudly, making the people next to Gert groan.

"You're your father's son." Gert laughed.

"I have to take over for Marc on the bad jokes," Michael said. "We were the bad-joke triplets."

"I noticed that you and Lachlan are both starting to look a little like Marc," Gert said.

"Lach has to finish his punk phase first," Michael said. "And since he's only thirteen, the worst is yet to come."

They looked over at Lach, who was dancing up a storm with his grandmother.

Michael told Gert he would see her later, and then he went to talk to other people. She didn't know if he really would.

At the end of the reception, the boy next to Gert gave her his number. Gert felt eons older than him, but he might make a good date for someone else. She'd save the number for Hallie or Chase.

The sky was getting darker as people began to leave.

Gert stood motionless by the tables, looking around the lawn. She took everything in like a snapshot, fearing she'd never see any of these people again.

She watched Mrs. Healy up on the hill, talking to one of her granddaughters. Eddie and Christine were transporting gifts to the hall. Patrick was wrestling on the lawn with his oldest son. Aunt Patty was debating something with the priest.

Should Gert go talk to them? They were part of five or six of her Christmases, birthdays, Fourth of July weekends, but most important—part of Marc. How could she make sure they shoe-horned her into their lives if there was no longer an official place?

Gert felt someone's hands over her eyes. She turned around.

"Boo," Michael said.

"You!" Gert said. "You have so many people to see."

"Not as important as you," Michael said, giving her a big hug. He was tall, like his brothers.

Gert laughed.

"I'm glad you came," Michael said. "I know it must have been hard for you."

"But I had to see you get married," Gert said.

"I'm glad to see you here," Michael said again. "I wanted to talk to you, but I didn't want to do it at the table." He looked down. "I'm so sorry Marc isn't here."

Gert said, "He's here. And he's proud of you."

Michael seemed to be blinking back tears. "If I have a son I'm going to name him after him," he said.

"Good."

"You're going to get an invitation soon," he said. "Jenny and I are having a Fourth of July party. Will you come?"

"Of course I will."

"Good."

The taxi dropped Gert at the hotel. When she got up to the room, Todd was in the shower. She took her dress off and laid it on the bed, relieved the day was over. Maybe she would bring Todd to the Fourth of July party. As long as she was still seeing him. She still had no way of knowing for sure.

She pulled on a sweatshirt. This felt good. Maybe they'd go down to the hot tub later.

Gert's cell phone rang.

"It's me!" Hallie said. She sounded excited.

"Why are you so excited?" Gert asked.

"Brett called. He wants to have dinner on Friday!"

"That's great!" Gert said.

"He apologized for taking so long to get back to me," Hallie said. "He said he's been thinking about what he wants."

"And…"

"He likes me, and he's not used to that. We're going to start seeing each other again. We both admitted to having played games. But I think we got to know each other. And I have to think that maybe we only played games because we cared. If we didn't like each other, we wouldn't have bothered, right?"

"Maybe," Gert said doubtfully, smoothing the dress out.

"If he says something phony, I'll call him on it," Hallie said. "I'm not going to be afraid anymore. I don't want to be the woman who's always making excuses for her jerky boyfriend. But I want at least to give him a chance to be honest."

"Good for you!" Gert said.

"Uh…so in case it doesn't work out, did you get me names from the wedding like you promised?"

Gert laughed. "I met a med student who's a friend of Michael's."

"Hubba hubba."

"He's young," Gert said, sitting down on the bed. "But legal."

"Sounds good."

Todd came out of the bathroom wearing a towel and rubbing the side of his head with a different one. Gert laughed because on a list of movie clichés that she'd once gotten as an e-mail forward from Hallie, it said that men coming out of a shower were always rubbing the side of their heads with a towel.

"What's so funny?" Hallie asked.

"Nothing," Gert said. "I have to go. Todd and I are taking a nighttime tour of Boston."

"You brought Todd to Michael's wedding?"

"He came up here with me, but he stayed at the hotel," Gert said. "And I'm glad he's here."

Todd knelt down and kissed her on the cheek. He smelled like soap.

"All right. Call me when you get home."

Gert hung up. She looked up at Todd.

"Excuse me," she said. "Can I borrow your towel? My car just hit a buffalo."

"I think it's 'water buffalo,'" Todd said, smiling. "What's that from, anyway?"

*"Fletch,"* Gert said.

"Overrated," Todd said.

It was cool out. The boat passed through the harbor. It was a large two-decker, with various couples, mostly older. There was a square bar in the middle of the ship.

Gert was near the railing, looking over the water. Orange lights shone across the surface, shimmering over the ripples. Todd was standing behind her, holding her around her waist. He felt strong.

"What's that clock?" Todd asked.

"I don't know," Gert said, looking at the building with the lit-up round clock. "Marc would know. He knew everything about Boston."

"Did he have an accident?" Todd asked.

Gert turned around and looked at him. "What?"

"Oh my God," Todd said. "I meant, 'Did he have an accent.' A Boston accent. I'm so sorry."

Gert looked at him for a second.

"I didn't mean to say that," Todd said.

Gert laughed. "You poor thing."

Todd was quiet. His arms felt more tentative around her. "I really didn't mean it…."

"I've done things like that," she said. "It's okay."

"I really am sorry."

"You're being silly. Don't worry about it."

He held her firmly from behind again, and she was glad. She looked back over the water. "I guess he might have had an accent, at one time," she said. "But he expunged it. His mom has one pretty bad."

"Well, Boston's a great town," Todd said. "I would have married him just for the town."

"I'm sure your homeland of East Grass Patch, Virginia, is equally charming," she said.

"East Grass Patch? I've never heard that one. I'm from Emporia."

"Sounds like a supermarket."

"Don't mock my town. Hometowns are like little brothers. Only you can pick on your own."

She liked that line, and smiled. "I won't make fun of Food Emporia ever again," she said.

"You should never make fun of any place unless you've been there." He put his chin on her shoulder and whispered in her ear. "I have a week off next month. Do you want to come down there with me?"

Gert turned to look at him. "Do you want me there?"

"Yes," he said. "I'd *love* to have you there."

"I'd be meeting your parents."

"If you're up for the challenge," he said.

"*Is* it a challenge?"

He laughed. "Of course not," he said. "When they see how much I care about you, they're bound to care about you just as much."

Gert smiled. It was the sign she'd been waiting for.

"Besides," Todd said, "thanks to my brother, who's brought home every purple-haired girl to ever set foot in Staunton College, they'll be pleased as punch to meet you. I thank Bill every day for blazing this primrose path for me."

She laughed.

At night, as they were quietly changing for bed, facing in opposite directions, Todd said, "Do you need to go to the grave before we leave?"

She turned around. He was still facing away from her, changing. She knew it had probably been a difficult thing for him to ask. But it was the right thing, too. She found that Todd was becoming increasingly intuitive about her.

"Would that bother you?" she asked him.

"No," he said, but he still wasn't facing her. She knew that he must feel funny—it was sensitive material, and he wasn't an expert in handling it. But the important thing was, he had cared enough to try.

Todd headed into the bathroom. He said, "We can make a stop before we head home."

Todd waited by the road, outside the cemetery gate. Gert made her way past the rows and rows of graves until she got to Marc's.

There were purple flowers on it.

Gert remembered the old woman.

She knelt down.

"Hi, Marc," she said. There were no motors or birds this morning. "Michael got married yesterday," she said. "I'm sure you were there. He's starting to look like you." She smiled. "I miss you. You know that. I miss you every day. I'm not going to stop."

She stood up. She felt sad. It felt like an ending. She wasn't sure why.

"I'll be back here on July fourth," she said. "I promise."

She thought of the July fourth photo she had of him at home, taken two months before he'd died.

She made herself smile. "I think about you every day," she said. "You know that."

She said goodbye and turned to walk away.

Before leaving, she stopped at Colin's grave.

"Hey, Colin," she said. "Nice Web site."

It was drizzling when Gert and Todd headed out of town. Small drops splattered on the windshield. The wipers swished silently.

The roads were slightly wet. Todd drove carefully.

They approached a railroad bridge, a small thick black one whose high metal walls had a fast food banner painted across. A freight train was stopped on top. The train was silvery, with vertical slits, and painted across it in red and blue was Union Pacific.

"Those are cattle cars," Todd said as they passed under it.

"I didn't know they still moved cattle by train," Gert said.

"How else did you think they move them?"

"Mooooove them?"

They were quiet for a few minutes. Gert thought about how important Todd's job was. No one really thought about it much these days.

They kept on through Massachusetts' small towns, heading toward the highway. Gert saw grassy yards, colonial homes, maple trees, supermarkets. She had that subtle longing for the suburbs again. Even though the city was convenient for now, it didn't feel like family. Marc's parents' house had felt like family. Her own parents' house felt that way. The city was rushed, tense, crowded. It was full of bars and clubs: bars on the windows, clubs on the steering wheels. And it felt transitional.

"Did you think they seemed like a good couple?" Todd said, out of the blue.

"Who?" Gert asked.

"Michael and his wife."

"Why do you ask?"

He shrugged. "I've been to three weddings in the past two years," he said. "One of them was fun, but the other two were so serious, I didn't even get the impression that the couple liked each other. It seemed like a chore meant to satisfy their parents, not the happiest moment of their lives. At the wedding I went to last summer, the best man gave this long speech and said he knew the groom's bachelor days were over when the groom turned to him and said, 'I really like this girl.'"

Todd shook his head.

"And?" Gert asked.

"I don't know," Todd said. "I just expect a guy to say more

than that about someone he's going to spend the rest of his life with."

"So you were disappointed," Gert said.

"I guess, a little," Todd said. "I mean, 'I really like this girl'? Is that the best you can come up with for someone you love? It seems like getting married should be about more than that."

"Maybe guys don't always gush to their friends about girls," Gert said.

"I gush about you," Todd said.

"No, you don't."

"Sure I do. I say that you're smart and witty and beautiful."

She blushed. "You don't say that."

Todd nodded. "*Those* are the things you say about someone you want to spend the rest of your life with."

She looked at him, but his eyes were on the road.

"Hey, we'll be passing Darien in a couple of hours," he said.

"We told you," she said. "It's Dari-*anne*."

"Just for that, we're not stopping at the diner for coffee."

# Chapter
## 23

Gert and Todd were sitting on the couch reading the Sunday paper. Sun streamed through the windows and bathed the coffee table. Neither of them had to go anywhere for the entire day.

Todd's toes wiggled on the table, in white socks. Gert noticed he had the comics open.

"One time," she said, "Marc was reading Blondie, and he decided we needed to make a Dagwood sandwich right that afternoon."

Todd said, "Sounds like fun."

"It was."

They were quiet for a moment.

"Speaking of the comics," Todd said, "did I ever tell you my theory about why comic strips are like freight trains?"

"I couldn't imagine there could be one."

Todd laughed. "There is," he said. "They're both colorful and have this great link with history. Some of these comics have been running since the Depression. They've got the same characters and a story that goes back seventy or eighty years." He put the paper down for a second. "There's something great about that, you know?"

She did.

That night, Todd went to bed early because he had to go to work at 5:00 a.m. Gert wandered alone through the house. She made her way into Marc's trophy room, or whatever it should be called—the extra bedroom, the study, the would-have-been-baby's room.

She wiped the dust off the top of the computer and stood there a minute. She felt full of love for so many different people. She didn't know if she had to choose only one.

She noticed, through the window, that in the house across the street, something was moving.

The little blond-haired girl was peeking out, poking her fingers through the blinds.

The girl had a look of wonder on her face. Gert knew why. It had gotten very warm that day. Spring was finally there. Gert figured the girl was thinking that she might like to go out and play tomorrow.

Soon the girl would be old enough to go to school. Gert would see her walking in the street, holding her mother's hand. *Wouldn't Marc be surprised to see her old enough for that?* Gert mused. The girl would proceed through elementary school and high school. At some point, someone might tell her that in her early twenties, she would meet a great guy, marry him and have kids. The girl might even hear it so often that she would come to expect it.

Gert wondered if the girl would meet her future husband in school or at work, whether she'd become an artist or office manager or doctor, whether she'd experience her first kiss in her backyard or under the elevated subway station or on some far-off college green. Gert wondered if she herself would still be living on the same block as the girl by the time the girl was that old. She doubted it.

Then again, there were no guarantees. Gert had thought there were, once—she'd thought her condo was just one on a series of steps, a temporary place and she'd split in a few years. Now she had no idea how long she'd stay. Now she didn't know anything for sure.

She still believed, though, that she would leave fairly soon. Being in Queens felt like living with someone but not marrying them; an intermediary semisettledness, but no real commitment. Manhattan was like singlehood. Gert wanted to be where life was a little slower. She hoped she'd have someone to go back to the suburbs with.

It was true that if she moved there, she and her significant other might go entire weekends without passing more than three other people in the street. But she still thought she'd be happier.

*Sooner or later,* she thought, *we all pair off.*

The little girl disappeared from the window. Gert's gaze wandered upward, toward the roof, and it was only then that she realized that the Christmas lights were gone.

On sale in April from Red Dress Ink

# My Fake Wedding

by Mina Ford

Katie's given up on love…
so she'll make the perfect bride.

When Katie's gay best friend suggests that she
marry his Aussie lover so that he can stay in the
country, she agrees. After all, things are looking
a little bleak for her on the love front. But just
as she starts trying on white dresses, romance
comes from the unlikeliest source. Will Katie
let the man she loves ruin her wedding day?

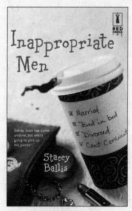

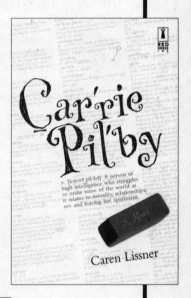